About the author

Anne Harris was born in New Zealand but has resided in the USA since the mid-1980s. A lover of finding what is over the next hill, she has lived in five of the fifty states of the USA and visited almost all of the others. She has had several different careers along the way, including banking and teaching, culminating in ordination to the Episcopal priesthood in 2008. Along the way she has written hundreds of thousands of words, in one form or another. *Bound by an Oath* is her first published novel.

BOUND BY AN OATH

Anne Marie Harris

BOUND BY AN OATH

Vanguard Press

VANGUARD PAPERBACK

© Copyright 2025
Anne Marie Harris

The right of Anne Marie Harris to be identified as author of
this work has been asserted by her in accordance with the
Copyright, Designs and Patents Act 1988.

All Rights Reserved

No reproduction, copy or transmission of this publication
may be made without written permission.
No paragraph of this publication may be reproduced,
copied or transmitted save with the written permission of the publisher, or
in accordance with the provisions
of the Copyright Act 1956 (as amended).

Any person who commits any unauthorised act in relation to this
publication may be liable to criminal prosecution and civil claims for
damages.

A CIP catalogue record for this title is available from the British Library.

ISBN 978-1-83794-224-4

This is a work of fiction. Names, characters, businesses, places, events
and incidents are either the products of the author's imagination or used
in a fictitious manner. Any resemblance to actual persons, living or dead,
or actual events is purely coincidental.

Vanguard Press is an imprint of
Pegasus Elliot Mackenzie Publishers Ltd.
www.pegasuspublishers.com

First Published in 2025

Vanguard Press
Sheraton House Castle Park
Cambridge England

Printed & Bound in Great Britain

I dedicate *Bound by an Oath* to my husband, who urged me to write this book and who guided me through numerous bouts of self-doubt, anxiety, and petulance. A history teacher, his knowledge of world history is prodigious, but after researching and writing this novel, I undoubtedly now know more about the process of building Roman roads than he does! Many humble thanks to my partner in life for his unceasing support of my numerous endeavors, literary and otherwise.

Chapter One

The Most Intelligent Person

The year was four hundred and sixty-two. Frater Paulos was sitting in the orange garden of the monastery in Ravenna, as he did in the late afternoon almost every day. He had lived a long life, and by virtue of his age he was allowed to take his rest before Vespers wherever he wished, rather than in his cell like every other monk at the monastery. His life had been filled with travel and excitement, which was most unusual for a monk in any century, but was especially so for one living only four hundred years after his Lord had walked on this earth. Fra Paulos was an exceptional monk. He had never sought the excitement of journeying far away, but rather he had been unable to avoid it. What he really preferred, even more so in his old age, was the calm and quiet of the routines and patterns of monastic life. Walking the hall and cloisters from cell to chapel, and chapel to refectory, in silence, was the way of life he loved best. And remembering (or perhaps it was dreaming about) the person he had loved as much as he had loved his Lord.

Above all, the monastery garden was a place of deep peace for him. He knew that being outside, with the sky forming a serene blue canopy above him, and from where he habitually sat, laced across with a tracery of leaves, allowed him to commune more deeply with God than he was able to do anywhere else, even in the chapel. In the garden he felt more strongly connected to the celestial, physical, and spiritual worlds, which he thought of as a Trinity of Being. He welcomed that connection, because there had been periods of his life when it had been sorely missing and he had felt out of balance with his creator and with the world. At that time of the day, he could either be found sitting in contentment among the orange trees and the marsh irises, thinking, remembering, and praying, or under the arches of the cloister, if the weather was inclement.

Fra Paulos was a renowned storyteller in the monastery at Ravenna. Heaven knew, he had a plethora of stories to tell. Fra Luke, one of the younger monks, attempted to join Fra Paulos in the afternoons whenever he could slip away without being noticed. He found much pleasure in listening to his older brother's tales; almost as much pleasure as the old man found in sharing them. He fancied that one day he might get to travel and meet interesting people as Fra Paulos had done. It was rumored that Fra Paulos had only divulged a tiny fraction of the events and secrets of his life and Fra Luke hoped to be the one to hear them all.

On that afternoon in late spring, when the air was deliciously fresh with the scent of the orange blossoms, and the light was just beginning to lose its midday clarity, fading softly and gently, like the colors of a day lily toward evening, Fra Luke passed quietly through the big oak door and entered the garden to spend some time with his elderly mentor.

After sitting in companionable silence for several minutes, he posed a question for his friend to answer. The question was something that had been brewing in his mind for some time. He was unlikely to ever have such adventures as Fra Paulos had undertaken, and participating in them from the dreamlike territory of his mind was as close to being there as he could reasonably expect. He turned his face, which was still youthful with its smooth, unwrinkled skin like the marble complexion of a Greek statue, toward the creased and withered face of his friend.

"Of all the people you have known, my friend, which man was the wisest and the most intelligent?"

Fra Paulos considered the question. He had a ready answer, but he guessed it was probably not the answer that Fra Luke was expecting. He guessed that Fra Luke had the name of some very famous person on his mind, perhaps even the Pope, and that he was going to drop that name into the conversation at the time he judged best for its maximum effect.

Fra Paulos had known his younger brother since he had arrived at the monastery in the hills of Ravenna as a young man, barely out of adolescence, seeking his vocation, and that was several decades ago. One of the things he knew about this younger brother was that Fra Luke was a notorious name-dropper. He would have you believe that he had met a goodly number of very high-profile people in his life. He had come from a well-respected Roman family where he might have met some famous people in his childhood, but he had not spent more than a few months outside of the monastery since he entered, and it was hard to see how he could be as well connected as he would have you believe. It was Fra Paulos's opinion that Fra Luke dropped names with some frequency simply because he needed to feel important; and because he knew Fra Luke cared about him, he humored him as much as possible. After all, it was a rare person that did not desire to be respected, and he himself had nothing to prove to anyone any more.

Unlike Fra Luke, and unlike most other monks at that time, Fra Paulos had traveled from Ravenna to Rome several times and from Rome to Britain, riding the arduous and dangerous trails through Gaul, three times, although he had never once volunteered to leave the monastery. He had always been summoned by a senior in the church, and he was bound by an oath of obedience to his superiors to do whatever he was asked to do. Fra Paulos had met the Pope when he was summoned to Rome before his first missionary trip.

The young Paulos had presented himself to the monastery when he was seventeen years old, even younger than Fra Luke had been when he began to seek his vocation. He knew that a life of prayer and meditation, and of helping others, was what he was put on the earth for. He had known it almost from the time his voice had broken. He was the last son of a family of five sons and three daughters, and so it was acceptable to his parents that he should enter a monastery rather than stay and help the family to earn their living making clay pots. He was the family's gift to the church. Both his mother and his father were thrilled that he was interested in the things of faith. His mother, in particular, was proud to have a son in the church, and told repeated stories about him to anyone who would listen.

And, fortunately, it had been the right decision for him. Fra Paulos had blossomed under the tutoring of the abbot, showing a keen intellect and a prodigious memory. He found he was a natural scholar and he had learned very quickly. He had mastered the Gallic language and learned to read and write as well as the abbot himself, which made him a very valuable member of the community. And he had not been bothered very often by the itch to bed a woman or to sire a son, as so many men did. Some of his brothers at the monastery fought with their natural desires every day. Fra Paulos may have had other issues, but lust was not one of them, at least not in the early days.

He had, in fact, loved a woman. He still loved her, truth be told, but he did not tell many people that fact, for fear that they would misunderstand. While the church might have had a different opinion, in the innermost part of his conscience, the part that was between God and himself, he did not believe that his love for her was a sin. What he felt for her was the deepest admiration, empathy, and compassion. It was said by some that the Lord Jesus had loved Mary Magdalene in the same way. But to be on the safe side, Fra Paulos prayed every night for forgiveness for his earthly love of a woman. That way, should he die in the night, and should he have been mistaken and his love was a sin after all, his soul would be shriven.

To Fra Luke he said, "Which man was the wisest and the most intelligent? Dear Brother, wisdom and intelligence are not often found in the same individual."

Fra Luke blushed. He did not like to be corrected, and it was his misfortune to often hear reprimand and correction when it was not intended. He looked down at his rough, sandaled feet to hide his humiliation, and spoke quietly.

"Of course, that is very true. Pardon me, Brother, for my oversight. Except…" He paused. "It must be said that I do not believe it to be true in your case, Fra Paulos." A small smile escaped from his lips at the little piece of flattery that he had used with the full intention of oiling the wheels of his relationship with Fra Paulos. He did not think his mentor had been serious when he made the comment, but he added the exception just in case. "But if we must choose from the two, for the sake of argument, let us settle on intelligence then. Who is the most intelligent man that you ever met?"

It was Fra Paulos's turn to smile. His brother's choice of intelligence over wisdom only served to emphasize his callowness. Wisdom was by far the greater virtue, as Fra Paulos had learned. He looked off into the distance, his cataract-clouded eyes missing the olive groves and the upright, dark green yews on the distant hills, but seeing far more in his memory than was actually in front of him in reality.

"Fra Luke, you might be surprised to know that the most intelligent 'man' that I ever met was a woman."

There was a silence as Fra Luke took in what his mentor had said.

"A woman?" He said the words in such a way that he was not really asking a question. He was making a statement that made clear how ridiculous he thought it was that a woman might be the most intelligent person Fra Paulos had met. Fra Paulos was still looking into the distance as he focused his mind on the one he was remembering from his distant past.

"Yes. A woman," he said softly.

"And who was that woman?" Fra Luke's mind was abuzz. He considered several possible scenarios, with lightning speed, as he waited for Fra Paulos to answer. And then he thought of the most likely possibility, and his face lost its puzzled look and his eyes regained their glimmer. "Was she perhaps a Roman matriarch?" After his initial disbelief, which had almost made him lose interest in knowing the answer to his question, he realized that there might still be a good story to be heard after all. It could have been the case that Fra Paulos had been burning a candle for some local woman all these years. If so, that would be something very juicy and entertaining to mull over and to embroider in his mind.

The older man looked up. He had a secret or two, but whatever Fra Luke was imagining might have gone on between him and a Roman matriarch, Fra Luke was going to find that the truth was very different.

"No, indeed," he said with a smile. "There has never been a Roman matriarch in my life, intelligent or otherwise. This woman was not of our people. She was the leader of the Cantii, a tribe of Kentish men and women." There was a deep silence from Fra Luke that indicated his complete lack of comprehension. The spoken words fell between them as if they had been the barks of a dog: there was sound and there was intended meaning, but they might as well have been yaps and whimpers.

However, Fra Luke was not a stupid man, and after a few moments, what Fra Paulos had said made sense to him, and he gave a short laugh.

"Oh! So, you met her on one of your missionary trips, then! I am anxious to know why you say she was the most intelligent person you ever met. Could she be even more intelligent than Pope Leo, the Holy Father?"

He sounded incredulous. It seemed likely that Fra Luke had been going to mention the Holy Father as the most intelligent acquaintance of his own, as Fra Paulos had suspected. Fra Paulos smiled inwardly, forbidding his lips to show his amusement. It had not been Pope Leo who had sent him to Britain, but Pope Innocent. He was so old that he had lived through at least six popes. He had completely lost count. But Fra Paulos did wonder if his brother was perhaps right to question him on his answer to the query. Perhaps no one could ever be wiser or more intelligent than the Father of the Church. Or perhaps a monk should never admit that anyone was, let alone a woman. And then again, perhaps Aethelreda of the Cantii had not been as intelligent as the Pope, technically. She was certainly not as educated, but she had been the most canny, curious, and clever person that he had ever met, and far more enjoyable to spend time with than anyone else that he had ever known.

His mind wandered to the day that he had first met the most blessed child of God, who was named Aethelreda of the Cantii. It had been on his first missionary trip to Britain. He had been sent there by Pope Innocent, who was concerned that after the Roman legions had left the island, the local tribes would be left to warfare and terror, just as Christianity had begun to gain a stronger foothold. And the Pope had a more personal reason, too. He had a brother, a Roman legionnaire who had remained in Britain after the troops had returned to Rome. The Pope had not heard from him since.

Fra Paulos and his fellow monk, Fra Augustus, who was sent to accompany him, and their small band of sailors and guards numbering fourteen in total, had arrived on the coast of Kent just the day before he had met Aethelreda. He could still see the coastline in his mind's eye as clearly as he had on the day that they drew near to it. There had been a dense fog somewhere between the coast of Gaul and where they finally landed, but it had cleared just an hour before they arrived at the small, pebbled beach.

The shoreline was shingly, but it had allowed them to land with surprising ease. On their port side they had missed an outcrop of rocks with tidal pools fringed with green seaweed by just a few yards. Augustus and Paulos bowed their heads in a prayer of gratitude for their safe arrival. The cove they had entered was sheltered by headlands on either side, with distinctive chalky white rocks rising out of the sea. Between the headlands, the land sloped gently down to the coast, with thick woods that grew almost to the seashore.

Evidently, they had landed on a part of the coast that was not populated by the local people. They had expected a party of people gathered on the shore to meet them, perhaps with weapons, but instead they had landed completely without witnesses. They had anchored their boat and pulled their cargo ashore, set up camp, said their prayers of thanksgiving, and turned in for a fretful night of sleep, all without seeing a single Briton. It was indeed a curious and unexpected thing. Some wondered aloud if they had actually reached their planned destination, or if they had gone completely off course in the fog.

Their captain, Quintus, swore loudly when he overheard the questions about the exact location of their landing. It had certainly crossed his mind that they might have gone off course in that thick fog, and if so, who knew where they were, or what might become of their little expedition? He knew that would be an ominous start for the Pope's mission. But Quintus was not one to admit mistakes, and he did not take kindly to the suggestion that he had sailed into the wrong bay. As their captain, he needed to have the full trust of his crew and passengers. He trusted his own navigational skills, despite the peculiarity of their circumstances. They had never let him down before.

"We are," he proclaimed in his loud seaman's voice, "in Kent, by the blood of Jove!" And no one dared to challenge him further after that. Even the two religious brothers let the pagan curse pass without reprimand.

It was with some relief to all of them, especially Quintus, that, the following morning, shortly after daybreak, the sound of hooves was heard, and their guard hastily got into formation to protect the two Christian brothers from whatever evils might be coming.

A small group of men, mounted on rough ponies, came out of the woods into sight. There were about eight of them, and as they came closer, Fra Paulos realized that they were riding in phalanx around a woman in a long, dark brown cloak, with a ring of gold, like a simple crown, on her brow. They stopped at a safe distance – about fifty feet away – and stared balefully at the Romans. It seemed that they had known the Romans were there and had come to find out who they were, and whether it was safe to approach them.

For what seemed like a long time, both groups were at a stalemate. The woman sat on her horse, surrounded by her guard, and Fra Augustus and Fra Paulos stood behind their guard, wondering who would make the first move. To calm himself, Fra Paulos was mouthing the twenty-third psalm, "Yea, though I walk through the valley of the shadow of death, I will fear no evil," and trying to take it all in. It was his first foray into the unknown world of the Britons. He supposed he was as well prepared as any Roman could have been, but he felt very insecure. He was painfully aware that the success of their mission might rise or fall at a moment such as they had just encountered. How terrible it would be for the Church of Rome if their expedition was over before it had really begun.

The Kentish men were short and stocky, with dark curling hair. They wore breeches of leather with tunics and cloaks of rough woven cloth, in earthy colors. They were armed with long wooden spears; and a dagger in the hand of each of the men closest to the woman warned the interlopers that they meant business.

The woman, almost certainly their queen, wore a light purple gown under her cloak, as delicate and pretty as any Fra Paulos had ever seen in his home country. But the most startling thing about her was not the color of her robe, but the color of her hair. It was a most peculiar light-yellow color, like the oat straw from the fields. It was pulled back from her fair face, parted in the middle, and plaited into two long braids that fell over her shoulders and down her chest. Paulos had never seen hair of that color before, although he had heard that the hair of some of the barbarians was light gold. It mesmerized him.

Fra Paulos realized that, as they were the interlopers in someone else's country, they needed to somehow show the Britons that they meant no harm. He hoped that the local people would recognize from their homespun tunics and their tonsures that he and Fra Augustus were religious men, not soldiers like the others; but the more he thought about it, the more he doubted that would be true in this faraway place. The precariousness of the situation made his heart beat as hard as if he had just run a mile uphill carrying a heavy load. The sweat was beading his upper lip and his breathing was labored. He knew he was going to have to make the first move, and that he would be taking a huge risk. He was not a military man. He was a man of prayer. But the Holy Father wanted their little mission group to reach out to the local people and offer them the protection of the Roman Church, if they would convert to Christianity.

With a silent prayer, he moved out from behind the guard and slowly opened his arms to the Britons so that they would see that he was not armed. It was a posture that reminded him of his Savior's outstretched arms on the cross. Fra Paulos did not labor under any illusions that he would save these people – he knew that only God could do that – but he hoped the Britons would read his outspread arms as a benign gesture. No one else moved. Turning his head carefully to speak to his guard, Paulos said in a voice that was much calmer than he thought it would sound, with his heart beating as loud and fast in his ears as it was, "Put your weapons down."

They did so, carefully. But still none of the Kentish party moved. Everybody waited, nervously. Finally, the young woman at the center of her group must have decided that it was safe, and she took things into her own hands. She dismounted from her horse in one smooth movement and handed the reins of her mount to her nearest escort. She took a few confident but short steps in the direction of the Romans, and then stopped again to reassess the situation. By then, Paulos could see her clearly. She was indeed wearing a slender crown of hammered and inscribed gold. She had bands of gold around her wrists, and her garments were of beautifully woven cloth with some decoration at the hem. She was clearly royalty. But as Paulos took a few careful steps of his own toward her, he noticed that there was something disturbing about her eyes. They were a light color, as blue as the silks he had seen in the markets of Rome. He sucked in his breath in an involuntary rush. He had seen eyes of a similar color in a beggar at the monastery gate in Ravenna. That beggar, holding up a clay cup for alms and staring at nothing at all, had been blind. He feared that the woman's strange eyes meant that she was blind, too. But in the next moment, he realized that there was nothing at all wrong with her eyesight. She looked right at Paulos, plainly seeing him, and her eyes were clear and shining, not milky like those of the blind beggar.

Then, in a surprisingly trusting gesture, the young woman put her hand on her chest, smiled, and said in a firm, deliberate voice, "Aethelreda."

Paulos was profoundly relieved. If he was not mistaken, she was telling him her name. He smiled back at her, touched his own chest and said, "Frater Paulos." Then, pointing to Augustus, he said, "Frater Augustus." Augustus bowed his head as a gesture of respect to the fair young woman.

Aethelreda looked at Paulos again and she said, pronouncing the two words distinctly, "Frater. Brother." She pointed at two of the young men who were guarding her and said, "My brothers."

Paulos did not speak more than a dozen words of the language of the Britons, but it seemed to him that she had recognized the word 'frater', and was telling him the word in her own language. At first he was astonished, but then he realized that after all the years of Roman occupation, it was quite likely that the locals could speak some Latin, even if they had not had much contact. He smiled and nodded to let her know that he understood.

The young woman, obviously glad to be in command of the situation, then introduced a few of her guards by name, each time turning to Paulos. Then she did a surprising and charming thing. She touched the head of her steed and said in her own language, "My horse," and laughed, as if she fully realized that identifying a horse was an amusing thing to do in the midst of making the introductions of men. She looked back at Paulos, waiting to hear what he would say. Paulos laughed, too, in relief and delight. He believed he knew what she was doing! She was teaching him words in her own language. He pointed at the animal and said the animal's name in Latin, "Equus."

That opened the floodgates for Aethelreda. She seemed to abandon any fear or reserve she might previously have had that these strangers might be enemies. While her men looked on anxiously, she went around naming a dozen objects – man, woman, boot, belt, earth, grass, leaf, flower, hand, arm, nose, and eye. After each word she looked at Paulos, who then told her the word in Latin. She was clearly excited by the process of learning the language. She seemed to be filled with an internal energy, an energy that Paulos was to see often as he taught her Latin, reading, a smattering of mathematics, and philosophy over the time that he knew her.

And so began the relationship with a remarkable young woman who was the most intelligent person that Frater Paulos was ever to meet.

***

Back in the monastery garden, Fra Luke was deeply engrossed in what he had heard about a woman who was as intelligent as a pope. He would have loved to have heard more, but Fra Paulos had become lost in his own thoughts, and it seemed kinder to let him be, rather than to interrupt them for his own selfish interest.

Fra Paulos shifted uncomfortably on the wooden bench. His hips and back were aching terribly. It was getting cooler as it was still early spring, and he was growing tired. He had lived eighty-four years of a life that had been filled with wonder, and he had lived them fully, and sometimes now the days were very long. He had begun to think that he would meet his Lord soon, and he was not reluctant to do so. He thought that he was as ready as he ever would be.

The Vespers bell rang, announcing evening services in the chapel. He turned to Fra Luke and said, "Go along, my brother. I will follow you shortly." But he did not follow. He did not want to stop remembering those weeks that he had spent with the amazing young woman who had eaten up knowledge as if it had been food for a starving prisoner.

For the first time in his life, he ignored the rules of the monastery and allowed himself the luxury of staying right where he was, while the others said their prayers and then went to dinner.

Chapter Two

Augustus Becomes Impatient

Fra Paulos waited a few minutes in the garden after Fra Luke went off to the chapel for Vespers. He heard his brothers begin the chanting of the first psalm for the evening. The melodic rhythm of their voices washed out of the chapel into the early evening air, floating, as ethereal as the mist that rose in the hills at dawn. It was a soothing sound, an evocative and holy sound for a man who had spent most of his life working, eating, praying, and sleeping in the rhythm of the monastery. He felt God draw near in the tones that he heard. He tried to guess which psalm they were chanting and had decided it was Psalm 86, but when the chanting stopped abruptly, he realized that he was mistaken. Psalm 86 was a much longer psalm. Perhaps that had been the psalm they had sung in morning chapel, or yesterday evening. It was so hard to keep events discrete in his mind these days. Without the regular repetition of the Daily Office, some days he would hardly have known whether it was day or night.

In his head he had been singing the words of the psalm along with the brothers, or of what he thought they were singing. When they had left off, he continued to recite the psalm, even though it was obviously not the psalm appointed for the service, because it did not seem right to leave it unfinished. He knew most of the psalms by heart after so many years.

"For Thou art great; Thou doest wondrous things; and Thou alone art God." At verse ten, his feelings overcame him, and he burst into audible song in his reedy, octogenarian voice.

"I will praise thee, O Lord my God, with all my heart: and I will glorify thy name for evermore."

He ended with the Doxology praising Father, Son, and Holy Ghost, with his heart full of gratitude. He felt around for his sturdy olive-wood walking stick, which was where he had placed it at the foot of the bench a full two hours ago, picked it up with difficulty, unable to contain the small grunt of discomfort that escaped from his throat, and then very slowly and very carefully he stood up, fighting off the stiffness in his body and the dizziness in his head that was afflicting him more and more often these days, and he began the slow walk back to his cell.

He had not gone more than a dozen shuffling steps when, as if out of the sacred air exhaled by the Holy Ghost, Bertrand the porter appeared at his side and took his left arm, gently but firmly. The porter had, in fact, noticed the figure of Fra Paulos on the bench when he first took his spot in the garden that afternoon, and had been watching out for his return to the main building. He knew that evening services had started. Although it was most unusual for Fra Paulos to be late for chapel services, Bertrand and everyone else was prepared to make exceptions for one as old and revered as he was. He was a little worried that Fra Paulos might have been feeling too fragile to join the community at prayer. That day was certainly not far away, if it had not already arrived, and he knew it.

"Fra Paulos, you are not at Vespers?" His voice was gentle, inquiring.

"Not tonight, Bertrand. Tonight, I am communing with God in solitude, in the beauty of the garden."

"Ah, I see. May I take you to supper, and then let Abbas Matthaeus know of your whereabouts?"

"Bertrand, you are a kind fellow, but no. That is not necessary. The abbot will be able to imagine why I am not with the group, and Fra Luke can explain the details. But if you would escort me to my cell, I would be most grateful."

"May I bring you something to eat in your cell, then?" This was most certainly not standard monastery practice, unless a brother was too ill to join the group for meals, but Bertrand loved the old man and would have cooked him a meal by himself, if it had been necessary. He was willing to take the punishment if Abbas Matthaeus was in a mood and decided not to allow the exception for the oldest member of their community. That would have been unusual, but it was known to happen on occasion. The abbot was human, after all.

Fra Paulos was looking straight ahead. He paused. He wanted to say, "No, thank you," since he had no desire to eat anything, but because he feared that his abstention from prayers **and** from supper might make the brothers worry too much about his health, he said, "Perhaps just a little bread and a cup of wine?"

It was on the tip of Bertrand's tongue to say, "Just like the Last Supper of our Lord," when he realized that it might, in fact, be Fra Paulos's 'Last Supper' before he went to meet his maker, and so, tucking away the thought with a shiver, he merely smiled and said, "Of course, my dear brother. I will bring them to you."

Fra Paulos lay on his narrow bed, fully clothed. He did not remove his sandals, nor his outer tunic, as was his usual custom before going to sleep; neither did he kneel on the stone floor for his final prayers of the day. He was so very tired. His head was swimming from the effort of getting back to his cell. He had been so thankful for Bertrand's help.

The Gallic man had been with the brothers for so long now that Paulos hardly remembered a time when he did not guard the door to the monastery. Bertrand always kept an eye on his whereabouts, in case he stumbled or became disoriented, which sometimes happened these days, when he would find him and return him without making a fuss, so that no one else knew quite how much he depended on his help. To be dependent was horribly embarrassing for a man who had traveled far and wide in his prime and had never been lost, not even once!

All the same, it would have been a very bad thing if he had fallen on the way back from the orange garden, and not been found until the next morning with his lips turned blue and a rime of frost in his hair.

Fra Paulos lay on his back in his narrow bed, said a prayer for the end of the day, and let his mind wander freely. As was the case most nights, into his head swam the face of Aethelreda of the Cantii, with her hair as yellow as the dried grasses on the Ravenna hills in late summer, and her eyes as blue as the agate in the Pope's tiara.

The last time he had seen her had been his third missionary trip to Britain, when he had found her still ruling her people, and with hair no longer golden but as silver as the moonlight reflected on a lake. Even so, she had been beautiful to his eyes. They had sat by her hearth and talked until everyone else was asleep, and then they had remained together, on the bench by the fire, until they had fallen asleep in each other's arms, where they were found by Aethelreda's servant in the morning. Paulos guessed that the servants thought they might have behaved as man and wife when they were left alone. After all, when Aethelreda had recognized him in her doorway, she had cried out and flung herself into his arms as if he had been a lover returning after a long absence.

But his relationship with Aethelreda was different from most relationships involving a man and a woman. From the time they had met, they had been drawn to each other, that was true, but at first it was simply mutual admiration. He was fascinated by a woman who was as smart as any man, and as tough. She was a leader of her people. She was a nurturer and a warrior, both. He knew of no one in Ravenna or Rome who filled those dual roles. Even the Abbess of the convent in Ravenna was not the proud leader that he saw in Aethelreda, who was also much fairer to the eye than the stout Abbess.

Aethelreda was equally enthralled by Fra Paulos. He was a man who was learned, and yet he treated her with respect and gentleness. She had not witnessed or experienced such behavior from the men among her own people. And even though she knew that Paulos did not think so himself, he was a fine looking man. He was tall and vigorous, with a head of dark hair, only very slightly disfigured by his tonsure. His features were balanced, his nose strong but not too big, his eyebrows not too bushy, and his teeth were white and regular. She thought he was fair to the eye, and she told him so, to his acute embarrassment.

It had taken him a little while to realize that Aethelreda had no idea about the lifestyle of a monk, although there was no reason that she should have known. Before the Roman occupation, the Britons had their own religious men and women, but they had still married and had produced children. The fact that he had sworn an oath of celibacy was shocking to her. She could not comprehend why anyone, man or woman, would deprive themselves of so basic a need. By the time her hair was silvered with age, she had experienced enough of the cruelty of men to understand why a woman might choose celibacy over being the object of some man's lust for power, but for a man to choose celibacy remained a mystery to her.

The first time that he and Fra Augustus had traveled to Britain, because of coming into contact with Aethelreda and her people, they had stayed near their original camp on the coast for most of the first week after they arrived.

They were only allotted six months for their mission. It was supposed to take a week, possibly two, depending on who they met on the way, to get from where they landed on the coast near to Duovernum Cantiacorum,

where it was hoped they would find the Pope's brother and also some local Christians who would contribute to their mission to convert the holdouts from the faith. After the first three days of stasis, Augustus complained. It had been his understanding that they would not have to go in search of the locals. He thought they would confront the Roman travelers. But no one had come to see them except for Aethelreda and her men.

After a spirited discussion, Paulos agreed that they could leave two guards at camp and the rest of the men could go on excursions of not more than two hours' duration, to see who they could find. But to everyone's disappointment, they found nothing, and no one. Aethelreda's settlement must have been very carefully hidden away from view, and they must have landed on a very sparsely populated part of the Kentish coast. Augustus was frustrated.

Paulos had been spending most of his time teaching Aethelreda Latin, and simultaneously learning the Kentish language. They spent a good part of each day wandering in the woods together while they apparently identified trees and birds, and shared each other's words for the creatures that they discovered. Their sporadic laughter could be heard by those in the camp. The two clearly delighted in each other's company. Augustus burned with resentment when he heard the whispered rumors. He would never have suspected that his studious and serious and devout brother would fall prey to a woman, and a heathen one at that.

On the fourth evening, Augustus was so disappointed by the lack of contact they had made with the locals that he pulled Paulos aside and reminded him that their mission was not to bond with one family and one tribe (in his mind he thought, "especially not with one woman"), but to evangelize all of the Kentish people, as they made their way to Canterbury where Pope Innocent's brother had last been seen. He owned the fact that he was impatient to move inland and meet whoever was placed in their way by the providence of God. He also admitted (to himself) another reason he was anxious to meet the locals. They were living on very sparse rations, only supplemented by a few fish and a couple of rabbits that one of the guards had caught the night before. Augustus hoped that a visit to a Cantii settlement might provide a better variety of food than the ground grains mixed with water that they had brought with them, and which they heated over the fire and ate twice a day.

Paulos tried in vain to convince his brother that his contact with Aethelreda would yield fruit but required some patience. He was well aware that they needed to move on, but he hoped that some proficiency in the local language would be a huge advantage and would help them all to expand their influence beyond the small, isolated Kentish tribe they had discovered (or rather, which had discovered them) to the Britons in general. He felt that the appearance in his life of a Kentish woman who was teaching him her language was a gift from God. What he did not see was that it was obvious to all how enraptured he was with the beautiful Kentish Queen, and that his enthrallment was like a spoonful of salt in a war wound for Augustus. Augustus himself was a plain man. His childhood bout with the pox had left him scarred, and his hair was thin so that his tonsure did him few favors in assuring people of his masculinity. It galled him that the woman did not seem to know, or else she did not care, that Paulos was a celibate monk who had taken a vow of chastity. And it galled him even more to see that Paulos was not trying very hard to impress such a fact on the woman.

Augustus was a thinker and a planner, a quiet man; and it was his cordial relationship with Paulos that had pushed the Pope toward including him in the mission, since they would be thrust together for the duration of a long and arduous journey, first diagonally across Gaul on horseback, and then across the ocean to the island occupied by the Britons. Paulos's companion would need to be the kind of person who would adjust calmly to possibly dangerous and threatening situations, and at the same time who would be steady in his friendship and support. The Pope thought that Augustus would fill both of those roles.

He also knew that Augustus owed a debt of gratitude to his own brother, Flavius, and would do his best to find him. As far as the religious mission they were sent out on, the Pope was confident of the success of Paulos to charm the local people. He was charismatic and outgoing. But he was less sure of Augustus. His hope was that the two of them would support each other as a team and win over all the heathen hearts to Christ and come back with good news about his brother.

Augustus was angry at being held on the coast by a woman who, as far as he could tell, was only the queen of a very small group of people. He could not even persuade the woman to take him and show her settlement to them, although he had tried. But he was not going to give up. He quizzed Paulos about her origins. Was she truly the leader of her tribe? How, then, had that come about? Was it common among her people to be led by a woman? He had heard of Boadicea, Queen of the Iceni and known by her own people as Boudicca. He knew that she had given the Romans an enormous amount of trouble, but that had been over four hundred years before. He also wondered why Aethelreda was so light of hair, and eyes, and skin, when her men were all much darker. He wondered if she was not, in fact, a Briton at all, but the offspring of a Viking raider.

Paulos had, by then, a vocabulary of several hundred Kentish words, but he was by no means sure of the grammar of the language and could only ask Aethelreda the most basic questions. And even then, when he asked something like, "Are you the leader of your people?" and she replied, "Yes," he could not work out how to ask her if it was a common situation among her people. And even if he could have done that, he would not have been able to understand an answer of more than a few words. The desire for such information had to be set aside for the time being.

Paulos could answer a few of his men's questions about her leadership, however, and he did so. He had found out that Aethelreda was the daughter of a Briton named Carvilius, the previous leader of her people. Her people were the Cantii. Her father was dead, and so was her mother. That was the sum total of his knowledge of her origin at that time.

Six days into the mission, Augustus took matters into his own hands. Instead of going with the others on yet another fruitless search for a settlement of Kentish people, which was making him more and more angry, he followed Paulos and Aethelreda into the woods at a distance.

Carefully staying out of sight, he watched the two of them walk a good way together, without conversation, and without communication, except for once when a bird called out a loud, trilling, bell-like call and Aethelreda, turning, grabbed Paulos's hand and said, "Wood warbler."

Fra Augustus stifled the urge to snicker. He spoke and read ecclesiastical Latin, which was the Latin that was used in the church and spoken in the monastery. In ecclesiastical Latin there were no 'w' sounds. The words 'wood warbler' sounded like silly gibberish to him. Her familiarity with Paulos also annoyed him. No one grabbed a monk's hand without permission.

The two walked on, unaware that they were being followed. They ducked under low tree branches and skirted around the occasional stump of an ancient fallen tree, with Augustus following at a distance, until they came to a small glade, which was dappled with sunlight. The observant Augustus wondered whether the trees had perhaps been thinned out in that area to allow access to a very large, very old oak tree that stood at the edge of the glade. Augustus knew that the ancient people of Britain had worshipped trees. He felt the hairs on his arms rise at the thought of what might have happened in that place. Somehow the pagan gods of the ancient Britons were far more terrifying than the heathen gods of his own people.

Paulos appeared unconcerned that he might be entering a place of pagan prayer. He had only given a quickly passing thought to why the woods had thinned out to create such a pleasant little grove, and had not let the thought settle in his mind. It had become hard for him to attend to anything else when he was with Aethelreda.

Fra Paulos and Aethelreda chose a spot and sat down on the ground, side by side, close enough to each other that they could have touched, but yet they did not. They sat, both appearing to simply be enjoying the pleasant sunshine, the bright birdsong, and the soft spring air. Augustus waited tensely. Between bird calls it was so silent that he was afraid the couple would hear his breathing. He hoped that he was not going to witness his brother break one of his monastic vows, which was what he fully expected to see, but the two continued to sit in silence, with neither one looking at the other.

Augustus was just about to turn and head back to camp in frustration when Paulos pulled his breviary out from where it had been tucked inside his habit. Augustus watched as the two of them bowed their heads and Paulos read a prayer from the book. From the easy, relaxed positioning of their bodies it was obvious that it was not the first time they had prayed together. Augustus felt a wave of shame pass through him as he watched the innocent tableau in front of him. He wondered why he would have doubted a man as stalwart in his faith as Paulos.

When the prayer was over, Paulos showed the rather battered little book to Aethelreda, pointing to the words, one at a time, while he pronounced them. Augustus realized with relief and amazement that he was teaching her to read!

Augustus's first emotion was relief, but fairly quickly that was followed by impatience and anger. It was not so much that Paulos was teaching a woman to read, which was a skill that was totally unnecessary for a female, or that it was a sin to be teaching in an unsupervised situation with one man and one woman alone together, or even that they might be meeting in a place filled with pagan spirits; the issue for Augustus was twofold: that it was being kept a secret from him, and even more so, that it was wasting precious time for everyone!

Chapter Three

The Bath

Finally, Aethelreda conceded that the time had come to show the Romans her village, which they called Lower Combe, named for its location in a small valley, hidden away from the main trails and roads. She left in the hour before dawn and arrived mid-morning with several men and several extra ponies for the Romans to ride on the return journey.

She would have shown the visitors her community sooner, but she had held back. She was not certain of her motivation, at first. It was not, she felt sure, that she did not trust the men, although they were not all as trustworthy as Paulos and Augustus. Several of the men had told her by gestures and body language that they would have taken her if she had been willing. She was not willing, and she made sure to never be alone with any of them, save Paulos. No, it gradually became clear to her that the delay was because she knew that the Romans would move on once they had seen her village, and met her people, and she wanted to learn as much from them as she could before they left.

Her grasp of Latin had burgeoned in the short time that she had been in the company of the learned Paulos. For his part, he was astonished at the speed with which she had learned. Her memory was prodigious. She knew three times as many words of Latin as he did of Kentish, and that was not without a massive effort on her part to pass on her language to him. He seemed to find her language a difficult one to learn. She had also begun to read! It was her pride and joy to be able to decipher the marks on the paper in Paulos's little book. She felt powerful in her knowledge, and she wanted so much more.

Aethelreda was the leader of her people although she was only young. She had figured she had been on this earth fewer years than she could count on her fingers and toes. She was perhaps eighteen, but she was not sure, and neither was anyone else. Her people had tried to get her to take a husband because she was already past the age when most young men and women chose a mate, but she was too busy learning how to lead her people, and besides, they were an isolated group and almost all related in some way. She met men from other groups on market days, but there was no one that she felt was suitable for her, despite many men's attempts to woo her, and many of her people's attempts at matching her. She was looking for someone strong, intelligent, someone who would respect her, and whom she could respect, equally. She had met all the likely candidates from among her own people. That meant she would have to look further abroad to someone from another tribe, or even from another country.

Her father, Carvilius, had suffered from the same problem when he was searching for a wife. In the end, he had taken for wife a woman from the neighboring Cantiaci group. She had grown up with them, but she was not one of them. She had been left behind as an infant by a group of Nordic raiders who had planned to settle in Kent, but had been driven out by the Britons. The young child's mother had been killed in a skirmish, and the girl was being cared for by a local woman on the day the Norsemen left the inhospitable shores of Kent to return to their home. Not being able to locate her on the morning they planned to leave, under cover of the darkness, they decided that she was better off with the Britons, and left her behind. The Cantiaci named her Merewenne, which meant 'maiden', and raised her as one of their own. She had the flaxen hair and blue eyes of her Nordic people. Because of her coloring, some thought she was a witch, and Aethelreda's father had certainly been bewitched by her. But she had been a good wife to him. She was fiercely strong and had borne him ten children before he died.

Aethelreda was their first child, and she had inherited the flaxen hair and intense blue eyes of her mother, who had loved her unreservedly. Merewenne had steadfastly insisted that she herself should rule

Lower Combe when her husband had been killed those two summers ago. She saw no reason why the role of tribal leader should not be filled by an intelligent, strong woman like she was, or like her first-born, and had often said as much in clan meetings. It was a known fact that they were not the only tribe to be led by a woman. Merewenne had several much younger sons, and there were some older male cousins, who were not widely respected because of their dissolute living habits. Merewenne was a force to be reckoned with, and her will prevailed. She ruled well, and she raised her daughter to be a ruler after she died.

Then Merewenne had been taken by a fever last summer. That had been a huge blow for Aethelreda, to be left an orphan at such a young age and expected to become the leader; but her mother's Nordic blood ran strongly in her veins. She did not mourn for long and she did not shy away from leadership, but moved into the role of tribal chief as if she had been born to it, which indeed she had.

The Romans were eager to finally see a village in Britain. They had been led to believe that the Britons had been completely Romanized and lived in towns and cities like those of the Roman Empire. They imagined great stone buildings, plazas, arenas, and that they would be surrounded by luxury. Aethelreda and her men led them by a tortuous route to the small village, hidden in a valley, about five miles from the coast. It was a wonder to Quintus and the others that they had not come across the village in their explorations, but it was just outside the travel restrictions that Paulos and Augustus had placed on them, and as they found out, the people of Lower Combe did not want to be discovered. Quintus was also suspicious that they had been led on a circuitous route so that they would still be uncertain of the location of the village, even after they had visited. He had to admire the craftiness of the Kentish people. They were not as simple as they appeared.

When they finally arrived, the village was not at all what they expected. It was as if they were stepping back into the past, and it was nothing at all like the towns they had come from around Rome. The men rode into the stone-walled enclosure behind Aethelreda and her guards. Her people looked up from their tasks as they rode in. Most bowed or nodded in respect as they paused in their digging and planting. Several appeared to be dyeing cloth in large wooden vats, and further away, citizens were tending their sheep and goats. Many of them dropped what they were doing and came closer to see the strangers who were following their queen, but they kept at a respectful distance.

Within the enclosure there were perhaps eight or ten large circular thatch-roofed dwellings that seemed to house both people and animals, and several rectangular smaller ones. The whole complex appeared to consist of dwellings for fewer than a hundred people, men, women, and children. It reminded Paulos and Augustus of some of the primitive farming communities in the remoter parts of their own country, except that the buildings of Lower Combe were round, whereas their own were rectangular.

They soon discovered that the main industry of Aethelreda's people was weaving and dyeing the wool that was shorn off the sheep they raised. They made and sold woolen cloth to other tribes in the area at combined markets which took place on each new moon.

Paulos was astonished at the variety of colors that he saw in the cloth that they made. He inquired after the dyeing process because he knew that they had no exotic powders and dyes from the East, and yet their cloth was as vibrant as any he had seen in Rome or Gaul. He discovered that the lavender, like that of Aethelreda's gown, was made by dyeing the fabric twice. It was dyed once with the leaves of the woad plant and then given a second dyeing with a solution made from the roots of the madder plant. The double-dyeing made that fabric more expensive than some of the other colors, and it was prized by royalty. The dark brown color worn by many of the villagers came from walnuts, which were plentiful, the yellow from the flowers and stalks of the weld plant, and so many other hues that almost every color of the rainbow was represented in the array of cloth that Paulos could see. There was even a light bright blue cloth that matched the color of Aethelreda's eyes.

He took it all in. He knew that many of the Britons had embraced their Roman conquerors and had taken up the Roman way of life. But he also knew that Aethelreda's people had not done so. They had remained steadfastly apart and had clung to the old ways of living. He had supposed that people who had so recently been living the life of a primitive people, circumscribed by the resources in their immediate location, would be living lives of austerity, with very little choice in what they ate, how they lived, and what they wore. It appeared that he had been wrong in coming to that conclusion. It seemed that they had made conscious choices about what they would embrace of the foreign culture, and what they would turn away from. It also seemed that their own culture was not as primitive as he had believed.

The Romans were treated with suspicion at first by Aethelreda's people. She had told the Cantii that the men, who had been observed on the coast on the afternoon that she had sent people to gather seaweed, were not a threat to them. She told them they had come to talk about their God, and that they were peaceful men. These facts she had gleaned from her talks with Paulos.

Her own people had secretly watched the Romans set up their encampment from a hidden vantage point, and then they had returned to Aethelreda with a report of what they had seen. They told her that the group was a small one, therefore not likely to fight or invade. It was even suggested that they might have arrived unintentionally, perhaps having been blown off course. Paulos smiled when he heard that detail. Captain

Quintus did not smile when the story was relayed to him. But even with Aethelreda's encouragement that the visitors were benign, the hatred of Romans ran deep in the Cantii, and they were very cautious toward the visitors.

Fra Paulos noticed that Aethelreda was clearly the leader of the Cantii. He observed that her people deferred to her, but there were other men who seemed to be held in high esteem as well. Two men in particular seemed to want to be included in the decision-making, and the whole group did not noticeably relax in the presence of the strangers until they had heard from those men that it was safe to do so.

The men were cousins of Aethelreda, the sons of King Carvilius's sister, and they were a constant challenge to her leadership since they believed that even though Aethelreda was Carvilius's child, they were men, and hence were more suited to leadership than she was. It gave Paulos cause to worry on her behalf when he noticed that it was only after the Cantii had heard from the two men that they accepted the Roman visitors. Only then did the women smile and the children come near with curious looks on their faces.

Someone asked about the peculiar haircuts of Paulos and Augustus. Paulos could tell what the man was asking when he made a circular motion with his index finger on the crown of his own head. Aethelreda gave him an answer that Paulos did not understand, but it made her people laugh. Paulos discovered later that she had said they had a bald spot on their heads because they had so many big thoughts that their hair had fallen out! He did not particularly enjoy being laughed at, but he realized that the monk's haircut was rather strange the first time you saw one. Once he explained that some monks in his home country shaved their heads as a sign of humility, since a shaved head was often an attribute of a slave, most people saw the significance.

But it was a step too far for them to understand that Christians saw themselves as servants of Jesus Christ. In any case, given a few more weeks, neither he nor Augustus would be identifiable by their tonsures, having given up the task of shaving since they had arrived in Britain. He hoped the Lord Jesus would forgive them. They had lost some soap supplies on the journey over when it was accidentally washed overboard while Paulos was shaving Augustus's pate, and it was just too uncomfortable to scrape the dulling blade over a bare scalp. Paulos was not interested in self-mortification, and neither was Augustus. They would resume the tonsuring once they had returned to their home.

The visit to Lower Combe was a successful one if you did not count the scowls of Aethelreda's cousins. The Cantii begged the Romans to stay the night so that they could cook a feast for them, and for themselves. It had been a long time since they had had any significant reason to revel. They did not often have visitors. A deer was killed, and the smell of the meat being seared over the cooking fire was truly delicious to Paulos's men, who had not had fresh-cooked meat in several weeks.

It did not take much to persuade them to stay, although Paulos was worried about his men who had remained on the coast, and he wished they could get a message to them, telling them of the delay. He hoped they were smart enough to stay where they were and would not go running off into the woods in search of their leaders. They had been told to stay put for twenty-four hours. Paulos also felt rather selfish thinking of them back at the camp eating stale grain and camp bread. He planned to ask if they could take a portion or two of the meat back for the guards.

The evening was rowdy. The Cantii had some kind of beverage that seemed to make them drunk very quickly, and they drank a lot of it. Aethelreda said it was made with grain and with honey and matured in barrels. She called it 'beer'. It was tasty and potent. Paulos and Augustus noticed that their men took advantage of the situation and drank plenty of the ale. The men also disappeared before the night was over and Paulos supposed each of them had gone to bed with a local woman of their choice. He remembered Aethelreda's comment that the clan was very close-knit and also closely related. He wondered if perhaps the spreading of their Roman seed was a beneficial thing for future generations, and he did not judge them for it.

Fra Paulos found himself in a difficult situation for a monk when, as the reveling died down and the revelers stole away to bed down for the night, Aethelreda turned her eyes on him and fixed him in her gaze. She was truly beautiful, he realized, even though he was not prone to make such judgements about women. The dim, warm light of the dying fire made her eyes look dark and her lashes cast a shadow across her cheek. She was relaxed and happy. Her smile was such that his guts twisted within him, and his heart did something peculiar when she turned it toward him. Reaching out her hand and taking his hand in hers, she asked in a soft voice, "Fra Paulos, would you join me in my bed tonight?"

Paulos's heart rate increased even more. He realized that he was being offered a valuable gift, and how he responded was crucial to his good relations with her, and also to their relations with the Cantii; but he was bound by his monastic vows to refuse her tempting offer. He felt like Adam must have felt when Eve first offered him the delicious fruit of the Tree of Knowledge.

"Oh, my dear Aethelreda," he stammered, "your offer is truly generous and so hard for me to resist. But I must. I have told you why." He spoke in Latin, and he could only hope that she understood. She and Paulos were able to communicate reasonably well by then, in gestures, in broken Brittonic on his part, and slightly less stumbling Latin on hers.

What Aethelreda understood did not require interpretation. She understood that her offer, never made to any other man, was being turned down. Her cheeks flushed and she jerked her hand away in anger. She was deeply disappointed. He had tried to explain before that he had made an oath before God that he would not lie with a woman, but she had never really believed his story. She did not understand why God would require that of any man. And even more importantly, she did not understand why any man would agree to such a thing. Her lips were tight with anger and her eyes flashed as she exclaimed, "Then I hope you will enjoy sleeping in the byre with the sheep and goats, because that is the only other place I will offer you!"

She was being petty, and she knew it, but she was personally offended by his refusal, and her reaction was purely automatic. It came from the place within her that was always fighting for what she needed in a world of powerful men. And there was another thing. Despite what Paulos had said, the more she got to know him, the more she thought he might make a good husband for her.

Paulos did not argue with the Cantii Queen. He had been caught in a very difficult situation. For him, there was no defensible response other than the one he had given to Aethelreda, although he found himself wishing it had been otherwise. His greatest fear was that by his refusal to sleep with her he had spoiled their beautiful relationship and he did not want to damage it further by arguing with her about the beauty and purity of the vows he had made when he became a monk. He sighed deeply and regretfully. The sheep and goats would at least keep him warm in the chilly British air.

The following morning, when all but Paulos woke with pounding heads, Aethelreda demanded a meeting with Paulos. One of her manservants went to the sheepfold to find him. He had had a cold and uncomfortable night, and his demeanor was not improved by being told to present himself before Queen Aethelreda, immediately. He was dirty, and he had not even had time to say his morning prayers.

Aethelreda's maidservant was brushing her mistress's light golden hair when he arrived, tagging along behind the manservant, smelling of sheep manure, hungry, disheveled, and very low of spirit.

She looked up as he entered and smiled sympathetically. Looking at him with gentle eyes, she said, "Oh, Fra Paulos! I am truly sorry. I should not have thrown you out last night. It does not look as though you had a very good night at all." There was more mirth than regret in her voice.

"It was as good as could be expected," he answered tersely. He felt disgustingly filthy and could hardly return her gaze as she looked him up and down with her clear blue eyes.

She smiled again, and gesturing toward her servant, who was placing supplies of some sort into a basket, she said, "I am about to take my morning bath. I believe that you also need a good wash. Will you join me?"

Paulos was startled. He could not believe the persistence of this woman. Apparently, his refusal to accept her advances the night before had not deterred her at all. Now she was trying to seduce him into her bath. He smiled to cover up his discomfort.

"I would very much appreciate a bath, certainly, but it would not be proper for me to bathe with you."

She gave him a sly smile that crinkled the corners of her eyes in a way he found most attractive.

"We Cantii often share our bath with others. There is no harm in it. I am just offering you basic hospitality, nothing more."

Paulos said nothing. He did not know a way to gracefully get out of the situation, especially after her reaction the night before, which he did not want repeated. As he pondered what to do, he found himself wondering how Augustus had fared that evening and where he was. It was only a little after daylight, and so he thought that perhaps he, like all the others, was still asleep. One thing he knew was that Augustus had not had to bed down with the animals, and so he was probably tucked up comfortably with the servants.

Paulos considered Aethelreda's request very gravely. There would be witnesses, and maybe if he remained partially clothed, and did not touch her, it would be appropriate. And if none of his people knew, he would be safe from questions and assumptions.

Holding his gaze with her astoundingly blue eyes, Aethelreda said, "Fra Paulos, it would be rude of you to refuse me! Even ruder than you were in refusing me last night."

Paulos flushed. "Aethelreda, forgive me if what I did seemed rude. A monk may not sleep with a woman, as I have told you. I could perhaps bathe with you, however, if it is simply an act of hospitality among the Cantii, as you say, and we are not alone together." Her eyes lit up. She spoke quickly to her maidservant and her manservant, and a stack of linen cloths and some bristle brushes with long wooden handles were rapidly gathered and placed in a second basket, along with a tunic which was held up to get the measure of Paulos and was presumably to replace his soiled garments. Then they all left the hut and walked to the edge of the river, as the sun came completely over the horizon and its light tipped everything with the mellow gold of dawn.

But when they reached the edge of the stream, they did not stop. Instead, the little bathing party turned upstream and walked for a few more minutes until they reached an area where the water came tumbling down from above, pouring over some rocks, and creating a series of small waterfalls. The ferns and mosses that edged the stream looked lush and luminous in the soft light of the early morning. The light spray from the carousing water misted those standing nearby.

Paulos was surprised by the whole early morning hike. By 'bath', he thought Aethelreda had meant a soak in a tub. Even in the monastery they had a series of bath rooms for the men in the community to use once a week. But for the monks, bathing was a private activity. He had heard about the bath houses in Rome where bathing was a communal activity and where men and women could bathe together, and he had been distressed by the whole idea, especially when he heard about the images of men and women engaged in intimate acts that were portrayed in the mosaics decorating the bath houses. He did not expect that situation to be played out in the culture of the Cantii, but he was even more distressed by the thought of having a small private tub, as he knew some Romans did, and being an invited guest to such a private ritual.

By contrast, the experience of bathing outdoors was much less intimate than what he had imagined, and he was glad that he had not made a big issue of it. With his back turned, he did not need to see Aethelreda at her toilette at all. Gratefully, he disrobed and let the water tumble over him.

Once the shock of the cold water was over, it was rejuvenating. The maidservant passed him a handful of some leaves and stems that she called soap wort, which produced a kind of soapy mixture when, as instructed, he rubbed it all over himself. Then the manservant scrubbed his back, torso, and arms with a long-handled brush until his flesh tingled and he felt invigorated and renewed. The whole experience was unexpectedly delightful, and he felt an upsurge of the joy of the goodness of God's creation when he came out of the water, as if he had been cleansed physically and spiritually. It almost felt like a baptism.

He made a short prayer of thanksgiving to God as he dried off with the linen cloth, dressed in the clean light brown tunic that the servant passed to him, and put on his own boots.

Looking around, he saw with shock that Aethelreda's maidservant was still grooming her hair and that his hostess was not yet fully clothed. At first, he looked quickly away, but he could not help himself and turned back to look at her again. She was sitting naked from the waist up while her wet, heavy hair was being braided. She seemed completely unconscious of her semi-nudity. Paulos looked at her with open admiration. She was beautiful and innocent, and he could not think that watching her was a sinful thing. He felt nothing but gratitude that God had created such beauty in a woman.

But then he became aware of a discomfort in his loins that was increasing as he watched her, and he began to feel anxious. He turned away, wondering what she had actually thought about his motives for agreeing to bathe with her. He was wondering that himself. Things were no longer as simple as they had been half an hour ago.

Like the first man, Adam, he found himself wanting to avoid blame and condemnation. He wanted to get back to the others before they knew what he had done. Whether it was initially innocent or not, the act of agreeing to bathe with Aethelreda had awakened self-knowledge for him. He could be aroused by a beautiful woman.

He knew that Augustus, in particular, would be stunned to hear what he had done, and Paulos found himself rather amused by that thought. Augustus had such a high opinion of him, looking up to him as a role model. Little did Augustus know that it could have been so much worse for his monastic vows than that innocent bath in the river, if Aethelreda had had her way.

And little did Paulos know that it **had** been so much worse for Augustus, who was, at that moment, waking up in the bed of a Cantii maiden. He had, like most of the men, had a little too much of the good beer the night before, and being partly inebriated, had allowed himself to set aside his inhibitions and be wooed by a pretty young woman with white teeth and lovely dark hair. The first thoughts of his foggy mind after his night of reveling was that he was unsure what had happened in her bed. He had no memory of what he had done, if anything. All he remembered was the sinking feeling as he lay down on the straw mattress and his head spun around and around. He remembered the woman's face over his, and that was all. He hoped that he had not made a fool of himself with her. He had never before been with a woman.

And then he condemned himself for not being more worried about the state of his immortal soul, if he had, in fact, broken his vow of chastity. He was going to have to confess his sins to Fra Paulos, no matter what – that was certain. What was also certain was that he could no longer be contemptuous of Paulos and his relationship with Aethelreda. He remembered that Jesus had said you could only throw the first stone at a condemned person if you yourself had not sinned. And he had most likely sinned.

***

It was a rather bedraggled group that rode back into the Roman camp later that day. The men who had been left guarding the camp were very glad to see them, even though everyone except Paulos looked decidedly worse for wear. They rejoiced at the gift of the haunch of deer that had been brought back for them, and immediately cut into it with their stout knives, despite the fact that it was not the customary time of day for a meal. All the others, except Paulos, made immediate attempts to bathe in the stream and then spent the rest of the day resting in the shade and regretting that they had drunk so much of the ale.

Augustus thought that Paulos was surprisingly understanding of their behavior. But when he said his confession to his brother that night and heard Paulos's confession in return, he understood. The two monks had, like all of the others, both been tempted, tested, and had only partially resisted. Both realized that they would have to do penance for their sins, and both were filled with remorse and with gratitude for the love of a God who was forgiving of the downfalls that so often overcame them.

Paulos rather enjoyed the regular act of confessing his sins to his brother Augustus. He found the practice spiritually freeing. First, the act of thinking back over the ways in which he had fallen short since his last confession was, in some mysterious way, a great relief for him. Not that he enjoyed thinking about his sinfulness, but rather that in doing so he felt that he was moving toward greater sanctification each day. He supposed that his satisfaction in the rite of confession might be evidence that he was too self-involved, but it was the verbalization of his shortcomings, followed by his petition for forgiveness, that made the rite so powerful. There was nothing that God would not forgive, if he was properly penitent, and starting afresh was a gift that only God could give.

Despite Augustus's frequent promptings, he had not mentioned Aethelreda in any of his previous confessions. He was certain that there was nothing that he had to atone for with regard to her. It was not a sin to look fondly at a woman who amazed him with her intelligence and her zest for life and learning. It was not a sin to walk with her in the woods and to enjoy the sound of her voice as she named birds, and trees, and wildflowers for him. It was not a sin to sit with her in a place that had an aura of spirituality that did not come from the God that he worshipped, even though he felt uncomfortable when he thought about that. It was not even a sin to wish to have more time with her, although he had to admit that whether it was a sin or not really depended on his motivation for wanting to do so. He was sure that he wanted only to learn more of the language of the Cantii. At least, he had been sure until that morning when he was with her as they bathed in the stream.

Augustus made his confession first. After the opening prayer and the required liturgical statements, he plunged right in.

"Fra Paulos, I am ashamed to have to admit this, but I was with a woman last night." Paulos said nothing, leaving a space for Augustus to go into more detail. "I might have sinned with her, but I cannot be sure."

Paulos looked quizzically at Augustus. He wondered how anyone could be uncertain of what he had done in bed with a woman. He was a tiny bit disappointed with Augustus, whom he considered his equal in so many ways, including intellectually. His confession and his attempt to ameliorate the seriousness of his sin was making him sound imbecilic.

Augustus continued, hesitantly. "I do not remember what I did after I went with her to her bed, but that is where I woke up in the morning. Clearly, I had much too much of that Cantii beer to drink than was good for me. It dimmed my moral judgement. I know I have some personal responsibility in what may or may not have happened, but I hope you will agree that because of the beer, my actions, whatever took place, were not really my own." Before Paulos could make any comments, Augustus rushed on, "And so, I confess to you that it was bad judgement on my behalf to drink too much beer. May God forgive me."

Paulos looked at Augustus's slightly flushed face. In the light of what he had done himself, he was mildly amused at Augustus's remorse and his self-justification.

"That is what you wish to confess? Drinking to excess?"

"I have no knowledge of any other sins. I sincerely hope I was steadfast."

Paulos spoke slowly to Augustus. He was frustrated by his brother's obtuseness. "Of course, if you had been truly concerned about what you had done, there was a way that you could have found out, and perhaps for the woman's sake you should have taken that recourse."

"You mean that when morning came around, I should have asked the maiden what had taken place?"

Paulos was relieved that Augustus had not completely lost his senses. At least he had apparently considered that option. Augustus flushed even redder and went on.

"Yes. I know I should have. And I considered it, but I found I was too embarrassed to do so. And so, like a coward, I left before she woke."

Paulos was taken aback by the cowardly and unmannerly behavior of his fellow monk. He found himself imagining what the maid would have felt when she woke in the morning to find herself alone and deserted. He imagined that would have felt terrible, regardless of whatever had happened the night before. His voice when he spoke to Augustus was curt.

"Perhaps, then, you had better confess to unseemly behavior with a maiden, behavior that you do know you indulged in; that is, running off and leaving her without a word. That was very, very uncivil, and exceedingly inconsiderate of her feelings."

Augustus gave Paulos a puzzled look. He found it very strange that Paulos thought it was the greater sin to run off and leave a woman after spending the night with her, than it was to actually spend the night with her. That was not at all what he had expected.

Paulos knew that Augustus would have been expecting him to say something more negative about his suspicious carnal behavior that night, but he decided to ignore it. He thought it better to bide his time until he had to confess his own sins to Augustus. But even though his own self-justification was no less twisted than that of Fra Augustus, he reasoned that the situation was different for him. He felt that he had done nothing wrong. He had not become drunk. He had not slept with a woman. He had been fully in possession of his faculties the whole time.

But even so, there was a doubt in his mind as to his own moral purity. After the event at the river, which he was coming to think of more as a baptism into a new life than a bath, he had allowed thoughts to occupy his mind that he should not have allowed. He was, even at the same time as he was hearing his brother's confession, regretting that he had not spent the night in the bed of Aethelreda. He knew that if he had, unlike Augustus, he would have stayed awake and been aware of every moment that they had been together.

And in that moment, Paulos realized with clarity that perhaps he was the greater sinner of the two brothers. He also knew, with equal clarity, that he was not going to confess it, to Augustus, or to God, even though God surely was already aware.

What Paulos did confess to God, in the presence of Augustus, was that he had bathed with Aethelreda, at her insistence, and that he had enjoyed the experience. He did not mention how his loins had burned when he had seen her partially naked. Nor did he tell Augustus that he had not been able to get the image of her beauty out of his mind ever since, and that he had not wanted to.

Chapter Four

The Brothers Are Uneasy

When Fra Paulos and his band of Romans departed from Lower Combe, they left trouble behind them at the village of the Cantii. Their presence had stirred up old animosities toward the outsiders who had only so recently departed from their four hundred years of occupation of the land. The Cantii had always stayed separate from the cultural colonizing of the Romans. They had continued to live in the style of their fathers and grandfathers. They had resisted the temptation to trade with the imposters. They had refused to learn their language. They had kept their old gods. And the arrival of their former enemies, who they thought had gone away for good, made them very uneasy.

After their night of revelry, Aethelreda's cousins, Segovax and Lugotori, had woken, groggy and befuddled. They did not need to expend any unnecessary energy trying to find out what others in the village had done, because their own servants were a mine of information about who had done what and with whom the night before, and they enjoyed every minute of the time they spent reciting other people's actions to the brothers. It was with much satisfaction that the two of them learned Fra Paulos had spent the night with the sheep and the goats, rather than in the bed of their cousin. They had seen a look in their cousin's eyes when she turned them toward the dark and handsome man named Fra Paulos. It was a look that worried them. They could see that she was besotted. They were certain that she would have picked him for her bedmate after the torches were extinguished that night.

And her obvious attraction to Fra Paulos was a problem. In their opinions, he would not be a suitable mate for their cousin, for a number of reasons, but primarily because both Segovax and Lugotori needed to be in control of whomever she chose for her mate. If they were not, then there would never be a possibility of unseating Aethelreda and ruling in her place.

They were therefore very much relieved to hear that she had fallen out with the Roman visitor the night before. They both wanted a much less threatening man for their cousin, someone who would do their bidding. The Roman monk was much too knowledgeable and cunning, and his henchmen all looked fit, and well trained in the military arts. They were always ready with their thrusting spears and their short swords.

The cousins had their own supporters, but the military knowhow of the Romans was legendary, and combined with those villagers who sided with

Aethelreda, they were unlikely to succeed against them, should they attempt to take power.

If Aethelreda married that man and the foreigners all stayed in their village, the two of them would sink down much lower in the line of succession. They had already lost much time by letting the girl take the leadership role for as long as she had. In that time, she had gathered around her many loyal servants who would back her against them if they dared to vie for control. The longer she was leader, the more loyal the Cantii would become. That was the way of the Cantii. That was how it had been with Carvilius. By the time he died, you would have thought that he was a god in the eyes of most of his people, a fact that the brothers found sickening.

And so, their pleasure in finding out that Aethelreda had not lain with Paulos was based on sinister and selfish motivations.

Unfortunately for them, their satisfaction with Aethelreda's rejection of Fra Paulos was short-lived. Their servants were quick to follow up with a tale that disturbed them, leaving them even angrier than they had been before speaking with their informers. They were told that Aethelreda had asked Fra Paulos to bathe with her that morning, even though she had tossed him out the night before, and that he had agreed to do so. They had been seen heading off to the waterfalls where Aethelreda liked to bathe.

It sounded to the brothers very much as if the dispute between Aethelreda and Paulos had been settled and that their bad feelings toward each other, their tiff, had been smoothed over. That was not a good thing. That was very likely the precursor to the two of them getting together with even stronger passion than if they had not argued. It crossed their minds it was entirely possible that Aethelreda had staged her anger with Fra Paulos the night before, in order to make his submission to her will the more glorious for both of them. She was clever enough and self-serving enough to have done that.

With no time to waste, the two presented themselves almost immediately at the door of Aethelreda's quarters to find out the truth.

They bowed with feigned humility to the porter, as he announced their arrival and gestured for them to enter Aethelreda's great room. A small fire was burning in one of the hearths across the room, to overcome the chill of the morning.

Her quarters were very comfortable. Every time he entered, Lugotori noticed the spaciousness of the great room, with its higher roof than any of the other dwellings, the wooden carvings of complicated interlaced vines and leaves that adorned the walls behind the benches, the thick sheepskins on the generously sized chairs by the hearth, the herbs and rushes on the floor that were freshly strewn at this time of year and smelled so sweet. His own quarters were much more humble and plain. That did not seem right to Lugotori, who of the two brothers was the one who cared the most about the physical comforts of wealth and power. Segovax cared only about the power.

Aethelreda gestured to the two men to be seated, one on her left and the other on her right, with their backs to the door. They took their seats.

The brothers were alike in stature, stocky and strong, with thick, wavy hair that they wore below their shoulders, and a bristling masculinity that surrounded them like an aura. Even though Aethelreda was taller than the average Cantii woman, almost as tall as Fra Paulos, in fact, sitting between the two of them she appeared small and delicate. It was easy to see that the two men were brothers because of their likeness. But it was also easy to tell them apart, because Segovax had been born with a strawberry mark on the brow over his left eye.

Segovax was two years older than Lugotori, and he was the spokesman.

"Cousin, that was a rousing celebration last night," he said cheerily. "I trust that your guests felt honored by our hospitality?"

"I believe they did. I know they enjoyed the meat and the beer."

"As did we both. It has been too long since we were able to carouse together."

Aethelreda knew there was a covert criticism of her leadership in that seemingly innocent statement. She had put a stop to the monthly gatherings that they traditionally enjoyed after each market day, because too much of their inventory of cloth disappeared after such festivities. It had not been a popular decision, and Segovax and Lugotori had opposed it. She knew what Segovax was hinting at, but she remained silent.

As surreptitiously as she could, she looked to see if her guard was paying attention. She hoped that there would not be a violent eviction of her cousins that day, although it would not have been the first time that such a thing had happened. Aethelreda was relieved to see that the guard's body was stiffly at attention and his hand was on his dagger. He was clearly listening to the conversation and on edge; ready to move at the slightest threat.

"We heard that one of your guests was not invited to your bed last night and instead spent the night with the livestock." Segovax smiled, but it was an unpleasant smile. Lugotori snickered.

Holding her regal pose, Aethelreda replied, "He was invited. He did not wish to join me." Aethelreda looked straight ahead at the space between the two men.

Lugotori cut in abruptly, "In truth, I find that hard to believe. And also, despite that, you still invited him to **join** you at your bath this morning? Did he '**join with**' you after that? Did you lie with him?" His tone was sneering.

Aethelreda gave the man a scornful look. "I do not have to answer such impertinent questions. Who shares my bed, or my bath, and with whom I spend my time, these are all things that are my decisions to make." She kept her voice calm and even. She did not wish to escalate the argument. She continued, "And **if I think** anyone else needs to know, **I will tell them**."

There was more than a hint of challenge in her voice, and Lugotori stood up, suddenly. The heavy carved oak stool he had been sitting on rocked back from the force of his movement, but did not fall. The expression on his face was ugly, and his complexion was flushed with anger. He deeply resented being spoken to in such a way by any woman, and he had never come to terms with the fact that this particular woman was his leader.

"Cousin, as your **advisors**" – he laid heavy stress on the word – "we advise you to speak plainly to us."

Aethelreda understood the underlying threat. She did not consider them her advisors, and had told them so many times, but if it helped to keep the peace that day, it was fine with her to humor them. They were close relatives and everyone in the village had to live and work together. If they could do so in harmony, it was to everyone's advantage. But at the same time, she would not be bullied. Turning calmly to Lugotori, she said, "What would you like me to speak plainly about? I have told you that I invited Fra Paulos to my bed, and he refused to come. He says he is a monk. I do not fully understand what that means, except that he has made some kind of promise to be obedient to his god. He has given away all of his possessions, and he is never to lie with a woman. As far as **I** know, he has not broken his vows." Aethelreda's voice was still calm, although a little louder than before. Another guard had appeared at the open doorway. Clearly, Aethelreda's men knew that she was likely to be threatened. Neither Segovax nor Lugotori could see the doorway. Aethelreda could. She had chosen her guests' seats strategically.

Lugotori clenched his jaw. Clearly, Aethelreda was not going to back down from her position of authority. He was still standing, and he moved menacingly toward Aethelreda. With an animal-like growl, he made a motion as if to strike her with his fist for her insolence. His brother leapt to his feet and, grabbing his arm, interceded before Lugotori could make contact with Aethelreda's person. At the same time, both of the guards rushed to Aethelreda's aid. There was a short scuffle, but the two guards had the advantage of seeing what was going to happen before it took place. They grabbed the two brothers and forced their arms behind their backs, walking them swiftly out of the room. The would-be over-throwers left without violence.

But from that time forward, Aethelreda understood that Fra Paulos was a marked man. Her cousins had ways of making things happen that she neither initiated nor endorsed. She was always acting on the knife's edge of power. She knew she was going to have to get to Fra Paulos and warn him that her cousins wanted to be rid of the Romans. She also knew that that was going to be exceedingly difficult to do, without her cousins' knowledge.

And then another possible outcome to the problem came to her quick mind. What if she seemed to play into their hands and told Segovax and Lugotori that she was thinking of leaving with Fra Paulos? Maybe they would be flushed out as the throne-hungry churls that they were. Maybe their delight in her departure would show her people that what she had been saying for the last two years was true, that they were a danger to her future success as a ruler. Maybe that would change the balance of power more to her advantage. She would then 'change her mind' and stay.

She knew that the Cantii had chosen her as their leader after her father's death, because that was a compromise of the traditional way of her people. The next ruler came from the loins of the former ruler. That she was a woman had caused some momentary concern, but her siblings were much too young, and if the oldest son had been raised to leadership, he would have needed an adult to guide him for several years, which would have had the same effect as if Aethelreda had ruled as Queen from the outset. And so Merewenne's wishes that her oldest child, Aethelreda, become the ruler prevailed. Her nephews were in line to lead only in the event of Aethelreda's death, or departure, and the demise of her siblings, although an overthrow by sheer power was not unknown, and had always to be guarded against. Hence the cousins' careful planning and low profile for the last few years.

As Aethelreda's quick brain considered the options, she wondered if she might try to persuade Paulos to talk with her cousins so that it looked like she really was planning to leave.

As a plan to secure her leadership for the foreseeable future, it was multifaceted, and therefore complicated. First, Segovax and Lugotori would have to believe that she meant to leave with Fra Paulos. Then, the temporary joint leadership in her absence would have to be discussed. Finally, Aethelreda hoped that the cousins would be able to be persuaded to see how impossible joint leadership would be without her ameliorating presence. That was the thorniest piece of the whole plan. Her cousins were hardheaded and power hungry, but they might be persuaded to rule jointly if that was the only option apart from allowing Aethelreda to stay in power.

The fact was that Carvilius's daughter, and her leadership, provided the only hope of stability and peace for the Cantii. Aethelreda would have to persuade them that if she stayed, they would be promoted to the rank of Lord, and given voice and vote at the table when decisions were made. It was risky, but it was a compromise she could live with. Assuming all of those elaborate details could be ironed out, she would be persuaded to stay with her people and rule. The only negative was that she would have to let Fra Paulos go for the time being.

Later that afternoon, she summoned the two cousins back to her quarters. She had increased her guard to four hefty, well-armed men. The cousins were ushered in as before. They took their seats as before. A maidservant was standing by with a large jug of beer. Aethelreda offered them some of the beer and they accepted. Once they were noisily imbibing, she began to speak.

"My dear cousins, I do not want to be in conflict with you. My father, the great and beloved Carvilius, was your uncle and he loved you both, almost as much as he loved his own children. We have grown up together. We are kin." The men were silent. Her opening salvo was meaningless to them. They knew she was exaggerating. They simply wanted to get rid of their cousin and take over leadership of the Cantii, by any means possible, at that point.

She continued, "I was not entirely honest with you when we spoke before."

Lugotori looked pointedly at his brother. Was she going to admit that she had, after all, slept with the Roman? That would be one of the few times that he had been right, and his brother had been wrong. That would be too, too sweet for Lugotori, who was always a distant second behind his brother.

"Although we have not yet lain together as man and wife – I was not speaking falsely about that – I do want to be with Fra Paulos. More than anything, I want to go with him when he rides to Canterbury, and then to go on with him, over the sea to his home in Rome. The two of us are in agreement on these things." She thought that her cousins would not be puzzled as to why a monk would take a woman back to his home country as a bride. She knew that their experiences with the Christian religion were very limited.

But she was wrong. Segovax leapt to his feet.

"What?" His face was white, but with shock and anger, not with fear. He could not believe his ears. He never would have thought that his cousin would give up her leadership of the Cantii for such a trivial reason. He leaned toward her, expostulating, "He would break his vows to be with you? What kind of a man is this monk? And what about you, Cousin? You would leave your people and your village to be with him?"

Aethelreda looked down at her feet in mock shame. There was a part of her that was surprised and impressed that Segovax had understood about a monk's vows and that he was capable of such deep thought.

"Please do not think that this has been an easy decision, but sometimes a woman has to make such a choice in order to be with the man that she loves."

Aethelreda had no intentions of leaving her home or her people, and it was terribly sad to her to see how radiantly happy her two idiot cousins had become at her announcement. Lugotori could not control the stupid grin that covered his face. Segovax still looked angry, but she knew he was simply processing the change in the only way a rash and irascible man could. She had always thought they would make a total hash of ruling the Cantii, and now she was certain of it.

"You would leave your people for a Roman?" Segovax could not let it go. Though his eyes were bright with the thought of his cousin's departure, Segovax's voice was dripping with hate. No one hated the Romans more than he did, as he had listened to his father's tales of how they had gained more and more control and as he himself saw them take over more and more of the land of the Britons.

Aethelreda had hated Romans, too, until she met Fra Paulos. Looking up with feigned shyness and trying to summon a blush, she said, "I would not leave my people for a Roman, no, but I would leave my people for a man that I love." She was playing a role, but as she said the words of the script she and Paulos had worked out between them, she wondered if that was, in fact, the truth now. Until Fra Paulos came along, she would have believed to the core of her being that she would never desert her people for a man. She had been raised to be more loyal to the Cantii than that. But her cousins glanced at each other. They sensed a way out. They smelled a victory. Segovax was determined to capitalize on the moment.

"Who would rule the Cantii after you leave? Your brother Toberonn is not strong, and Wilfrid and the others are still too young."

Now it was Aethelreda's turn to capitalize on the moment. Looking him fully in the face and making her expression as warm and sincere as she could, she moved on to put the second piece of the plan in place. "Cousins, as you know, I can nominate a ruler in my place." The two looked blankly at her. That might have been true in theory, but it had never been done, as far as they knew. She went on, "If I so rule, I believe our people would accept you two as their leaders in my place. You have your own supporters; of this I am very aware."

There was a stunned silence. Neither Segovax nor Lugotori had expected Aethelreda to offer up her leadership without a fight. The air was electric with the sudden possibility of dreams coming true. Both Segovax and Lugotori were nearly bursting with the miraculous ease of their overthrow. The gods must have been on their side for once. And yet her offer made some sense. If she wanted to leave her home and her people, it was better that she selected her successor rather than leave a period of uncertainty when all kinds of unrest would gush up to the surface like pus leaving a newly opened abscess. Aethelreda continued, "I will ride to the coast to see Fra Paulos tomorrow and to bring him back so that we can call a meeting to explain everything to the village, and we can say our farewells together."

The two merely grunted. They could not believe their luck, but they could not risk saying anything for fear that she would hear the unbound joy in their voices. They both recognized the need for dignity under the circumstances. When it came down to it, if they could become leaders without bloodshed, everyone was better off.

The next day, Aethelreda rode to the coast with a small guard and returned with Fra Paulos and the other Romans, minus Captain Quintus and two men who remained on the coast to keep their ship safe.

Aethelreda explained her plan to Fra Paulos, who was rendered almost speechless by the complexity and cleverness of it. She had no difficulty convincing him to return to the Cantii village, even though he expressed his suspicions that her cousins might stage a coup while they were within the stone walls of the settlement and kill them all. It was certainly a risk, but he understood Aethelreda's need to quench the fires of discord that were smoldering, due to his earlier visit, and he felt partly responsible for the unrest. It was not a feeling that he enjoyed. He hoped that by passing through on their way to Watling Street, which was the Roman road that would take them to Canterbury, he would help to calm the situation and not stir up any more trouble.

Fra Paulos knew the time had come to move on to Canterbury. The idea energized him, but at the same time he felt a deep sense of sorrow and a restlessness that he could never have predicted, and that he could not explain. He was self-aware enough, however, to know it was related to the fact that he would not see Aethelreda for months, and he was already planning how soon he could return. He did not mention his desires to anyone, least of all to Augustus, who was focused on getting to Canterbury as single-mindedly as a falcon that had spied its prey and was circling in for the kill.

Augustus had a good reason for wanting to get to Canterbury, and it was not because he wanted to remove Fra Paulos from the temptation of being near a beautiful young woman who had set her sights on him; nor was it because he needed to remove himself from future occasions when he might meet the woman he had shared a bed with. Augustus was a man who kept his word, and he had given his word to the Pope. For his part, Pope Innocent had sent the mission to Britain for a deeply personal reason. His own younger brother, Flavius, had been a part of the Roman army that was stationed in Canterbury before the withdrawal from Britain. Flavius had become a Christian several years before, under the influence of some of the local holy men, and when the troops returned to Rome, he had stayed behind to help evangelize the Britons. No one had heard from him in two years, and the Pope was worried.

In the days before he entered the monastery, Augustus had been in the Roman army along with Flavius. He had admired him greatly. Flavius was a man you could depend on. He made few promises, but when he did make an oath, he always kept his word. He had a stronger sense of honor than anyone Augustus knew. Flavius had helped Augustus out of a bad spot more than once in those earlier days when they were both soldiers, rolling around Rome together like carefree adolescents.

Flavius had once taken the blame for a fracas that had broken out in a drinking house which had actually been caused by Augustus. It would have been one infraction too many for Augustus. He would have been discharged from the army if he had admitted it was he who had thrown the first punch. Flavius, on the other hand, had a clean slate. He also had a brother who was, at the time, a high-ranking Cardinal of the church. Nevertheless, Flavius had acted with great selflessness, and since that time Augustus had always felt that he was in his debt. If Augustus could find Flavius and report back to his brother, who was now the Pope, he felt he would have righted some of the wrong he had done to Flavius in allowing him to take the blame for his own folly.

The days spent in the camp on the beach had been an agony of waiting for him. But there was also a problem about returning to the village for Augustus. There was a nagging worry about what had happened in the bed of the maiden with the curling dark hair he had spent the night with. Going back to the village would mean that he would have to see her again, and who knew what that might lead to?

There was for all of them an overarching issue with how well the Cantii people would receive them now that it was known that Aethelreda was attracted to Paulos. The villagers were not united in their feelings toward the two of them. Many who supported Aethelreda as their rightful leader wanted her to take Fra Paulos for her husband and for the other Romans to stay and to assimilate into the simple life of the Cantii people. One woman in particular was hoping for the return of the gentle, sandy-haired monk with whom she had shared her bed, although Augustus was going to take pains to avoid her if he could. Those people who hoped for assimilation of the Romans and a mate for Aethelreda would not be a problem when they returned, but when they headed off to Canterbury there would be a big uproar.

But there were others in the village who felt very differently. They wanted the Romans to move on to Canterbury immediately. To them, the only good Roman was the one that was as far away as possible. When they had received word, a few years previously, that the Roman garrisons in Rutupiae had packed up and left, they had celebrated for a week. But the recent circumstances they found themselves in, with Aethelreda so clearly admiring Fra Paulos, meant that they kept their opinions largely to themselves. They were in a bind as to what would be done if Aethelreda left with Paulos, which was one of the rumors floating around the village. Most of them did not believe that was likely to happen, and they were praying that it was not so. Aethelreda's loyal servants, however, saw the angry faces, and heard the mutterings of others, and reported them to their leader.

A small number of villagers wanted Fra Paulos to take Aethelreda with him on the trip to Canterbury, and then back to Rome, never to return. Those friends of

Segovax and Lugotori were the most dangerous ones of all. They pasted smiles on their faces and went about their daily lives as inconspicuously as possible, waiting for their time to come.

Chapter Five

Enacting the Plan

Aethelreda, Fra Paulos, and their entourage entered the village without incident. There were many blank faces among those who witnessed their return, but no one showed any obvious animosity. They were keeping their feelings hidden. All except for Sigeburg, whose eyes shone when she saw Augustus. But Augustus pretended not to have seen her. His spirit was deeply troubled by what he had done, and he was still working through what his actions had meant for him and for his future.

Segovax and Lugotori were nowhere to be seen. Upon inquiry, Segovax was out hunting for game and Lugotori was probably with him, though no one was sure. Sometimes, it was said, Lugotori spent time by himself, collecting reeds and other herbs to bring back for cooking and to use about his small quarters. There were rumors that he often took a young woman with him on such gathering expeditions. It was known that she often stayed with him, and why he had not taken her for a wife was puzzling to many. It was suggested that

Lugotori was not as strong and virile as he liked people to believe.

With the first part of Aethelreda's plan in place, the real negotiations for changing the leadership began at dinner that night. She had organized a second feast for her guests, much smaller in scale than the first. She, Paulos, Augustus, Segovax, Lugotori, and her servants dined on pheasant, roasted vegetables and herbs, in her personal quarters, a smaller room that opened into the great room where large banquets were held. More of the excellent beer was served, but everyone, save Lugotori, drank sparingly. It seemed important on such an occasion to keep a clear head. Lugotori had intended to be wise and drink little, as his brother had advised, but he had very little self-control when it came to drinking, and by the time they were ready to discuss the future, he was already a little loose and giggly.

Aethelreda was regal in a beautiful blue dress that reflected in her eyes, turning them into small pools of deep water. Her clothing glinted with royal subtlety from the gold thread that was woven into the hem, the elaborate silver buckle, and her fine coronet of engraved gold.

She opened the discussion by saying how glad she was that Segovax and Lugotori were willing and able to lead the Cantii in her absence. She ignored the obvious matter that they had always wanted to rule in her place and kept silent about her personal belief that they were not suitable as candidates to rule because they were both hot-headed and unstable. Lugotori was unable to control his snickering laugh, but Segovax looked suitably serious.

Aethelreda went ahead to reveal the next step of her plan. She was surprised by the calmness that she felt within her. She had prayed to Lugus, the druid god of courage in war, asking him for courage, but she was half-hearted in her request. She did not want the situation to turn into a war. But instead of courage, what she felt was peace, which made her wonder if Paulos's God had everything under control and her audacious plan was assured of success because of his God's support. She said a silent prayer to Paulos's God that all would be well. Then she cleared her throat and raised her cup.

"Let us drink to the future of the brave Cantii people!" Everyone held their cups up high and then took a sip from them. It was a perfectly general toast that everyone in the room could ascribe to, though there were many different beliefs as to what the best path to the future was. Aethelreda looked around the table before continuing.

"As we all know, my decision to go to Canterbury with Fra Paulos will not be a popular one. I know full well there will be some who will be very angry when I leave and will demand a meeting to decide who will lead them. It would be their right. Leadership has always been a community agreement, when direct succession is not possible. But, as of now, I am still the leader of the

Cantii, and I intend to introduce a new way. I will tell the people that as their chief I have the right to name a successor. It is an ancient right that my father told me about. I will announce to them that I have thought long and hard and I have decided to pass the leadership to the two of you, to be shared equally. I will tell them that is the best way."

Paulos looked greatly concerned to hear her announcement. He looked for all the world as though it was the first time that he had heard it; not, as was the case, like it was something that he and Aethelreda had planned out so carefully the night before. He leaned forward as if to speak. Aethelreda picked up her cue.

"What is the matter, Fra Paulos?" There was worry in Aethelreda's voice, even though she knew what he was going to say. She was as believable in her role as a departing, regretful leader as Paulos was in his role as the innocent Roman visitor.

"I am sorry to say that leadership shared among brothers is often not a good solution." There was a silence in the room. The brothers looked at Fra Paulos with something like contempt, and Segovax made a disgusted noise in his throat. But Paulos continued.

"May I share something from the Holy Bible about the problems that arise between brothers who both want to lead?"

"Of course. Let us hear it." Aethelreda was probably the only other person in that room who wanted to hear the story, but no one dared to contradict her.

Fra Paulos continued, "There is a story that has come to us from ancient times of two men who were brothers. As is the way with brothers, they were in competition with each other. The older brother was a farmer and the younger one was a shepherd. They played one parent off against the other to try and earn their favor. They even tried to get God, the Almighty One who is the creator of all things living, to favor one of them over the other."

Lugotori shot an impatient look at his brother and turned to Paulos. His speech was slightly slurred from the effects of the alcohol. "If you are trying to get us to believe in your god, you might as well stop there. We follow the old gods, like our father before us, and his father before him. And right now there is a more urgent problem than who is the best god – a problem that has been caused by you. We are trying to work out who will lead our people if Aethelreda runs off to Canterbury with you."

There was a certain logic in what Lugotori said, despite his inebriation. Paulos was sorry to have to pass up the opportunity to evangelize, but it had to be done for the success of their long-range plan. He replied carefully, "I am not trying to convert you, Lugotori. In fact, I am on your side here. The most urgent need is to work out a leadership solution that will be the best for the Cantii people. I am simply passing on some ancient wisdom by telling you what happened to two brothers who were in competition with each other. When you have heard what I have to say, I think you will agree it is a story that might apply to your situation."

Aethelreda interjected in an authoritative voice, "Let the monk speak. I believe there is wisdom in the writings of the ancients. Let us hear the whole story." Her voice did not invite any argument. Lugotori's brow furrowed, but he said no more. He was having trouble focusing as the beer took its full effect. Fra Paulos, without looking at Aethelreda, continued.

"The farmer's name was Cain and he took some grain and some fruit and burned it on an altar as an offering to God, according to the custom of his religion. It was an acceptable offering, made up of good grain and rosy apples and ripe berries, and it smelled pleasantly of the roasting grain as it burned." Paulos was embellishing the simple biblical story with details that he thought would appeal to the farming folk of the village, especially Segovax and Lugotori. Aethelreda had coached him with vocabulary the day before.

"The other brother was a shepherd. His name was Abel. He wanted God to favor him over Cain, and so he took the first-born lamb of his flock for an offering. He was taking a risk in doing so since from year to year no one ever knew how many lambs there would be, and his future depended on the annual increase of his flock. He killed the lamb and offered it on the altar. The smell of the roasting grain had pleased God, but the aroma of the roasting flesh was **very** pleasing to God." Here both of Aethelreda's cousins looked as though they were imagining the wonderful smell of roasting lamb. But little did they know that the story was about to turn toward the grim, as mankind's first murder was recounted in the ancient tale.

"Cain became jealous because he felt that God was favoring his brother's offering over his own. He arranged to meet with his brother in the fields, and there he killed him." Fra Paulos stopped talking. The cousins looked at each other in alarm. After a period of time had gone by and Fra Paulos had said nothing more, Segovax spoke up.

"Fra Paulos, what is the point of this story? Are you warning Lugotori that I might kill him? Because if so, that is sheer nonsense."

Paulos replied, calmly, "I have not yet finished the story."

Segovax looked annoyed. He pushed his cup away from him, roughly. "Well, let us hear it then. We do not have all day to sit around listening to old stories!"

And so, having prepared everyone, Fra Paulos went on to tell the climactic ending of the Biblical tale.

"God saw what Cain had done and he asked him where his brother was. Cain in return asked God whether he was supposed to always be looking after his brother. This is a question that applies to all of us, even today. Are we to be our brother's keeper, or our cousin's keeper?"

At this point, both of the brothers at Aethelreda's table shifted impatiently, as if they were about to stand up and leave. Segovax exhaled loudly in frustration, but Fra Paulos held up his hand in a motion that warned the brothers to stay put. Aethelreda kept her eyes on Fra Paulos, ignoring the rude interruption. He went on to finish his cautionary tale.

"God punished Cain for killing his brother by condemning him to a life of wandering. That was a terrible fate for a farmer who was not at all sure how long he could survive in the wilderness. He was used to the safety of his fields and his house and his garden." Paulos knew that the Cantii also preferred the safety of their fields and houses and gardens to the wandering life of a nomad. They had guarded their own way of life, fiercely, against outsiders. He felt certain that the cousins would empathize with Cain in his predicament.

"Cain begged God to reconsider, and God said… 'Whoever kills Cain shall suffer sevenfold vengeance.' And the Lord set a mark upon Cain so that whoever found him would not slay him."

Fra Paulos had quoted the words directly from the scripture. It was one of the many passages from the bible that he had memorized at the abbey. And for extra emphasis, at the words "the Lord set a mark upon Cain", he touched his own brow in exactly the same spot as the strawberry mark that was on the brow of Segovax.

At that gesture, both brothers sucked in their breath at the same time, and there was an electric silence while Lugotori stared fixedly at the mark on his brother's brow. Then Segovax stood up violently, overturning his chair with a clatter, and staggered out the door.

Lugotori turned his staring eyes to Fra Paulos. "Are you saying that God has marked Segovax? That he is Cain, and I am Abel?"

"No! Not exactly. What I am saying is that brothers who try to rule together will find it impossible because of jealousy, and violence will probably be the result, as it was with Cain and Abel. Because of that possibility, I am also thinking that is not a solution for the leadership of the Cantii if Aethelreda were to leave. I am certain, therefore, that although it pains me greatly, I cannot take Aethelreda with me to Canterbury."

Aethelreda burst out in apparent surprise and anguish, "No! Paulos, no! What are you saying? We must go together! We have discussed this and prayed about it. My future lies with you, Paulos!"

"Perhaps it does, Aethelreda, but not in the way we have been thinking, dear one. Perhaps we will be together at some later date, but I could not, in good conscience, bring disaster on your people by taking you away from them now. Do you see that?" His voice was emotional, and Fra Paulos took Aethelreda's hand and looked into her eyes, before he continued, "I have been wondering about another way that might help bring peace to your people. What if you and Segovax and Lugotori ruled together, with you as the Queen and the brothers as High Lords? You would have to apportion their responsibilities evenly but differently so that they would not be in conflict with each other. That would give them almost as much power as you have, and far more than they have right now. That would appease those who support leadership by your cousins, AND those who support your leadership."

Aethelreda looked pensive. "I do not know." There was a silence before she continued. "Perhaps. I think that might be done. It is risky, but it might be the perfect solution for us. What do you think, Lugotori?"

Lugotori was still reeling from the aftermath of the story which had seemed to condemn him to an early death. What with that and the beer, he hardly knew what to think. Also, he was not at all accustomed to making any decisions without his brother at his side. He spoke cautiously.

"I think perhaps that might be so, but we need to bring Segovax back and talk with him. He is superstitious. I think he is now afraid that your story will turn out to be true." The shock had sobered Lugotori and his speech was surprisingly clear and strong.

Fra Paulos allowed a small smile to cross his lips as he glanced at Aethelreda. "Let us hope not," he said.

***

In Ravenna, the night was passing quietly. It seemed that the whole universe was waiting on something as the stars moved imperceptibly across the arc of black that reached up and away behind them to the heavens.

Abbas Matthaeus had finished the final prayers of the day at Compline, and he had carefully arranged his departure so that he was able to surreptitiously tap on the shoulder of the man he knew to be closest to Fra Paulos.

"Come with me, Brother." It was all he needed to say. Fra Luke knew where they were going, and why. He had noted his dear friend's absence and guessed that the end was near.

Their sandals made soft scraping sounds and muffled slapping noises as they walked the stone-flagged path to Fra Paulos's cell in silence.

Abbas Matthaeus looked through the small opening in the door into the cell that Fra Paulos had made his home for over sixty years. He could see the simple crucifix on the wall, the prayer book on the table beside the bed, and the form of his beloved brother, lying on his back, motionless, his sandals still on his feet. He opened the door, as silently as was possible for a heavy door on iron hinges. Although the door creaked as if in pain, Fra Paulos did not stir.

The two of them entered. The abbot immediately went to the bedside and checked the status of the aged man. He noted the rasping breathing and the slack mouth. He knew that the time was not far away when Fra Paulos would step across the great divide between life and death. He leaned over the frail form in the cot and absolved him from his sins for the last time.

"Go gently, dear friend. May our Lord Jesus Christ absolve you from your sins and restore you in perfect peace." He made the sign of the cross over Fra Paulos, and Fra Luke made the sign over himself.

Then the abbot pulled a brass vial of holy oil from an internal pocket within the folds of his homespun habit and anointed Fra Paulos's brow with gentle hands, saying:

> "Depart, O Christian soul, out of this world;
> In the name of God the Father Almighty who created you.
> In the name of Jesus Christ who redeemed you;
> In the name of the Holy Spirit who sanctifies you.
>
> May your rest be this night in peace."

Both monks murmured, "Amen."

The abbot waited a while in silent prayer and then he turned to Fra Luke and said, "Fra Luke, would you sit with our brother a few hours? I think he will pass before the night is over. It would be a great pity if he had a moment's lucidity before he died and there was no one with him to hear his final words."

"Of course, Abbas. I was going to ask if I could do that very thing."

The abbot stepped quietly out of the room. Fra Luke gently removed the sandals from his brother's feet and took his place on the stool next to the bed. He folded his hands in prayer and waited.

Old Fra Paulos, in his liminal state, somewhere intermediate between living and dying, was smiling as he reminisced about those days so long ago. That whole plan to manipulate Aethelreda's cousins had gone so smoothly that he and Aethelreda had hardly dared to believe their good fortune. Thinking back, he saw God's hand at work in a powerful way. Why else would the two brothers give up the chance for shared leadership and agree to a plan that involved three of them? It was absurd. And yet that was what they did.

As the abbot left, the creaking of the door hinges and the thud as it closed awoke Fra Paulos from his journey toward the eternal. He opened his eyes and was grateful to see Fra Luke at his side.

"Fra Luke!" His voice was rusty, but surprisingly strong. He struggled to sit up, but finding it too difficult in his weakened state, he lay down again with a bubbly sigh. The fluid was accumulating in his lungs.

Fra Luke was startled into complete wakefulness by the dying man's voice. "Fra Paulos, you are awake! How wonderful! Praise be to God!" Fra Luke sounded surprised and glad, but he was actually electrified. Instead of slipping slowly away and passing to the other side, Fra Paulos seemed to be rejuvenated. Then he remembered that this often happened in the last hours of a person's life. People often rallied in order to say goodbye.

But Fra Paulos had closed his eyes again, and like his Lord had done at the end of his life, he said, "I am thirsty."

The echo of his savior on the cross telling his executioners that he was thirsty was not lost on Fra Luke. He felt the gravity of the moment.

"Here, my brother, sip this wine, or perhaps you would prefer for me to get you some water?"

"No. Thank you. Wine is sufficient to wet my lips." Fra Luke held the cup to Fra Paulos's lips and poured a drop or two into his mouth, sufficient to help him moisten his tongue.

"How are you feeling?"

"I am tired. I feel as though I have the accumulated tiredness… of my whole life… weighing me down… like a stone… Was it the abbot who was just here?… I thought I heard his voice… The absolution and the prayers for the dead, was it not?" The words trailed slowly out of Fra Paulos's lips.

"Yes, he was here, brother. He has given you last rites."

"Then I am ready." There was a period of respectful silence as each brother pondered his place in the universe. Fra Paulos knew that he was ready to move on to meet his beloved Lord Jesus. Fra Luke hoped that when his own time came, he would be as prepared as his fine friend and mentor. Then, with unexpected lucidity, Fra Paulos said, "Did I tell you what happened on my second trip to Britain?"

Fra Luke was shocked. Did Fra Paulos really want to embark on the saga of his life when he was so close to ending it? He stammered, "N... n... no! You did not. Do you wish to tell me now?" He sounded as incredulous as he felt.

And the old man closed his eyes again to better remember the events and adventures that took place on his second mission to the Cantii.

Chapter Six

Watling Street

Fra Paulos began to tell his story to Fra Luke, but his mind was not clear and his thoughts were jumbled.

"Canterbury. We were going to Canterbury to find Flavius… No! Wait!… That was our first mission trip… Did I ever finish that story? I fear I did not." Fra Paulos struggled to sit up, turning his head from one side to the other in confusion. He did not seem to see Fra Luke sitting beside him in the light of the small tallow candle that he had lit. Fra Luke took the old man's hand and stroked it gently to soothe his agitation.

"Whatever you wish to share with me, Fra Paulos, I am here to listen. Tell me about the journey to Canterbury."

Fra Paulos lay back down and looked at the ceiling. His hands picked at the sheets, restlessly.

"We left for Canterbury on a drizzly day. It was that kind of misty drizzle that so often dampens the spirit in Britain. Aethelreda sent two men to show us the way to Watling Street. We were not in the location that we had expected to be, you see, which would have been closer to Watling Street. We were about twenty miles south of where our Roman troops had landed in the invasion."

Fra Paulos's voice had started to fade after the effort of putting together so many consecutive sentences. Soon, Fra Luke could only catch a word here and there, and he gave up trying to put the words together to make sense out of the story. He gathered that Aethelreda had stayed with her people, although neither she nor Fra Paulos had wanted that to happen. He followed the sense of the rough journey from the village of the Cantii to Watling Street, through the thickness of the forest, and the misty rain that obscured everyone's vision.

While Fra Luke was struggling to put the pieces together in a comprehensible fashion, Fra Paulos was vividly reliving the journey in his mind. The pictures were appearing and disappearing like paintings on a plaster wall, or embroideries on a tapestry.

The hike with Aethelreda's men from her village to the road the Romans called Watling Street was a difficult one. As they struggled through the undergrowth and up and down hills, crossing numerous small rushing streams, Paulos's men wondered again if they were being led on a false journey in order to make it hard for them to find their way back. Paulos thought of the men they had left guarding their ship and hoped that was not the case, for their sakes; but the path seemed not to have been traveled very much, if at all, in recent years. They were so relieved to arrive at the road that led in a northwesterly direction to the city of Canterbury that when they stepped out of the undergrowth and on to the pavement, Fra Augustus called out a loud, "Praise to our Lord Jesus Christ!" – and all the men, even the soldiers, replied "Amen!" Their gratitude for the hard work of the legions of soldiers who had carved out the miles of road and paved the way for the future was deep and heartfelt.

It seemed like a small miracle to have flat stones under foot, and a level, rolling pathway to walk upon, even though in the two short years since the Romans had left the island of Britain, there were signs that nature was already reclaiming her domain by sprinkling dandelions and other wildflowers and grasses along the edges and in the cracks between the stones in the road. Small shrubs were growing again on the wide verges that the Romans had cleared for the sake of safety, so that the local people could not hide beside the road and ambush the soldiers as they passed. In some areas the verge had all but disappeared behind a tangle of long grasses and small trees and shrubs.

The fifty miles or so that they had to travel to Canterbury, or Durovernum, as it was called at the time, should have been easy and uneventful, except that they were unwelcome people in an inhospitable land. The sight of the six Roman soldiers, in distinctively Roman military dress, reentering the country they had previously conquered and then so abruptly left, was an immediate alarm to many. Even the fact that among them there were obviously two monks, holy men, clad in raw linen robes, did not do much to appease the situation. The suspicious Cantiaci would only surmise that it was a trap.

They had hardly walked a half day's journey when the first round of trouble hit them.

Just as they cleared the top of a long hill, men suddenly appeared on the other side, facing them. In that particular place the undergrowth on the side of the road had regenerated quickly since the Romans had left, so that there was some sparse coverage for men to hide on the verges. That, combined with the blind hill that the group was traveling up, made it a perfect place for a highway robbery.

The Britons had clearly been waiting to ambush Fra Paulos and his men, though who had informed them of the travelers' presence was a curious question. There were about eight Britons in the group, men in their young and middle years, variously dressed in the typical stockings and tunics, and carrying cudgels and knives.

The Britons had the element of surprise on their side, and they should have been able to overcome two monks and six Roman soldiers, but Roman soldiers are always vigilant, and well trained. They quickly put up their shields and surrounded the two monks, brandishing their long swords and with their short swords tucked into their belts, to be used in close combat. The Britons attempted to break their formation with loud shouts and vigorous lunges, as they rushed the Romans. But the Romans held their ground.

The fighting that ensued on behalf of the Britons was undisciplined and terrifying to Paulos, who hunkered down inside the protective ring of shields and prayed out loud from Psalm 91:

"Thou shalt not be afraid for the terror by night; nor for the arrow that flieth by day; Nor for the pestilence that walketh in darkness; nor for the destruction that wasteth at noonday. A thousand shall fall at thy side, and ten thousand at thy right hand; but it shall not come nigh thee."

His words were punctuated with the shouts and screams of the Britons.

But while Fra Paulos was praying for them all to be saved from injury or death, Augustus was experiencing different emotions. He found himself wishing that he had his own sword to help beat off the brigands. He discovered in that moment that a part of his life as a soldier had remained with him. The realization both shocked and energized him. He had a small knife stored with his possessions, but it was of no use tucked away in there. He vowed to always carry it on him, henceforth. He could not stand being vulnerable and useless in battle.

The Britons were undisciplined and fierce, and it looked as though they may have prevailed until a well-placed slice from the long sword of one of the Romans almost removed the arm of one of the Britons, and at his screams of agony they all retreated, melting back into the woods.

When it was over, the group gathered to catch their collective breath before continuing.

"Do you suppose that someone from Lower Combe passed the word of our journey to some tribe closer to Canterbury and encouraged them to ambush us? Maybe even to kill us?" Laurentinus, one of the Roman soldiers, asked.

"Why would they do that?" Fra Augustus replied.

"We are not very popular with some of the Cantii," another soldier noted wryly.

Laurentinus continued the conversation. "That is true, but on the other hand, what do they stand to gain if we never return? We left half of us on the coastline."

Here, Fra Paulos spoke up. "To be sure, there does not seem to be much to gain, unless there was personal hatred at the heart of the betrayal. Our deaths would be reward enough if that were the case. That would be my best guess as to the motives of these people. We have nothing for them to steal except for our weapons, and our lives. And as for the men we left at the boat, perhaps the Cantii planned to kill them, too.

"Or it is quite possible that someone in Aethelreda's village hoped to persuade Quintus and his men not to sail back to Rome before the leaves fall, as instructed, but rather to join the people of Lower Combe. They may be hoping that at least some of us stay with them."

Fra Augustus said, "Do you think anyone would be that conniving? That seems like a detail whose results would be too distant in the future to consider. Lugotori, in particular, does not appear to think very far ahead." Augustus did not have a very high opinion of the intellect of Aethelreda's cousins.

Fra Paulos nodded. "You are probably right. But Segovax, on the other hand – I could see him planning and waiting, as hotheaded as he can be."

It was then that they discovered that one of their number, Martialis, had been wounded. The man slumped alarmingly to the ground where he awkwardly took off his shield and pulled down the neck of his tunic. Despite the armor he was wearing, Martialis had sustained a wound in his upper arm, near the unprotected armpit, from one of the Britons' knives. He was in considerable pain, but tried not to show it, maintaining a stoic look on his face. But the fact that once he sat down he could not get up again told the truth about the seriousness of his injury. Fortunately, it was not bleeding very profusely, but the cut was deep.

Fra Paulos went into his bundle of personal belongings and pulled out a small skin of wine and a bandage. He poured some wine on the wound to clean it, trying not to notice that Martialis flinched as he did so, and then he carefully covered it with the bandage.

"We will need to be on the lookout for some lady's mantle. It is a medicinal herb that Aethelreda told me her people use to help wounds to heal, and despite the name, it is used for men, too. Martialis, you will need to keep this stab wound as clean as possible. It is deep and will become poisoned very quickly if you are not careful."

Martialis being seriously wounded meant that there were only five men to actively guard and protect the monks. They slept by the side of the road that night, under the trees, with one of the soldiers awake and on guard at all times.

Martialis was very stiff and sore when he woke the next day, but with a bit more of a cleansing with the wine that Fra Paulos carried for that purpose, and with some gentle movement of his shoulder and arm, Martialis thought he would recover quite quickly. He walked with the group the whole day, but as the day progressed, the wound clearly impeded him. Fra Augustus took Martialis's long sword, which was proving a heavy burden, leaving him with his short sword and his shield for self-protection. Eventually, Augustus took the shield, too, as Martialis's strength was fading, and he could no longer hold it. All of them kept an eye out for the unusual rounded leaves and small yellow flowers of the lady's mantle which Fra Paulos had described to them, but nothing was found.

By the end of the third day, Fra Paulos began to worry about the state of Martialis's wound, which was deep and nasty-looking. He poured more wine over the slash, although he had used more than half of the wine by that time, and kept it as clean as was possible under the circumstances. They had walked more slowly that day so that Martialis could keep up with the group, even though Fra Paulos worried that they would be a target for more bandits the longer they were on the road. They had aimed to walk fifteen to twenty miles each day, meaning that it would have taken them three, or at the most, four days to reach Canterbury. Fra Paulos estimated that they had walked much fewer than fifteen miles that day. He noticed that Martialis was obviously in a great deal of pain and his face was flushed with fever.

When they stopped and found a place to stay that night, it was Martialis's welfare that guided their decision. They left the road to find a hut or cottage to stay in so that he could have a comfortable night, and something more nourishing to eat than the crusts of camp-baked bread that they had taken with them, and the chunks of dried venison.

Both Paulos and Augustus knew that they would have to be careful who they approached in any town. They knew about the mansios that their own troops had built to house soldiers on their way up and down Watling Street, between Londinium and the port towns, but were unsure of the reception they would find if they tried to get rooms at one of them. If they were still operating, the landlord would have been shocked to find a group of Romans knocking on the door. They also feared that such establishments would have become run down since the troops had almost all been gone for more than five years by then. They knew that it was highly likely that the local people in those parts had as much animosity towards the Romans as the Cantii did, and if so, that they might find their throats slit in the night.

The two monks had often discussed how they had been quite wrong in what they had been led to believe about the acceptance of Roman culture among the Britons. They had been told a rather different story than what the reality turned out to be when they landed on the sandy beach of that small country.

It was general knowledge in Rome that the Britons had flourished under Roman governance, and that the local tribes had quickly acquiesced. There was talk of a rebellion way back in the beginning under Suetonius Paulinus, when the fierce warrior queen, Boadicea, had led her people in some successful skirmishes, but she had been well and truly put down, according to Roman historians, and there had been no uprising in the south since then. The Romans had gone on to establish and develop their own culture of villas and bath houses, public squares, monuments, and roads, all of which had immensely benefited the primitive Britons, as the story was told. Back home, even Romans like Paulos and Augustus, who lived in a monastery, benefited from living in stone buildings with flagged floors, glass in the windows, and walking on streets with curbstones.

Paulos realized that while the stories about the acceptance of the Britons he had been told in Rome may have been true in essence, these accounts were only a part of the story. The tales had not made any mention of the simmering resentment that had been just below the surface for nearly four hundred years, in the minds of the Britons, while their own culture was being suppressed. The Cantii were a prime example, but Paulos had heard from Aethelreda that there were far more people like the Cantii, further west in Britain, who had never accepted Roman rule and who had lived their own lives, following their own gods, and ignoring all Roman 'improvements'.

All of this meant that they had to be very cautious about who they approached for help when they left the road. There were a few settlements on the way between Rutupiae and Durovernum.

The problem was Martialis, who was suffering from his wound, and despite the tender care given him by Fra Paulos, and the prayers offered by Paulos and Augustus to their God, and those offered by the Roman soldiers to their various gods, he seemed less and less likely to make it to Durovernum.

After discussing various different scenarios and the probabilities of success, it was decided to send Augustus and Martialis to a Roman villa that was just visible from the road, to ask for aid. It was hoped that Martialis's condition would elicit compassion, even if the owner of the villa was not a Roman sympathizer.

They were met at the door by a servant who listened without expression to Fra Augustus as he pled for shelter and care for the wounded soldier at his side. The servant, perhaps unable to understand the Latin spoken by Augustus, suddenly turned tail and walked away, without a word or gesture, but he had left the door ajar and so it seemed likely that he was going to return after seeking out his master to obtain an answer.

Fra Augustus thought the act of leaving the door unguarded was very trusting of him. He did not immediately see the two large hounds, lying in the entrance way, just inside the door, but they made their presence known with bared teeth and deep growls when he attempted to push the door a little further open so that he could see inside. He backed out hurriedly.

Through the partly opened doorway he could see a glimpse of the interior of the villa and noticed that the floor was covered with beautiful mosaics and the walls were plastered and painted with colorful murals. The owner was obviously very rich and liked the Roman style. That was probably a good sign for the group, because a rich owner had obviously at least cooperated with the Roman administration and might not object to their presence as much as some of the Britons would.

Within moments, an older woman appeared at the doorway. Fra Augustus was no judge of such things, but he estimated her to be close to sixty years old. Her dark hair was well sprinkled with silver, like frost on a dark hillside. Her face was abundantly creased with lines, where she had smiled, and where she had frowned, over the years. But despite her obvious age, she carried herself with pride, holding her shoulders back and her spine straight.

The most welcome thing of all for Augustus was to see that she was beautifully dressed in an elegant mix of Roman styling and local fabric. Her gown was of the palest blue, almost white, and sleeveless. Over the gown she wore a leaf-green palla, a short, draped cloak that covered one arm, in the way of Roman women, and left the other arm bare, exposing the wide, silver, engraved arm bands that she wore. Even Aethelreda's lovely, embroidered gowns were simple and homespun in comparison to the stylish and expensive clothing of the matron of the villa. A fine white linen veil covered her silvered hair, which was braided and piled onto her head. Around her neck she wore a heavy silver necklace.

From her physical appearance, with its obvious connection to the Roman style of dress, Augustus dared to hope that she might be sympathetic to their plight, but then changed his mind when she looked coldly at the two men at her door.

"Yes? Is there something I can do for you?" She spoke in Latin that was accented but fluent and grammatically correct.

"We beg your mercy, Mistress," Fra Augustus began. He bowed deeply, and said a quick prayer for mercy, if not from the woman, then at least from his Heavenly Father. Looking back at the woman, and seeing no change of expression, he plunged ahead.

"We are here from Rome. We have been sent by the Pope on a compassionate mission. Two of us are monks of the Christian faith, and this man, Martialis, who is one of our companions and guards, was badly wounded when we were attacked on Watling Street by a crowd of brigands. We are in dire need of a roof over our heads, some bandages for our friend, and a bowl of soup, before we walk the last stretch to Durovernum."

"How many are in your party? I am not a mansio." She referred to the wayside houses that sheltered Roman soldiers on their marches up and down Watling Street. Her voice was sharp, and she seemed completely unmoved by the fact that Martialis could barely stand in her entryway. Fra Augustus found himself wishing that Fra Paulos was with them. He was the one with the silver tongue. He could have talked this fierce, intimidating matron into giving them shelter for the night, if anyone could. He sighed heavily.

"I am so sorry to trouble you, Mistress. There are eight of us, but we could sleep in your yard, as long as Martialis could have a bed. As you can see, he is very weak."

As if on cue, Martialis suddenly sagged and fell to the stone-flagged floor of the porch in a dead faint. The matron stepped back in alarm. Then she surprised Augustus by saying in a softer voice, "Bring him in. I will see what I can do, but it may not be much, and I do not want to be blamed if he dies."

Augustus was taken aback at the matron's bluntness, but relieved that she had offered to look at Martialis, at least. He picked him up as best he could without hurting his arm, while the woman called for her servant to help out. They carried him to a bed raised up from the floor on a wooden frame and laid him on it. His breathing was shallow, and his face was white. The woman carefully uncovered the wound and examined it with a face that left no doubt about her feelings. She was clearly repulsed by the state of it and turned aside as she pulled her palla over her nose. She announced, "This is not good. He needs hot water, lady's mantle, clean bandages, and prayer." She nodded to a servant.

Augustus spoke up. "Mistress, we can gladly provide the prayer to our Father in Heaven, if you can provide some hot water, lady's mantle, and bandages."

For the first time the woman seemed to take an interest in the man who had come to her for help.

"You are a monk, you say? From Rome?"

"Yes, Mistress. There is me, I am Fra Augustus, and there is also Fra Paulos. He is from Ravenna and I am from Rome. Pope Innocent has sent us to find his brother, Flavius."

The woman's face brightened even more. Something about the name had piqued her interest. "Flavius? I wonder if that is the man who is wed to my niece, Aeditha. He was a Roman soldier. Is your man Flavius a soldier?"

At the time, Augustus did not pay much attention to what the woman had said about possibly knowing Flavius; he was too focused on finding a safe place for Martialis to rest and recover. He answered without considering the repercussions of what she had said. "He was a soldier, but when our troops were sent back to protect Rome, he stayed behind, somewhere here in Britain. He was based in Durovernum when he first came here, but no one knows where he may be found today. He may be dead."

"I wonder...," she said thoughtfully, as her voice trailed off.

But Augustus's mind was solely concerned with Martialis. "Mistress, I am loathe to interrupt you, but Martialis may die if he is not treated promptly."

The woman looked at Augustus with pity. He seemed not to know how powerful she was and how her servants obeyed her slightest nod or turn of the head. He seemed not to know just whose villa he had been fortunate to stumble upon. Any other establishment in the town of Wingham would have given him a different reception. Rather than being invited in, albeit after a chilly reception, they would have been chased back to Rutupiae on the coast.

"My servants are taking care of things," she said coolly, and as she spoke a servant arrived with a bowl of steaming water in which some leaves were steeping, and a clean bandage.

The matron of the house took over the task of caring for the wound herself. She washed out the wound with the hot water and made a poultice with the leaves, which Augustus assumed were lady's mantle. Then she carefully bound up the wound. Martialis did not even move during the entire procedure. He was still unconscious. She turned to Augustus. "You had better tell your friends that they may stay here tonight. In the morning I will see you on your way. I doubt that Martialis will be able to walk, and you are still a good many miles from Durovernum, but in the morning we will see if we can provide you with a hand cart to move him in."

The change in the woman's demeanor was remarkable. Augustus was not sure what had caused it, but he was grateful. "Mistress, how can we thank you for your kindness and generosity?"

Her reply was immediate. "Perhaps you would mention my name to Father Oswald in Durovernum? He is a priest of the Christian faith and I have heard that he is a very holy man. You never know when you might need the services of a holy man."

Fra Augustus was taken aback. He had never thought of men of God as commodities for others to use when needed, but this woman appeared to think they were. As he turned to leave, the woman stated, "Tell your friends, and anyone else who asks, that you are staying in the house of Blaedswith, but do not be surprised if they want nothing more to do with you when they hear my name."

He bowed to her and left the room, puzzled by her cryptic comments, but anxious to tell his companions the good news about their accommodations.

Chapter Seven

The Truth About Blaedswith

Fra Paulos and the other men were relieved to hear that Fra Augustus had been successful in finding accommodation for them all. Fra Augustus explained what had happened at the villa in as much detail as he could. As they all approached the lovely house, there were several comments about how long it had been since they had been in civilization. Fra Augustus said nothing at the time about the questions that troubled him regarding the mistress of the house. But Fra Paulos almost forced his hand and caused him to speak his hesitations out loud when he asked the question that was on everybody's mind.

"Is the owner a Briton, or a Roman?"

Fra Augustus answered carefully. "Her name is Blaedswith, so I am certain that she is a Briton, but her house is just like any villa that you might find anywhere in the Roman countryside. There are fine mosaics on the floor, and paintings on the walls, and drapery, and linens of excellent quality. And there are proper beds!

However Blaedswith came by her wealth, there is no doubt that Rome was involved. And she hopes to capitalize on her friendship with us by gaining a good reputation with Father Oswald in Durovernum."

"Father Oswald? I have not heard Pope Innocent mention him, have you?"

"I do not believe so, but we should be able to find him if he is a prominent Christian, and I think he must be if he is known outside of Durovernum."

The group was welcomed quietly and without fuss into Blaedswith's villa by the doorman. The hounds were not visible in the entryway when the larger group arrived. Augustus assumed that they had been moved so as not to leap on the visitors, and he was relieved to note their absence. They reappeared at dinner time, looking more like family pets in search of a tidbit than guard dogs in search of a mouthful of enemy flesh.

Blaedswith appeared and introductions were made. She fixed her stern gaze on Fra Paulos. "So, you are the other monk?"

"Yes, Mistress. I am."

"I will ask you the same thing that I asked your brother Augustus. When you get to Durovernum, find Father Oswald and immediately tell him how my household was of help to you."

Fra Paulos noted the directness of the woman's words, but as he was a guest in her house, he felt he had better humor her. "Certainly. We would be glad to, when we get to Durovernum. But as for right now, our first duty is to have our guard Martialis back on his feet. I heard that you brought your healing skills to bear and treated him very well. How is he doing now?"

Blaedswith looked slightly startled at the mention of her 'healing skills', but quickly recovered her composure. When the time was right, she would divulge her connections with the old religion.

"You will be glad to know that he has regained consciousness, and has sipped a little broth, but his fever is still high. I am preparing a draft from a dried herb that I procured from Rome that will help to bring his fever down." She was leading them through the villa to the bedroom wing as she spoke. The halls were wide and elegant, with carved plaster cornices that illustrated fruits and leaves from local trees. The floors were made of marble and were cool beneath their feet.

They found Martialis lying on one of the comfortable Roman beds, raised up from the floor, with a linen mattress stuffed with wool, and a light woolen blanket covering him. Compared to how he had been sleeping in the camp on the beach, his accommodation at the villa was luxurious. He opened his eyes as they entered the room.

"Fra Paulos…" His voice was weak.

Although Fra Paulos was very glad to note the improvement in Martialis's condition, he knew that they were not out of the woods yet. He spoke gently. "Do not speak, Martialis. All of your energy must be directed toward your healing. The matron of this villa,

Blaedswith, has made a potion that will help to heal this wound. Please drink what you can and then we will surround you with prayer, asking our Father in Heaven and the Blessed Lord Jesus to grant you healing."

Blaedswith's servant held a cup of the strong, bitter-smelling liquid to his lips. Martialis struggled to swallow a few sips. It was obviously unpleasant, and he shuddered and screwed up his face at the taste of it. But Blaedswith spoke up.

"More! You must drink it all, Martialis," Blaedswith commanded. She was clearly used to being in charge, and to having her orders obeyed.

Martialis struggled mightily to get the potion into his body, and at last he lay back, utterly spent from the effort. He had been able to consume most of it, at least enough to satisfy Blaedswith, who placed the cup on the small table beside the bed. The two monks moved to his side and after each of them placed a hand on his body, they prayed out loud for his healing. The other soldiers in the room respectfully bowed their heads while the monks prayed.

Blaedswith stood aside and watched the tableau like a disinterested visitor. She clearly had nothing invested in the soldier's healing, nor with the God whose name was being invoked. Fra Paulos did not notice her standoffishness, but Augustus did. He wondered again who she was, and how she had come to be so rich. He thought about her eagerness to be thought well of by Father Oswald, whoever he was. It seemed unlikely that she was a Christian herself, judging by her reaction to the prayers. The numbers did not add up in his mind. Something was amiss, he was sure of it.

A servant arrived to announce that a meal had been prepared and served for them. Blaedswith led them to a separate room, beautifully appointed and decorated, with a large oak table and many chairs and a fire burning in the large fireplace.

The hounds were sleeping on the hearth. They raised their heads with interest as the group entered, but lowered them again when Blaedswith gave them a command in her own language. The men took their places around the table. Fra Paulos asked if he could say a blessing before they ate, and Blaedswith acquiesced. Again, Augustus noticed that she did not bow her head or shut her eyes as Paulos prayed, thanking God for the household that had made them welcome, and for Blaedswith, their hostess, as well as for the food which would nourish their bodies.

When the soup was served, Fra Paulos thought that he may have been a little too quick in assuming that the food at the villa would be nourishing. A bowl of greenish, rather watery soup was placed before each of them. It had obviously been brewed from herbs. The disturbing thing was that it was not dissimilar looking to the potion that had been given to Martialis earlier, although it did smell much better than his had smelled.

As if reading the men's minds, Blaedswith explained, "This broth is a kind of herbal tonic that will stimulate your appetite and keep you healthy."

Augustus pondered the fact that their hostess seemed to know a great deal about herbs. He wondered if she followed the old religion.

The men did not look convinced that the soup was healthy, and each of them made a very slow start on it, taking only tiny, reluctant sips. But they were relieved to find that it was actually quite tasty, and once they had reassured themselves it was not the same as the potion that had been given to Martialis, they consumed it gratefully. After the soup, Blaedswith's servant ladled out a hearty, satisfying stew of meat and vegetables that filled their stomachs and revived their spirits.

Served along with the meal, the guests were surprised to find cups of good red wine! Blaedswith made no excuses or explanations for the absence of ale and the presence of wine at her table, even though the visitors already knew that beer was the usual beverage served to accompany a meal in Britain. She and her husband had imported a great number of barrels of wine when the rumors were flying abundantly that the Roman garrison was going to be withdrawn from Britain. They had become accustomed to it rounding out their meals on a nightly basis during the latter years of their marriage, when they were comfortably well off, and even six years after her husband, Godefridus, had died, she still had several barrels in her cellar. Her guests were delighted to find themselves drinking Roman wine and sitting at a table set in a room that could well have been in their home country. It felt dreamlike after the rough, primitive life they had been leading since they left Rome.

Augustus finally plucked up the courage to say something. "Mistress Blaedswith, what a special treat it is to be served a very fine Roman wine, in a Roman villa, in a small town in Britain! I wonder how this came to be?"

Blaedswith looked annoyed by the question. She sensed the reason behind the enquiry. She could have sidestepped the question, but her nearly sixty years of living had taught her that it was sometimes best to be straightforward.

"My husband and I were helpful to the Romans when they were administrators here, as many of us were; all of those of us with good sense, that is. We saw no virtue in fighting such a vast power. We were rewarded for our loyalty to the Emperor."

That should have been all there was to the matter. The men clustered around the table, all of whom were Romans, should have understood the situation, and been grateful that some of the Britons collaborated so readily. It was in the interest of the Emperor, after all. But having spent time with Aethelreda and her people, their minds had been bent toward compassion for the native people of the land, the people who had been overthrown, subjugated, and repressed.

Blaedswith's answer made both of the monks, at least, bridle at the thought of such a lack of loyalty for her own people. The question rose up in his mind – what and who had the couple sold out, along with their own souls?

Augustus felt the anger rising from his chest to his throat, but common decency helped him to stuff it down. It would not be wise to prod at the conscience of a woman who was giving them shelter for the night and helping Martialis to recover his strength. If it had not been for Martialis, however, he might have said exactly what he thought. He hoped there might be another time to draw out the moral implications of Baedswith's behavior and set her on a better course.

Fra Paulos was thinking almost the same thoughts as his friend. Since spending time with the Cantii, he had learned how they had suffered when the Romans came. He knew that they had worked hard to stay separate from their overlords, and he had seen with his own eyes how they had rejected Rome's influence. He had come to admire their resilience and their loyalty. Even if he did wonder how anyone could give up the refinements of Roman culture that came with the invasion – underfloor heating from a hypocaust, for instance, must have been an enormous benefit in the wintertime, and beds raised up off the ground, such as the one he was looking forward to sleeping on that night, were so much more inviting of a good night's sleep than an animal skin on the floor. To refuse such advancements almost seemed like cutting off one's nose to spite one's face.

With feigned ignorance, Fra Paulos said, "Blaedswith. That is a Brittonic name, is it not?"

She gave him a sharp look. "Yes, it is. What of it?"

"I meant no harm in asking. I was merely interested in knowing what it meant." There was partial truth in what Fra Paulos said. He was also still trying to find out how a Briton had become so thoroughly Romanized and why she was clinging to Roman ways when others had so quickly tossed them off like uncomfortable and restrictive clothing.

"It means 'splendor and strength'." She almost sounded scornful as she spoke the words, even though the name was a fine one by anyone's measure.

Fra Paulos was concentrating on his cup of wine and said almost to himself, "A very fine name indeed."

It was Blaedswith's turn to look at her wine cup. Her face was somber, perhaps even regretful, as she spoke. "It does have a fine meaning. However, I am not sure that I have always embodied those characteristics."

Paulos was caught offguard by her sudden and candid self-disclosure. He thought quickly, and to give her the opportunity to recover her composure and so as not to back her into a corner, he said, "It seems that you have been splendidly strong since your husband died!"

But Blaedswith was not to be sidetracked. She looked at Paulos sharply and retorted, "He did not just die. He was killed!"

Perhaps it was the wine, or perhaps it was the fact that Blaedswith was in the presence of a group of Romans who did not seem to be a threat and reminded her of the good days of the past, or perhaps it was the presence of the holy men of God among them, but whatever it was, Blaedswith let down her guard and began to share some of her past with her visitors. She sat up straight in her chair and began to tell her story.

"My husband was a good man. He was kind and hardworking, but he was also a practical man. He saw what had happened to the others who kept up their resistance against Rome, and knowing it was futile, he went to the governor to offer his allegiance. He was, of course, required to contribute to the Roman purse.

"We grew good crops here in this part of the country – wheat, rye, and barley. We paid our taxes to the Roman governors, even in the years when there was barely enough for our own people. But what really caused the problem to escalate was the fact that we also had a silver mine." Blaedswith touched the beautiful necklace she was wearing.

"Our silver was used to make coins that were used by the Romans to buy goods from other parts of the Empire. In the early part of our agreement with them, we mined the silver and had plenty left after taxes to bring in our own goods from the other side of the world! But then the silver began to run out. It was only a small mine. The Romans thought we were holding back on the output from the mine and sent soldiers to extract the ore.

They made our agricultural workers labor in the silver mine instead of in the fields, and our crop yield fell even lower.

"This situation went on for years. The troops built us this villa and allowed us to import many goods from Gaul and Rome to make our lives comfortable. And we were very comfortable. But I should have realized that when we went to the governor, we were selling our souls to Orcus.

"Eventually, the hatred against us grew. We were seen as collaborators and traitors, and there was a revolt. Godefridus was killed by some of our own workers." At this point, Blaedswith looked up and caught the glance of Paulos, who was truly moved by the direction the story was taking. He fixed her with his most sympathetic look.

"Dear lady, I am deeply saddened to hear your story. But it is surely a blessing that you yourself managed to escape the anger of the local people, is it not?"

Blaedswith looked past Fra Paulos, into the distance. She appeared to be considering whether it was, in fact, a blessing that she was still on this earth. When she spoke again, her voice was low, almost as if she did not want to be overheard.

"My family is an ancient family of these parts. Our links to the Druid religion are strong, even now. I know a great deal about herbs and herbal remedies, which I learned from my mother and my aunts, and they learned from others before them. But most have given up the old religion by now and are fearful of its influence.

"Some of the people thought I was involved with druidic magic. It suited me to let them believe it. Thinking I was a druid made them afraid of me, and they have kept their distance, which was what I needed and wanted. But everything has a price. I have been vulnerable since the garrison left. Many thought I would leave myself, because I would never be able to manage this villa after the military support was gone. But I would not give them the satisfaction of seeing me fail." Blaedswith straightened her spine once more.

"And here I am, with the trusted few folk who stayed to support me." She looked around and nodded at the two servants who were sitting on the bench in the hall. They nodded back. There was a pause, and then she continued, thoughtfully, "Perhaps I did sell my soul to Orcus, or to the Devil, as the Christians say, because I find myself one of the unhappiest people on this earth. The Cantiaci, my own people, are afraid of me. I am neither Roman nor am I a Briton any more. I am not a Druid, nor a Christian, nor do I worship a Roman god. I have been vilified by everyone. Apparently, I am a threat to everyone. Father Oswald in Durovernum came to try to convert me. I sent him back, unrewarded."

The tiniest smile escaped from her lips at the memory of the disappointed priest. Fra Paulos found himself, against his better judgement, feeling glad for her impertinence. He had been worried about her state of mind when she spoke of her loneliness and how ostracized she felt. But obviously she still had some fight in her.

Both of the monks wondered what kind of reception they would receive from Father Oswald when they mentioned Blaedswith's name to him, assuming they could find him. Fra Paulos had a passing thought that he should try to convert Blaedswith to Christianity so that she could really impress Father Oswald, but he pushed the thought aside for its less than holy origins. Unlike many of his religious colleagues, Paulos believed that a person had to come to belief in Christ for genuine and pure reasons, not for political one-upmanship. Too much trouble had already been caused in Rome by that very thing.

Everyone except Martialis slept soundly that night. Their minds drifted off, carrying them in their imaginations back to Rome. Even the two monks had enjoyed more comfortable conditions in the monastery than they had experienced for the last few months since they left Rome.

But Martialis was feverish and had bad fever dreams. He tossed and turned and cried out loudly in his sleep. His clothing and his bed were drenched with the sweat that his body gave off as it tried to fight the poison and heal his wound.

Blaedswith's servant changed his tunic, and his bed covers, and made another potion from the Roman herb which Paulos learned was called feverfew. After a herculean effort which she was sure had awakened the whole house, she managed to get him to drink some of it, after which he was more settled for what was left of the night.

In the morning all awoke refreshed, even Martialis, though he was very weak.

Paulos and Augustus were profuse in their thanks for the hospitality that Blaedswith had shown them, and for her good care of Martialis. After the unpromising start they had made when Augustus and Martialis had first arrived, they felt they had been guided to that very house with that very mistress whose knowledge of herbal treatments had made all the difference for Martialis. To the two monks it had been clear evidence of the providence of God that they had been led to her villa.

It was quite miraculous how much better Martialis was after the ministrations of Blaedswith and her servant. He was still too weak to walk with them, when they set off for the last leg of their journey to Durovernum, but he no longer seemed in danger of dying before their journey was over, which was a tremendous relief to everyone. Blaedswith provided them with a small hand cart, of the kind that one servant would use to carry in a few buckets of vegetables from the garden to the kitchen, or some jars of water from the river. It worked very well to hold Martialis, and the soldiers took turns pulling it.

They made very good time for the remainder of the journey, with Martialis bumping along in the hand cart, and they came in sight of the wall and towers of Durovernum, known again as Canterbury, before night fall.

Chapter Eight

Canterbury

Passing through the gated wall into Canterbury was almost a disaster. Even with two monks and a sick man in a hand cart, the guards were not disposed to let them enter the city. It seemed that the presence of Roman soldiers was nearly as welcome as a man with the plague. (Fra Augustus made a mental note to find some less obvious clothing for the soldiers, although he realized that he would never persuade them to surrender their weapons or their shields, and that those two things would always identify the army to which they belonged.)

Paulos had hoped that they would be well received if the guards understood the reason for their journey, but the name Flavius meant nothing to the guards, nor did they seem impressed by the fact that the group was on a mission from Pope Innocent to find his brother. In the end it was by invoking the name of Father Oswald that they gained entry to the city.

The great irony did not escape the two monks that it was with Blaedswith's help that they made it inside the gates. If she had not mentioned Father Oswald to them, they would have been left outside to fend for themselves. On the other hand, if the Canterbury guards had known that Blaedswith had supported and aided the travelers, they might have been even less charitable than they were. Sometimes the ways of God were truly mysterious.

Canterbury was not a large town, but it had been thoroughly changed in the four hundred years of occupation by Roman troops and administrators. The former administrative center of the city was obvious to all, as soon as they were inside the gates. The wide, paved avenue led directly to it, passing between buildings with clay-tiled roofs. In the exact center of the town stood the broad city square, edged on one side with the governor's impressive home, on the second side by the quarters for the soldiers, and on the third side by the imposing three-storied, semicircular building that housed the arena. As they walked down the smooth, paved street, looking from side to side, no glimpse of a Christian church could be seen anywhere.

Paulos marveled again at the changes that his own people had brought to the people of Britain. But he also noted that although the soldiers had been gone only a few years, there were already signs of disrepair. Weeds were growing in the places where water gathered on the paved streets, and in some places on the tiled roofs.

Refuse was seen in some of the smaller streets. He listened to the sounds of the people talking as they passed a small group. The rushing, staccato, clacking language was harsh to his ears, still. He caught a few of the words. Most of them were uncomplimentary. It seemed hard to imagine, but it would take less than fifty years for the old culture of the Britons to rise again. Even the old gods would bubble up to the surface like gases filtering through the heavy layers of the mud in the swamp.

Finally, one of the soldiers thought he saw a cross on a building about a block away from the arena, and they turned down the side street to investigate. It was indeed a church complex that seemed to be comprised of Brittonic elements and Roman ones. The walls of the building were wattle and daub such as those used by the Britons, but the roof was made of red clay tiles such as those used by the Romans. The structure was rectangular in the Roman style, but with a semicircular apse at one end.

Fra Paulos knocked on the heavy wooden door of the church. The porter opened it and eyed the motley crowd up and down. The two monks stood at the front of the group and hurriedly explained their situation. The porter said he would go to get Father Oswald, and they were to stay where they were.

That was when Tiberius, who was taking his turn with the barrow, realized that Martialis had not said anything for the longest time and that his head was lolling to the side. To everyone's consternation, it appeared that he had fallen unconscious again, for how long no one knew, and no one could rouse him.

When Father Oswald, a barrel-chested Briton of middle age with a full head of chestnut hair, arrived at the door, what he saw was a disorganized mob of what appeared to be Roman soldiers, accompanied by two monks, and a dead man in a cart whom they were trying to resuscitate.

Father Oswald expostulated, "Are you bringing me a dead man? Because, if so, I am warning you that although I am a man of faith, I do not have the power to raise the dead! Only our Lord can do that." His voice was loud and deep, and there was a hint of mirth in every word he spoke.

The group arranged itself into some kind of order with the two monks at the forefront, and Fra Paulos introduced first himself, then Fra Augustus, and then the others, to the merry priest.

"We are sorry for the ruckus, Father Oswald. We had just arrived when we realized that our friend Martialis had fallen unconscious again. He was wounded in an altercation on Watling Street, two days ago. He was treated with lady's mantle and feverfew last night, but the feverfew potion must have worn off."

Father Oswald looked concerned. "Feverfew? Is that some kind of herb?" But before anyone could answer he continued, "We do not have any plant of that name in these parts. I wonder where you could have found it? But the sisters of the convent, next door, know all the local herbs and their uses. They will come up with something efficacious for your friend, I am sure. Please, please enter and know that you are welcome in the name of the Lord Jesus Christ!"

Father Oswald was a loquacious man, and his thoughts were wont to tumble out of his mouth in a long stream. He kept going with barely a breath. "Come in, come in, good people. We will look at your man and pray for him. Martialis, am I right? And we will see what else we can do. You are from Rome, you say? Sent by Pope Innocent? We do not have much contact with the church in Rome these days. We are on our own here in these parts. But that is not necessarily a bad thing."

As he talked, Father Oswald led the group briskly into the cloister and through a door into a hallway lined with small cell-like rooms. He motioned for Tiberius to place Martialis onto a small, hard bed in one of the rooms, and said to the others, "Please find yourself a cell for the night. We have plenty of room. Neither monks nor soldiers should be concerned about the comfort of the beds!" He then spoke quickly to the porter and asked him to get the sisters to come and look at the wounded soldier.

The soldiers peeled off and found their bunks for the night. They laughed together about Father Oswald's comment. The narrow wooden beds were certainly a class above sleeping on the ground as they had been in their camp at Lower Combe inlet, or even the workers' accommodation at the villa.

The two monks, knowing that there was a lot of hard prayer ahead of them, knelt on the floor in Martialis's room and immediately commenced their petitions. Fra Augustus felt in his bones that the night ahead would be the turning point for Martialis. He would either recover or he would die.

Two nuns arrived with all haste, recognizable by their simple brown tunic gowns and veils, carrying a leather bag of herbs and a mortar and pestle. They examined Martialis with similar results to those of the night before at Blaedswith's villa. Their faces puckered with distaste. They declared that the wound was nasty and that it needed to be cauterized, and Father Oswald immediately disappeared and reappeared with a sharp knife and a small bowl of glowing embers. The knife was heated in the embers and the wound was cleaned with the hot knife by one of the sisters. The smell of burnt flesh was nauseating.

Martialis did not move, even while his body was being mortified with a searing blade of iron. It was definitely something to be thankful for that he was unconscious, as far as the onlookers were concerned.

While the sisters set about preparing a poultice of the herbs by crushing the leaves and stems in the bowl of the mortar, Fra Paulos, Fra Augustus, and Father Oswald surrounded Martialis with prayer. Their voices rose and fell as each one put before God the fate of their brother Martialis, who had pledged to keep them safe, and pleaded with God, if it was at all possible, to spare his life.

While the sisters quietly prepared the poultice and applied it to the seared flesh, the men of God continued to pray. When the wound dressing was finished, the nuns joined the men on their knees. A ring of prayer surrounded Martialis all night.

In the morning, Martialis opened his eyes to find two nuns resting with their elbows on the foot of his bed, and three men propped against the walls, half asleep. He sat up, grimacing from the pain in his armpit, and exhaled loudly.

"Are you all taking a break from your prayers?" he asked.

The heads of the men jerked up and the nuns sat up straight. A befuddled chorus of "What?" and "Did someone say something?" gave way to a louder chorus of "Praise to the Lord".

"Martialis! *Deo gratias*! Thanks be to the Lord! You are with us still!"

Martialis chuckled at the cacophony. "I am indeed with you still, AND I am as hungry as a mountain lion. Can I get something to eat?"

There was loud laughter as everyone rejoiced in the raw humanity of a soldier, who had not eaten in three days, lustily requesting a meal. Father Oswald rushed out of the room to get some bread and water, and whatever else he could muster up. The nuns gathered their belongings and left. Fra Paulos and Fra Augustus felt weak with relief as they reviewed the events of the last two days with Martialis.

"Last night, I felt in my bones that you would turn a corner," Augustus remarked.

"Yes, but which corner would I turn? The one that led to life or the one that led to death?" Martialis was joking, which was a clear sign of his amazing recovery, but his question was a good one.

"Well, obviously God saw fit that you should turn the corner to life anew." Augustus's face was shining with joy.

Martialis reached out and grabbed his hand. "Thank you, Fra Augustus. You are a good man." He turned to Fra Paulos. "And you, too, Fra Paulos. I can never thank you enough for all the effort the two of you put in to keeping me alive, and for all the prayers to your God for healing."

Both brothers were glad of the gratitude their friend had shown. They did not necessarily expect such appreciation from their traveling companions. The soldiers who accompanied them had been selected by the Pope, and while they were undoubtedly good men themselves, they were not Christians. It was hoped by both Fra Augustus and Fra Paulos that all of them would convert to Christianity before their time in Britain was over. Fra Paulos seized the moment.

"I think our God..." He used Martialis's words and then expanded on them. "He is your God, too, Martialis, and there is no doubt that he has a plan for you. That is why you are here with us today. You have been close to death twice already, and he has spared you."

Martialis looked uncertain. "I may have to find out more about your God before I call him MY God. But if he has saved me, at the very least I owe him a serious investigation."

Fra Augustus broke in, "That is a fine starting point, my brother. We can help you to find out all that you want to know, but in the end, you must simply make a decision whether to be baptized and follow the Christian God, or not."

While Martialis regained his strength, and the soldiers were shown around the town by some men that Oswald trusted (which Paulos assumed meant that they stopped at the first alehouse they encountered), Fra Augustus and Fra Paulos stayed to talk with Father Oswald. They learned that Oswald was from Canterbury and had grown up within the city walls, and under the occupation of the Romans. They learned that he had no great love for the Romans and that he had seen it as his mission to convert as many of the Roman soldiers as he could, away from paganism and toward Christianity. He had spent several extended periods of his life living outside the protection of the city wall as punishment for what the Roman administrators saw as his insurrection.

At the mention of being outside the walls, Augustus brought up the fact that if it had not been for Blaedswith, they would have been barred from entering the city of

Canterbury. At the sound of the name Blaedswith, Father Oswald looked alight with curiosity.

"Blaedswith? Is that Mistress Blaedswith of Wingham?"

"I believe it is, yes."

"Ah. Blaedswith the Bold! I remember her so clearly. Is she well?"

"She is well. She remembers you fondly and asked to be remembered to you." Fra Paulos thought there was no point in saying that she had smiled with amusement when she thought of Father Oswald's attempts at evangelizing her. 'Fondly' was a word that had several meanings, and it was true enough in the context of her feelings toward the Christian priest. Father Oswald looked as if he knew that Fra Paulos was engaging in obfuscation of the truth.

"Mistress Blaedswith was a tough nut to crack, to be sure. She was such a puzzle. She was so strongly attached to her culture and religion that she would not listen to our stories about our Lord, and yet she and her husband, Godefridus, had fully embraced the Roman ways. I remember that she uttered what sounded like druid spells and curses at me when I brought up the name of Jesus." Father Oswald looked amused at the memory.

"What did you do, Father Oswald?" Fra Augustus was alarmed at the thought of being cursed by a druid, even though he knew that the God he worshipped reigned supreme over all other gods. He had to admit that he was intimidated by what he had heard about the druids, with their worship of nature and their human sacrifice. He remembered how it had felt when he stood in the ancient druid grove by the ocean watching Fra Paulos and Aethelreda and the hairs had risen up on his arms and on the back of his neck. He knew it was the old magic that he felt, and he wanted nothing to do with any of it. He felt sure he would have turned tail and run far away if the fiery Blaedswith had cursed him. But Oswald did not run away in fear. He took things in his stride.

"I crossed myself and kissed my scapular, pronounced a Christian blessing upon her, and left her house. Tell me, was it Blaedswith who gave you the feverfew?"

"Indeed it was. She was very compassionate towards Martialis." It was true that she had overcome her initial coldness to care for the soldier. Paulos thought it best to paint her in as positive a way as he could. It was always best to try to find the good in people, especially when you did not know the opinion of the person with whom you were speaking.

"I thought as much. She must still be practicing her crafts then."

Fra Paulos was surprised to hear Oswald say such a thing. It implied that he thought Blaedswith was following the Druid religion.

"I do not know that she has many people to practice them on. I think the townsfolk stay away from her. She said they were afraid of her and that she prefers that they leave her alone."

Father Oswald raised his bushy eyebrows and lowered them again. "That sounds very much like Blaedswith. I can hear her saying it. But you would be surprised what people will overlook when they are desperate for healing. I have no doubt that the people of Wingham still seek her out. And you would be surprised how much Blaedswith likes the payment she no doubt receives from the people she treats. Her love of fine things is what got her into the service of the Romans in the first place. I hope that one day she will realize that love is more lasting and greatly to be treasured than silver, and silks, and fine wines."

Fra Paulos had to admit that he had come to much the same conclusion about her character in the very short time that he had known Mistress Blaedswith, although if Father Oswald had said as much to Blaedswith, he completely understood her antipathy. He preferred to evangelize using more subtle and refined phrases.

Chapter Nine

Finding Flavius

Fra Paulos and Fra Augustus were already indebted to Blaedswith for clearing their way into the city of Canterbury, but they had not by any means discovered the depth and breadth of her influence in the surrounding area. If you mentioned her name to almost any random traveler, they would have been able to tell you at least that she was the mistress of the big villa at Wingham. If you engaged them in further conversation, the subject of how she had gained her wealth would have arisen, and the attitude of the speaker to the Roman occupation would have been laid bare. If you had spoken to a woman, she might have told you of Blaedswith's talents with herbs and healing, if she thought you were sympathetic to such practices.

After noon-day prayers in the church, attended by some of the local people, those who worked at the church, and the visitors, everyone gathered around the large table in the refectory for a simple meal.

During the meal, Father Oswald engaged in telling the tale of the development of the wattle and daub church that had been built in Canterbury. It was obviously a tale that he loved to tell. He was as complimentary of the Romans as he could be, since he had a group of them sitting at his table. He told them of how well the church had been maintained by the Romans when they were in control, and that they had been the benefactors of a beautiful tiled roof, and glass windows, which kept the weather at bay.

The church of the Holy Trinity, as it was called, had been decorated in the Roman style on the interior. The lovely mosaics on both the walls and the floor carried a Trinitarian theme, with motifs of three repeated throughout. On the floor near where he sat during the service, Fra Paulos had noticed a mosaic that portrayed three lambs surrounding a chalice, and painted on the wall was a deer hunt in progress, with a trinity of doves hovering over the men.

Fra Paulos had been delighted to see the local flora and fauna worked into the design in several places. He loved the sprigs of three oak leaves that were carved into the woodwork, and the three little wrens that peeked out of twists of ivy in several places near where he had been seated.

There had been a community of men living within the compound at one time, necessitating the dormitories and the refectory, but most of the local men had gradually defected and married local women, leaving

Father Oswald the lone cleric in charge of the facilities, with the help of a sexton and the nuns from the nearby convent.

When Father Oswald had finished talking about his church, Fra Paulos got a chance to insert a word or two. He explained to Father Oswald that they had been sent by the Pope to find his brother Flavius, and that they intended to be on their way the following day, assuming that Martialis was well enough to accompany them. Father Oswald made no comment.

"I hope finding Flavius will not be like searching for a needle in a haystack," Fra Paulos said.

Father Oswald gave a short laugh. "I think it will be a great deal easier than finding a needle in a haystack," he replied cryptically.

"Have you heard of this man? Is he living nearby?" Fra Augustus asked.

"He is known around these parts, although he does not live within the city," Father Oswald replied. He was withholding information until he was more certain of the validity of the men who were now under his roof. He wanted to know whether or not they would try to force Flavius to return to Rome, before he disclosed his location.

"Will you take us to him?" Augustus did not like to beat around the bush.

"In due course I will, Fra Augustus, but it is not in my interest to lead you to him until I am clearer about your intentions. He is an acolyte of mine. I trained him in the way of Our Lord, and he is dear to me."

The two monks looked startled. They did not often have their motives questioned.

"We mean him no harm, Father Oswald. We will not force him to do anything that he does not want to do."

Father Oswald still looked uncertain. It was hard to tell whether or not he trusted men who, although they were of the church, were also of Rome. Then he remembered their conversation about the Mistress of the Villa in Wingham. His expression changed to one that was quizzical, almost playful.

"You might be surprised to know that Mistress Blaedswith, about whom we have already spoken, is also connected to your quest to find Flavius." Both of the monks showed renewed interest.

Paulos said, "She did tell us that her niece was married to a man named Flavius, but we dared not assume it was the same man. Is it the same man?"

Father Oswald smiled congenially. "I believe it most certainly is. He was my senior guard when I traveled to Wingham on a mission just before we found out that the Roman garrison was leaving Britain. He was not a Christian at that time, even though his brother was a priest in the church in Rome, but I had been instructing him in the catechism and he was a willing and diligent student.

"In Wingham we met Blaedswith and her niece, who is a very beautiful young woman. Aeditha is the daughter of Blaedswith's brother, and she had been taken under Blaedswith's wing since her father had been killed fighting against the Romans. Even though her parents had not been lovers of the Romans, her aunt was glad to give shelter to her niece, since she had not been blessed with any children of her own. She was training her in the ways of her people, which, as you no doubt know, are not Christian ways." Both Augustus and Paulos nodded cautiously.

"Flavius took one look at Aeditha and was smitten by her beautiful chestnut hair (which, under her aunt's influence, she wore in a braided Roman style – an attractive style, I think, even though foreign) and her hazel eyes, and her fair complexion. I think it would be true to say that Flavius never took his eyes off the lovely Aeditha the whole time we were there. And Blaedswith took it all in.

"She was not upset at first. A good marriage to a Roman soldier rising in the ranks was quite acceptable to her and might have proved to be very useful. That was the way that Blaedswith thought, as I think you know. But when she found out that Flavius was a catechumen of our faith, she changed her attitude. She became scornful and angry. She knew that if Flavius converted, there was a very good chance that Aeditha would also. She also knew that losing Aeditha to the Christian faith would mean that her niece would close the door on her forever. She would not practice the old arts and she would try to dissuade her aunt from doing so.

"And, of course, whatever chance we might have had in converting Blaedswith was lost when Flavius swept her niece up with his Italian virility, and his sweet words, and married her.

"But there was also a great blessing. I was privileged to bring the two of them into the faith through holy Baptism, and then I joined them together in holy matrimony. And everything was moving along as smoothly as the cloth in a well-oiled loom until it was announced that the troops were leaving Britain. By then, Aeditha was with child. She did not want to leave her home and she persuaded Flavius to stay with her. He would apparently do anything for her sake, then as now.

"As you might imagine, the couple were not in such an advantageous position after the army left. Flavius had pulled some strings to get himself set up with a house and an income, but he had to go into hiding because, in effect, he was a deserter from the army. And even though his older brother was the Pope, there was no way he could use his influence to keep him and his wife and child safe, once the Romans had left.

"And now, as I tell you all of this, I find myself wondering what Blaedswith is planning. She knew that by giving you my name she was connecting us all together. She knew I would be able to tell you where Aeditha is. And she is still, despite what she may have said to you, a powerful woman. I would not be surprised if she is having us watched so that she can find her niece and get rid of her husband, and take her back to Wingham, although may God forgive me for saying such a thing if it be not the truth."

After Oswald had told them the whole story, they sat in silence, trying to digest it. It seemed entirely possible that Blaedswith had some plan, but Fra Paulos was still puzzled about her desire to have Father Oswald know that she had offered hospitality to their group. It did not seem to fit in with anything else. He looked steadily at Oswald and said, "I know that you understand Blaedswith better than I (certainly I have only known her for the briefest of moments), and you and she are both Britons, but I am struggling to understand why it was so important to her that you knew it was she who gave us shelter in Wingham."

If there was more to the story than Father Oswald was letting on, he did not give away any secrets at that time. The expression on his face was as normal as if he was contemplating a bowl of ordinary stew. His reply was carefully worded.

"She is a complex woman. I imagine that she wanted me to know that she was not entirely without compassion for others. When we were last together, we discussed many of the attributes of Christianity, such as loving your neighbor and caring for the poor. We spent a long time discussing the Christian virtue of poverty, and she had argued forcefully against it, saying it was stupidity to voluntarily give up the comforts of life. She argued that she would never give up what she and her husband had fought so hard to get. I could not convince her of the freedom and lightness of spirit that comes from giving up attachments to material things.

"As for why she wanted me to know that she had helped you, perhaps she wanted me to know that she did possess the attribute of compassion, even though she is not a Christian. Perhaps she wants to reopen the pathway to her future with Canterbury and her daughter? I do not know, but I would wager a very good dinner on the fact that we will see her, or her representative, very soon."

***

Tossing on his narrow bed in his cell in Ravenna, Fra Paulos found himself pondering the two women he had met in Briton – Aethelreda and Blaedswith. They were so very different. It was not just a matter of age, although that certainly did have a major effect. Whereas Aethelreda was young when they first met and had most of her life still ahead of her, Blaedswith had lived most of her life and was coming to grips with what she had done in her past life that might affect how she was received in the next one.

But it was more than just age and experience that made the two women different. There was something elementally disparate in their characters, at their very core. Aethelreda was always open, delighted by life, and willing to take chances. She was unafraid of making mistakes, quickly tossing off any regret and considering the results as opportunities to learn for the future. She had remained that way over the more than thirty years that he had known her.

On the other hand, Blaedswith was closed, secretive, and unwilling to do anything that might change the way things were. Ultimately, their differences made one woman a joyful person and the other a fearful one. And yet the two women had ultimately found each other, because of him, and each one of them had supported the other and championed each other's causes.

As he thought of the two of them, Fra Paulos sighed as deeply as he could with his lungs nearly full of fluid. His breathing had deteriorated so much that what he had meant as a regretful sigh sounded more like a prolonged gurgle.

He had long recognized that one woman had been a delight to be with, and the other had been a trial. And yet Paulos had not given up on Blaedswith. After all, she had befriended and supported Aethelreda, and because of that act of love he had tried to the end to reach her. He had tried to persuade her that she was a beloved child of the one true God, and that God would forgive her and enfold her, and welcome her home, no matter what she had done, if she was truly repentant.

It had taken her a long time to learn to forgive. He had spent many years worrying that she would go to her death reaching out to Arawn, the Druid god of the dead, and finding no one there.

***

Finding Flavius turned out not to be very difficult, thanks to Blaedswith and Oswald. Persuading him to return to Rome, on the other hand, turned out to be impossible.

Because there was a lurking suspicion that Blaedswith might be having them watched, Father Oswald took only Augustus and Paulos with him when they set off to find Flavius. Oswald also took the precaution of putting caps on their heads and staffs in their hands as a kind of disguise, and he walked to Flavius's dwelling by a circuitous pathway. They passed out of the city gates and walked through a patch of woods, with scattered cottages throughout. They continued on through some fields, and then doubled back through the woods again, finally crossing a good-sized stream at a rocky ford.

On their arrival at his cottage outside the city wall, Flavius answered the door but closed it behind him and stood tall, with his arms folded, barring the way inside the modest dwelling to the intruders.

If the Romans had financially contributed to his stay in Britain, he had not used the money to buy a lavish villa such as the one lived in by Blaedswith. He apparently had different values. Flavius was dressed like a Kentish man in a simple homespun tunic with woolen leggings and rather clumsy leather boots. His hair, once trimmed short in the way of all Roman soldiers, had grown and curled around his ears and over his shoulders.

"My dear Flavius," Father Oswald began in his cheeriest of voices, "I come here with a delegation from your brother, His Holiness Pope Innocent, inquiring after your wellbeing."

Flavius swept his eyes over the disguised Romans. "Father Oswald, I respect and honor you. In fact, I owe my soul to you, and I love you as my Christian brother, but I will not allow these men in my home. I know they did not come to this country alone, and not one of them is welcome here, not even if they are monks." Flavius had been able to tell, somehow, perhaps by the bearing of the two men, that they were monks, or perhaps he simply knew his brother would have sent monks to find him, rather than soldiers. He looked hard at Augustus and Paulos, but did not recognize either of them.

"You can pass the message to my brother that I am well and happy, and that I will not be returning to Rome. I love my life here with Aeditha and our children. We do not need the luxuries of Rome, nor anything else, to be contented and happy."

The two monks bowed. There was no need to try to persuade Flavius. It had been understood that if he was alive and staying there voluntarily, he would most likely not want to return to Rome. All Pope Innocent wanted was to know that he was dead or alive, and if alive, that he was healthy and happy.

Augustus spoke. "Brother, we are happy to pass on that message!"

At the sound of his voice, Flavius suddenly realized who was hidden in the rough clothes of a Briton. He stepped forward and dropped his arms from their defensive position.

"Augustus? Is that you?"

Augustus stepped forward with a grin. "It is the very Augustus who was once your comrade in arms!"

"Brother!" Flavius burst out, and moving to him, he enveloped the man in his muscular arms. The two of them slapped each other on the back and laughed with joy and delight. The whole atmosphere had changed in the single beat of a bird's wing. After the inhospitable greeting he had given them, Flavius was quick to invite the men into his dwelling, and to share his food and drink with them. Flavius was quick to give honor where honor was due. Turning to Augustus, he said, "I have to say that it was a stroke of brilliance on my brother's part to send you as an emissary, Augustus! Anyone else would have been sent packing from this house. We have to be careful who we allow under our roof."

"I, too, thought it was a smart move," Augustus said, "although I had no desire to travel all the way from Rome to this... this island, to find you. But it has turned out that traveling with Fra Paulos has been a better experience than I had feared." He had been going to cast aspersions on what he saw as the godforsaken nature of the place where he found himself, and thought he had stopped just in time to prevent insulting his friend, but Flavius was quick to pick up on his hesitation.

"This island is a beautiful place to live, my friend. You might not yet appreciate its gentle climate and its fertile soils, and its running streams, but life can be truly fruitful and fulfilling here, and the life of a small farmer is far less driven than the life of a soldier. I make my own decisions about what to do and when to do it. I till the soil and plant the vegetables. I make and mend the walls to keep the wild deer out. I help the sheep to give birth. I find myself content."

As he spoke, a baby stirred from the crib at the other side of the room and began to fuss. Aeditha, who had served the men with cups of ale, and who had been sitting quietly as they talked, quickly rose and scooped up her baby. Aeditha was as lovely as Father Oswald had described her. She still wore her dark hair in a braided Roman style, which served to emphasize her feminine beauty, with her high cheekbones, straight nose, strong jaw and slightly cleft chin.

Augustus watched the pleasant domestic scene as she settled in the corner to nurse her infant. He was surprised at how much yearning he felt, deep within himself. He had never realized how much he wished to have a son like that little lad of Flavius and Aeditha: he who was a spiritual father to all, but who would be a physical father to none. He pushed the thought aside. He had made vows to be totally devoted to God, for a lifetime, and he intended to be obedient and faithful to his savior. With a twinkle in his eyes he said, "Yes, I can see that life has been fruitful for you! How many children do you have, Flavius?"

Flavius threw back his head and laughed. "Just three, but we hope for many more. Our children have given my life so much meaning. I want them to grow up here and appreciate all that their people, Aeditha's people, have become over the years."

They sat in Flavius's cottage and talked for hours, with the toddlers and the infant each demanding their share of attention. They reminisced about their time together as soldiers and caught each other up with what had happened to them since they had last been together. Paulos talked about his life in Ravenna.

As the time came for them to leave, Flavius asked Paulos, "Now that you have found me, is your mission completed?"

"In a sense, it is," Paulos replied. "And yet we have not yet had a chance to talk to any of the people about God, which was also part of our mission."

Flavius smiled and caught the eye of Father Oswald. "I think you will find that they have mostly heard the good news of the gospel, thanks to Father Oswald. I thank Father Oswald every day for reaching out to me when I was lonely and desperate, and for telling me about God. Except for my brother, I had not spent much time in the company of Christians until I met him, and who listens to a brother who is fifteen years older than you are?"

Father Oswald had been listening with obvious pleasure while Flavius complimented his efforts. Then he turned his merry eyes to Paulos and said, "And yet there is still much work to be done! The old religion has a deep hold over the Britons, and many have returned to it since the Romans left. I would welcome both Fra Augustus and Fra Paulos to stay and work with me to encourage more people to take up the Christian faith. I do not believe it is in opposition to many of the good things from the old faith, and where it is, Christianity is the gentler, more loving option, in my opinion, and it is very much to the advantage of the people to follow the one true God."

His invitation left the two monks with a decision to make. Logically, it seemed like the better option for them to pick up the reins of the horse that Father Oswald had ridden, and to help him expand his work, than to strike off on their own into areas that might rather kill a Roman than sit and listen to him preach. They thought that by aiding Oswald, a known holy man, they could all go further afield and plant the seeds of the gospel where they would yield good fruit.

But logic was not the only thing motivating Paulos. He wanted so very much to be back in Lower Combe, at the side of a certain golden-haired woman that the conflict caused his brain to ache. He wanted to be with her so badly that when he thought of her, he felt physically ill with longing.

Before they left Flavius and his family, Paulos spoke quietly to Oswald.

"Father Oswald, would it be the right thing to do to warn Flavius about Blaedswith, since we have good reason to believe that she might try to steal Aeditha away? I feel some personal responsibility since I may have set a trail right to her doorstep, despite the precautions that we took."

Oswald pursed his lips thoughtfully before he replied.

"I do not think that we were followed, but perhaps it is better to be warned about something that might not happen, than it is to be left in the dark and to suffer the consequences. Even though Blaedswith is Aeditha's aunt, and until Flavius came on the scene, the two of them were close," he added.

The fact of the matter was that all the men thought that Aeditha belonged with her husband and that Blaedswith had no hold over her niece. Because she was married, her allegiance belonged to her husband, not to her aunt who had raised her. Flavius understood that universal truth, but he knew that it did not preclude the fact that Aeditha had loved her aunt and felt a depth of gratitude to her that caused conflict between her and her husband. He was wise enough to know that relationships are seldom ever based on a one-to-one ratio with the facts.

Paulos wondered how much of the break in Aeditha and Blaedswith's relationship was caused by Aeditha leaving with Flavius and how much of it was caused by Blaedswith trying to control her niece. It seemed to him that the latter was just as likely as the former.

Augustus was very considerate of the feelings of Flavius's young wife and warned Flavius, out of Aeditha's hearing, that Blaedswith might be planning to try and get her niece back. Flavius could then do with the information whatever he wanted; ignore it and not involve his wife, or act on it and tell her what was going on. But at least he could be on the lookout for strangers in the area.

Chapter Ten

A Decision Is Made

Flavius was a smart man. He knew that harmonious relationships within the household involved respect between both of the partners, and full disclosure of the facts. In that respect he was a man far ahead of his time, but he had seen how such a pattern had been successful in the hierarchy of the army. When the visitors had left, he pulled his wife aside and spoke to her.

"Aeditha, it seems as though your aunt has never given up on trying to find you. She has probably been following the visitors who came today, and is very likely not far away, hoping to connect with you. Fra Paulos seems to think so, at any rate."

Aeditha was cradling their youngest in her arms and rocking him to sleep. The other two children were playing at their feet. She passed the infant to her husband. Her face was serious.

"Flavius, my place is with you, and I will never leave you. You know that, do you not? You sacrificed so much to make me your wife and stay with me. I was never as grateful for anything as I was when you decided to give up your place in the army and start over here. I know that you had prospects in the army. You were an immune and on your way up the ranks because you were so well thought of and highly skilled in building, and in managing other soldiers. You gave up the chance to become a centurion. It was a lot to ask of you, and you did it willingly.

"But when I let myself brood on it, I admit that there is sadness for me being here in Canterbury, because we have had to be estranged from Blaedswith, who was so good to me. I thank the good Lord for Father Oswald and the church! Without them we would have been quite alone.

"You know, Flavius, that I love my aunt, and I am glad that she has not given up on me; but it is also true that she never gave you a chance. I have never been as happy as I have been since I met you and we began our life together. Surely, she should understand that I love being with you, and that I belong with you.

"There is no way that I would voluntarily leave you now and go to live with her. Remember that, in case I am abducted and carried off to Wingham! Blaedswith is determined and fierce, and she has friends who can make things happen, as we both know. But I do wish that the two of us could be reconciled. I think of her as a mother, not an aunt."

Flavius listened to his beautiful young wife with open admiration showing on his face. She had indeed made many sacrifices to be with him, perhaps as many as he had made to be with her. She would have had all the creature comforts of life had she stayed with Blaedswith in Wingham. And she would have had the companionship of the older woman. Instead, she was raising a brood of children, alone, in a house that was not much more than a hut with a dirt floor, and he had never heard her complain.

The Christians, and Flavius counted himself among them, all claimed that love was the greatest of all virtues and the strongest. According to them, love could help a person to endure many hardships. A part of him wanted to believe in the truth of what they claimed. Another part of him did not want to test its validity. The old Roman in his soul was still quite superstitious. He did not want to anger any kind of God, Christian or Roman, by being too sure of himself. He felt certain that he would not have to wait too long to see what was going to happen next. If Blaedswith or her kin were lurking anywhere around, they would play their hand within a day or two, otherwise they risked being discovered.

Flavius and Aeditha knelt at their bedside and prayed together every night, but that night they prayed more than usual, and with more than the usual fervor. The words of the great prayer that was prayed in the church throughout the season of Lent came into Flavius's mind, and after offering God thanks for the events of the day, he opened his heart and mind to let the words of the Great Litany of Lent flow through him.

"O Lord, deliver us from all evil and wickedness, from sin; from the crafts and assaults of the devil; and from everlasting damnation."

Aeditha, with her hands clasped in front of her and her head bowed, prayed the responses, "Spare us, Good Lord."

Then Flavius continued, "O Lord, deliver us from violence, battle, and murder, and from dying suddenly and unprepared."

"Spare us, Good Lord."

And so they prayed, through all the petitions that Flavius could remember, until his mind was calmed.

Finally, they joined together in the prayer that they called 'The Lord's Prayer', after which they checked on the children, and pulled the bed covers over themselves in preparation for the night's sleep.

***

It was no surprise to anyone when a day later a stranger knocked on the door to the dwelling of Flavius and Aeditha. After a slight delay, Flavius presented himself, but he opened the door only partially and he stood firmly on the threshold.

"Yes?" His tone was threatening.

"Master, are you Flavius of Rome?" The man was a Briton and he spoke in the language of the Britons.

Flavius took a wild guess that his hometown was Wingham. Flavius answered tersely, "No. I am Flavius of Canterbury. Who wants to know?"

Just a few yards away, Flavius saw movement in the undergrowth. This man had not come alone, which was what he had suspected. "What do you want of me that you knock on my door while others hide in the bushes? Show yourselves, you scoundrels!"

Flavius's voice was rough and loud. He hoped that Aeditha could hear him from inside. She had been nursing her infant when the knock on the door came, but she had hurriedly gathered the children, hushing them, and getting ready to exit through the small door on the other side of their house (an architectural detail that Flavius had insisted on, for ventilation).

The plan for her escape, even before Augustus had arrived with his news, had been discussed many times. She was to run with them into the woods until she got to the house of another parishioner of Holy Trinity who had been forced to live outside the walls of Canterbury because of a long-ago misdemeanor. There they would seek shelter until it was safe to return. Aeditha was no soft townswoman. She was strong and knowledgeable about living in the woods, and could take care of herself and the children, even if they had to spend a night or two out of doors.

She heard Flavius, understood, left the house with the children, and melted quickly out of sight, her soft footfall barely bending the twigs, and making not a sound.

The man at the door answered, "We come from Wingham, and we mean you no harm. Mistress

Blaedswith wants simply to know how the Mistress Aeditha fares. We shall take back a message when we have seen her for ourselves."

The room behind Flavius was deathly quiet. There were no sounds of children playing, chortling, or whimpering. There were obviously no young children within its walls, and the man from Wingham noticed.

"Where is Aeditha, and where are your children?" he asked sharply.

As Flavius was thinking of his reply, the man in front of him gestured to the others in the bushes. They immediately stood up and started to move rapidly toward the back of the house.

Then the man in the doorway spat violently on the ground in front of Flavius, turned, and went after the others.

Flavius stood uncertainly in the doorway for a moment or two. He hoped his hastily enacted plan would keep Aeditha and the little ones safe. He would know soon enough.

A short while after Aeditha's departure, a young woman arrived at the door of Flavius's cottage, out of breath, to tell Flavius that Aeditha had arrived and had been quickly hidden in a cart, along with the children. They had gone immediately into the city, where they would take shelter with a friend of Father Oswald's. The plan had been executed smoothly. Flavius was full of gratitude for the community that surrounded him and his little family, even though they lived outside the walls.

He wished he could tell his brother, the Pope, how grateful he was to now be a part of the religion he led. He hoped he could send a message back with Paulos and Augustus that would set his brother's mind at ease.

In a day or two, Flavius would go into the city and seek out his family. Then, when it was deemed safe, he would return with them to their cottage. He hoped life would resume at its former pleasant, rural pace. There was a part of him, though, that was worried that Blaedswith would not stop at one attempt to get her niece back, now that she knew where they were located. The only way to prevent that from happening would be to move his family back inside the city walls. Or, and the second possibility hit him hard, maybe they could go back to Wingham, together, and be reconciled with Blaedswith.

Paulos also had a hard time sleeping that night. He tossed and turned in his small monk's bed at Holy Trinity, running various scenarios through his mind. He had spoken with Father Oswald about joining in with his missionary efforts and had been enthusiastically received.

Father Oswald needed help and he was overjoyed to think the two monks might join him in his ministry. The British cleric's mind ran ahead to imagine how many new Christians they might baptize with the extra help, and how large and successful their community might become. Perhaps Canterbury would become a center of the faith for the whole land. What a joy it would be to send word to the Holy Father that their community had been revived.

In the morning, Paulos arranged for a messenger to ride to Lower Combe and to tell Aethelreda and his own men that he and Augustus would stay in Canterbury to help the Christian community there, for the time being. He wondered if his heart would ever feel normal again, but he had to go on with life as if nothing had happened. And he did.

A week later, a messenger arrived from Lower Combe. He passed the message to the gatekeeper, who took it to Holy Trinity. Father Oswald delivered it to Paulos. The message had been stowed in a small leather pouch.

When Paulos received it, he had no idea who it was from. He pulled a piece of parchment out of the pouch and unrolled it to see his own lettering of the alphabet across the top and Aethelreda's careful copying of his letters underneath. It was the parchment that he had given her to help her learn her letters. Then, below the alphabet, perhaps printed in the juice of some dark berries, using the quill pen he had given to her to practice with, Aethelreda had written a short note in neat letters with rather childlike spacing. She wrote the words in Latin – 'Paulos, when will you come to me' – and she had signed her message with a simple initial, 'A'.

It broke Paulos to read those poignant words. He had to bite his lip to prevent it from trembling and to control the tears that welled up in his eyes and wanted to run down his cheeks. There were just six simple words written in a language that she was still learning, and yet there was such longing expressed in them. And the words drove into his heart and connected with the same longing that was buried there within him.

But with all that had happened, it now seemed unlikely that he would return to Lower Combe. He thought it would be much more practical to ask his men to sail up the coast to Rutupiae and leave for France directly from there when their six months was over. That would mean that he might never see Aethelreda again. He understood, in his mind, that the better course of action would be to go back to Rome and leave Aethelreda to rule her people and to make her way without him, but he could not get rid of the heavy aching feeling in his chest when he thought of leaving her. He was coming to see that the mind and the heart were not separate entities, that the one was tied to the other like an elaborate piece of weaving. The mind and the heart were as essential to living as the warp and the weft were to a good piece of linen. They worked together to make up the fabric of life.

He took his time to write his reply.

'A, my beloved, I cannot come to you yet. Be patient. God is doing a work here that I must be part of. Peace and love to you, my dearest. I will see you again some day. P.'

He prayed as he rolled up the parchment and placed it in the pouch. He prayed that Aethelreda would understand. He prayed that she would never forget him, even if they never saw each other again. But, above all, he prayed that he **would** see her again. He could no longer imagine a life that did not include her. That was a problem for a monk; but, somehow, he hoped that God would understand.

Chapter Eleven

A Visit to Wingham

Fra Paulos had not seen Aethelreda again on that first mission trip. It had been a terrible decision to have to make, but in the end his life-time vows seemed to be more important than his recent 'infatuation' with a young woman. That was what Augustus had called his relationship with Aethelreda, when he had been trying to persuade him to finish the mission and return to Rome. The word had hurt. But Paulos did feel the conflict between his desire for Aethelreda and for his church down deep in his soul, and he was finally persuaded to keep his vows.

    He and Augustus had stayed in Canterbury and worked with Father Oswald, preaching and teaching the local people. They had also gone outside the city walls and heard confessions, prayed for healing, and baptized many, young and old. The Christian community was expanded while they were there by several dozen souls. He and Augustus hoped the Pope would be pleased with their efforts. Paulos fervently hoped he would be, because he feared that the bringing in of Christian souls had cost him his friendship with Aethelreda.

Flavius had helped them with the mission at first and proved that he had the makings of a good missionary; but a few weeks after Blaedswith's attempted kidnapping of Aeditha, he went himself to Wingham to visit his wife's aunt to see if reconciliation would be possible. He did not want to spend the rest of his life looking over his shoulder to see who was creeping out of the woods like a crazed barbarian, waiting to attack him and carry off his wife and children.

He and Aeditha discussed the possibilities of moving back to Wingham and living near Blaedswith. Aeditha acted as if she was dubious about the whole endeavor because she did not want to hurt Flavius, but she felt a sense of loyalty to the aunt whom she had deserted, and she secretly hoped that they would be reconciled. Flavius left Canterbury to visit Blaedswith and discuss their return, with Aeditha's blessing.

He received a very frosty reception from the servant who opened the door to Blaedswith's villa. The servant recognized Flavius from the last time he had been there, several years ago by then. Even though he was wearing British clothing, and had let his hair and beard grow, Eadric had an excellent memory for faces, and had fully expected that Flavius would come back some day. He eyed Flavius coldly and said, "My mistress will not want to see you. Leave now, before she sets the dogs on you."

From behind the servant, Flavius could see the huge dogs and hear their menacing growls. He wondered if the dogs were responding to Eadric's tone of voice, or if he, the outsider, was emitting some odor that displeased the animals. He heard Blaedswith call out from one of the interior rooms, "Who is there, Eadric?"

"Mistress, it is the husband of your niece." Behind him, the dogs were still growling and beginning to salivate in their eagerness to get at the visitor.

"Vesta, Jupiter, be silent!" their mistress commanded, and the dogs immediately slunk out of sight. Blaedswith came into the entrance hall. To Flavius's surprise, she invited him into the villa with a cordial smile. He did not expect kindness from her and was momentarily taken aback. But he did not trust her. He feared that her smile could only mean that he was playing into her hand, in some way. He entered her house, but he kept his hand near the dagger in his belt, and he kept a wary eye out for sudden movements from any direction.

"To what do I owe this visit?" Her voice betrayed no anger or bitterness, but neither was it warm or hospitable. She was keeping her true feelings hidden behind forced neutrality.

"I am here of my own accord." Flavius thought it best to get things out in the open and let her know that he had Aeditha's blessing. But Blaedswith took what he said and heard the exact opposite.

"Aeditha does not know you are here?"

"She knows, but it was my idea to come, not hers." Flavius tried to keep the impatience out of his voice.

"So, I ask again, to what do I owe this visit?"

They were still standing in the entrance hall. He could see the lovely colors of the walls, ceilings, and furnishings through the opening into the next room. He had forgotten how luxurious Roman life could be. He thought again of all the creature comforts that Aeditha had given up to spend her life with him. Looking at the villa he had just entered, he was surprised to find that he missed them himself.

"Mistress Blaedswith, my wife" – he looked at the ground and corrected himself with emphasis – "**your niece**, really desires your company." That was the best he could do. It was the truth, but it sounded weak in his own ears. The problem was that he was admitting that he had done the wrong thing in taking her away from her family, and Flavius hated to be wrong. He expected Blaedswith to sneer, but there was no reaction from her. She looked at Flavius blankly. She had no intention of helping him overcome the uncomfortable situation he was in, because, as far as she was concerned, he had made his own bed and she hoped he would have to lie in it for quite a while longer.

Blaedswith made Flavius extremely nervous. He was not too manly to admit that he was afraid of her because of her curses. He had heard that they were powerful. The rumor was that she had killed a man by calling down some ancient curse upon him. He did not for one moment think that was true, but he was still wary of what might happen. Blaedswith's lack of response forced him to stumble on.

"I... I... uh, I wonder if you would permit her to come and stay a while with the children? We have three beautiful little ones. They are your great-nieces and a nephew, our youngest." He was in danger of rambling on to cover his nervousness, but Blaedswith cut him off.

"She is welcome here, any time, as are the children. But you, Flavius? I'm afraid you will have to find accommodation somewhere else. I do not want you under my roof. And as a former Roman soldier, I do not know where you might find shelter. The people of Wingham have a strong dislike of your people."

Flavius was tempted to remind her that she had become, to all intents and purposes, a Roman herself, and was equally disliked, but he had to choke down his retort for his wife's sake. To his surprise, his voice was gentle, but firm, when he replied.

"I would accept that, Mistress, for Aeditha's sake. Perhaps I could find work in the area I am a competent builder and administrator, and we could eventually relocate to be near to you. I do not know how realistic that is, but it is my goal for the future."

Blaedswith had not expected to hear Flavius say anything like what she had just heard. She had imagined that she would have to get Aeditha back through subterfuge and force, not with the blessing of her husband. And she had never contemplated that the whole family might move nearby. For a second the surprise registered on her face, but she quickly recovered her composure.

"I have no idea how realistic that would be. It might not be realistic at all at the present time. You will have to assess that for yourself." Then she added, as if it was an afterthought, "I have room for Aeditha and the children, though four more mouths to feed will be a challenge. I would expect some financial recompense to cover the costs. How you propose to do that is up to you."

Blaedswith knew that Flavius was by no means rich, and he knew that she knew his status. He and Aeditha just made ends meet where they were living in Canterbury, where they were known and where they were surrounded by a community that looked out for each other. Father Oswald had made sure that they lacked for no bodily or spiritual need. Moving to Wingham would leave them cut off from that Christian community, but it would reconnect Aeditha to her family. He had imagined that they would be supported by Blaedswith, at least until he could get on his feet. It had always been a risk, and with Blaedswith expecting something remunerative out of the deal, she had made it even harder.

Flavius felt the anger rising up within him and he turned to the door. He did not think he could choke down the insult of being asked to pay to return his wife to her aunt. He knew it would be best to leave right then, and try to cool his temper, even if he smashed something with his fist while he was walking down the road in a rage. He needed the time to think things through. Blaedswith did not prevent him from leaving.

As he strode angrily toward the road, he realized that he might as well take the opportunity to walk into the town of Wingham and see what there was to see and who there was to meet.

The moment he left, Blaedswith realized that she had made a strategic error. She ardently desired the return of her niece, and the idea of grand-nieces and nephews running through the villa, calling to each other and tumbling with laughter, brought her great joy. For all of her hardness and spite, there was a mother inside her, wanting a family to love and nurture. She turned to her servant and with her hands cupping her cheeks in distress, and her brow deeply furrowed, she said, "Eadric, I think I have made a mistake."

Eadric bowed slightly. "Mistress, he will come back."

"How can you be sure?" There was anguish in her voice. Blaedswith hardly ever showed her true feelings to anyone, but Eadric was one of her most trusted servants, and she sometimes let down her guard with him. He was as much her friend as he was her servant.

Eadric replied, "Mistress, I watched him leaving. This was not the end that he desired, either."

"But he is a proud Roman. He might find it very hard to come back here and face me again."

"He might. That is true. We could wait a day or two and if he does not, perhaps you could go to him instead?"

"Perhaps I could." Blaedswith did not sound as if she was convinced. As mistress of the villa, she did not often venture beyond the confines of the property. They had most of what they needed within the walls and boundary ditches of the farm. Her servants went into the city for the rare supply that was needed from the weekly market, or occasionally when the mistress had a hankering for some of the fresh oysters from Whitstable. She did not admit it to Eadric, but there was no way that she would go in search of Flavius.

Once Flavius had cooled his temper, he enjoyed the walk into the town. The day was warm, with plump, rounded clouds sailing across the light blue sky. Flavius had come to think of that particular hue as Kentish blue. The skies in Rome were of a different shade of blue, more intense somehow, and yet often, ironically, washed out with the heat. He did not miss that scorching heat. He loved the mildness of the Kentish climate. He loved the trees in Kent, too. The large oaks and elms were majestic in their height and span. He often pondered how many years it had taken them to reach that size. He was awed by their ancient heritage. He fully understood the inclination to worship the spirit of the trees.

His step had lightened to a jaunty walk by the time he reached the town, and his spirit had revived.

Wingham was a pleasant market town situated about a mile south of Watling Street, on the banks of the small but pretty River Stour. It was obvious that Roman soldiers had constructed many of the buildings in the town. Flavius smiled in recognition of the rectangular structures with clay-tiled roofs. He noted, however, that some of the tiles on a few of the older buildings looked as if they needed to be replaced, as weeds were taking hold in the cracks.

Several roads met in the town center, and he was pleasantly surprised to quickly find a small church identifiable by the wooden cross erected on the eastern roof ridge. It was situated centrally between two of the roads on the town square. He guessed that Father Oswald's efforts had not been in vain. The fact that there was a church also meant that there was a community that he and Aeditha could belong to.

On that warm day, after his walk, Flavius was just as happy to find an open alehouse on the town square as he was to find a church, and he went in to buy a drink. He also hoped to meet some of the locals. He was not worried about being ill-received, as Blaedswith had suggested he might be, because he felt sure that they would not know he was a Roman with his heavy beard and dark curling hair, at least until he spoke. He had learned the Brittonic language while still in the army, and Aeditha had worked on his pronunciation since then, but it was still recognizably different from the local accent.

He ordered a cup of ale and sat on a bench by the wall near the door to drink it. Two older men were sitting on the other side of the room. They nodded to him in greeting and he nodded back.

"Visiting our fair town?" one of the men asked.

"Seeing my wife's family," he answered.

"And who might that be?"

Flavius realized he might be on very dangerous ground if Blaedswith was right in her assumptions, but he lacked the kind of devious mind that could spin a tale of any convincing kind on such short notice, and so he kept to the basic truth.

"My wife is Aeditha." He was counting on a fifty percent chance that they would know who she was. And they did.

"Aeditha? She that is niece to Mistress Blaedswith?"

"The same."

"How fares Mistress Aeditha?"

Flavius was relieved that the mention of Blaedswith's name had not shut down the conversation or resulted in his being thrown out of the tavern. Instead, they had ignored the mention of the mistress of the villa to inquire after his wife. He took it as a good sign.

"She is well. We have three babies to add to the family."

"Three! You are working quickly, young man." The speaker smiled and winked at Flavius. The other man, who had thus far been silent, suddenly spoke up.

"I reckon I know who you are. Are you named Flavius?"

"Yes, that is my name. I used to be Flavius of Rome. Now I am Flavius of Canterbury." He hoped that would satisfy the men that he no longer identified as Roman.

The first elderly man said, "No wonder, then, that your speech is strange. It is on account of your Roman accent."

Flavius smiled. "I suppose it is. To whom do I have the pleasure of speaking?"

"I am Petros, and he is my brother, Andreas."

Flavius registered surprise. "But those are Roman names! How did you come by them?"

"They are the names we chose at our baptism when Father Oswald baptized us in the River Stour, out there." He gestured out the door to the river. "But Roman names they are not. I was Seanu and I am named for Saint Peter, and my brother was Aedelheard, and he was named for Saint Andrew."

Flavius grinned broadly as he put the facts together while the older man spoke. All the marks of the influence of Father Oswald were present.

"He baptized me too, and Aeditha though we did not take for ourselves Christian names. That makes us brothers, in the church."

"Indeed it does! Welcome to Wingham, brother Flavius!" Petros grinned as broadly as Flavius. Then Andreas spoke again.

"And we are also related because we are Aeditha's uncles. Her father was our brother." Andreas, the quieter of the two brothers, was the one who Flavius realized he should listen to. He was the one controlling the amount of information that was shared. He had just divulged the most sensitive fact so far.

Flavius asked carefully, "Does that make Blaedswith your sister?"

"It does. She who turned her back on her family."

Flavius was momentarily lost for words. The last thing he wanted to do was to alienate himself in any way from Blaedswith or her family, especially not after the pleasant conversation he had just had. His heart had been light with the thought that moving with Aeditha and the children to Wingham might not be so challenging after all. But he did not know whether to speak in defense of Blaedswith or to agree with the elderly men. He rummaged through his mind to find the only good thing he knew about her that he could share with these relatives that he wanted to stay on the good side of.

"Mistress Blaedswith was very good to Aeditha. She treated her as if she were her daughter."

"True enough," answered Petros, sipping thoughtfully.

The younger brother was not as mellow. His voice was firm with condemnation when he spoke.

"But Blaedswith would have kept her from finding the true faith of Christ if she had stayed at the villa.

Leaving was most likely part of God's plan so that she could be added to the number of those who are saved. We are filled with gladness to hear that you and Aeditha have been baptized. Perhaps Blaedswith will see the truth before too long, as well, but she is stubborn." Again, Andreas had divulged an important fact. Religious beliefs were clearly a dividing issue in their family. There was a silence as the three of them sipped their ales and contemplated the future. Flavius broke the silence and changed the subject.

"Gentlemen, is there any work here in Wingham for a man who can construct stone walls and houses, and put his hand to many kinds of building?"

"You are planning on staying, then?" Petros asked.

Flavius hardly knew what to say. He did not know himself whether he would settle in Wingham. So much water would have to pass under the bridge before that could be accomplished. But Flavius had learned how to temper his plain soldier's speech in his time in Britain. Aeditha had taught him to say little and listen well.

"It is my desire to bring Aeditha back and stay in the area, yes." That was not giving anything away. But Andreas was quick to see through his attempt at skirting around the truth, which was that his relocation all depended on whether or not Blaedswith wanted it to take place.

"And what does Mistress Blaedswith have to say about that?" Andreas chimed in.

Flavius sighed. He could see that beating around the bush would not do any good with these canny men.

"She will gladly house Aeditha and the children under her roof, but I must go elsewhere."

Petros threw back his head and laughed. "That sister of ours! She will not desist. But in a year or two she will be glad to have you, Flavius! I know that the roof has already started leaking in one of the servants' quarters. No one here will go over there to fix it. As a matter of fact, no one here really knows how to work with those Roman tiles. We will need repairs in Wingham before too long, as well."

Andreas gestured to Flavius to sit on the bench they were occupying, and so he crossed the room and sat down.

"Brother Flavius, if you come to Wingham and Blaedswith still rejects you, you are welcome to stay in my cottage. It is very humble, but it would be a roof over your head. As for work, we know everyone in this town and can give you recommendations."

Flavius felt his spirits revive for the second time that day. He would need a place to stay and some work to earn money so that he could pay Blaedswith for the care of Aeditha and the children. After what he had seen in the village of roofs deteriorating in the Kentish damp, and after what Petros had said about Blaedswith needing help at the villa, he hoped that living apart from his wife and children would only be a temporary situation.

Andreas, however, was scandalized to hear what Blaedswith had planned.

Flavius continued, "I would be eternally grateful to you, Andreas. I may have to take you up on your offer for shelter and I am glad to hear that I might be able to find work. Mistress Blaedswith has asked for payment to help cover the expenses in sheltering my family." Flavius did not really know why he had told the brothers that incriminating fact. He presumed it would not come as a surprise to them that their sister was highly motivated by pecuniary matters, but Andreas's face flushed red and he stood up abruptly.

"What! That witch is planning to charge her own niece and family to live in that huge villa! She rattles around it all alone while people in Wingham sleep in hovels. That is just not right. Something will have to be done, so help me God."

Petros looked distressed by his brother's outburst. "Sit down, brother, and do not call our sister a witch. She may be contrary and downright unpleasant at times, and she may be much too concerned about her own comforts, but she would never harm anyone, and you know it."

Andreas sat back down in a huff. The three men resumed sipping their ale.

The proprietor of the alehouse wiped down the bar with a wet rag and pondered the men in silence. It looked as if there might be some upheaval in the house of Blaedswith.

Chapter Twelve

In a Cave

Instead of sleeping under the trees at the side of the road, as Flavius had planned to do before setting out for the return journey to Canterbury and his precious wife and family, he accepted Andreas's kind offer and spent the night in his cottage. It was the typical cottage of a Briton, with a few Roman updates such as a tiled floor and glass in the windows. But Andreas lived alone with only a manservant to help, and Flavius did not spend the night in luxury. He was surprised that he had enjoyed a very good night's sleep, however, and he awoke in the morning feeling refreshed and cheerful.

At dinner the night before, Andreas had told Flavius about a short cut back to Watling Street that would bring him close to his sister's villa and cut about half a mile off the journey. Andreas explained that he used it whenever he went to the villa, although he had not walked that way in quite some time.

Flavius set out in the morning, in high spirits despite the fact that there was a chilly drizzle. He was already imagining his homecoming with Aeditha and the children hugging him and crying with joy to see him safely home. He crossed the fields with his bag on his back and his hat catching the moisture so that it dripped on his shoulders instead of down his neck. He had left just after dawn so that he had a full day to travel and would get a good way back toward Canterbury that day.

All was going well until the weather took a turn for the worse and the drizzle turned into a downpour so heavy that Flavius could hardly see two feet in front of himself. That was when he lost his footing. He saw nothing in his way that would have caused him to stumble, but stumble he did, and suddenly it was as if the ground had opened up beneath him. He gasped and tumbled downward into the darkness.

His fall ended with a jarring shock as he hit the bottom of the hole into which he had dropped. The wind was knocked out of him, and when he was just recovering from that he realized that he was in severe pain. It was hard to see because only a little light was coming into the opening, but he knew from the pain that he had seriously injured his foot.

When his eyes had adjusted to the low light, he discovered that he had fallen into a small cave weathered out by water entering the crack which he had broken open when he stumbled into it. The crack was directly above him, about eighteen feet above his head. There was no way to climb out, even if he had not hurt his ankle and foot.

Flavius was prevented from feeling the direness of his situation for a few minutes as he was forced to turn his attention to his foot. In shock, he discovered that he could see one of the bones of his foot poking through the skin near his ankle. The sight of it made him feel faint. He felt even worse when he realized there was blood, too, and then again when the searing pain finally registered in his brain. But he had been a soldier and had seen much worse injuries in his lifetime. He chided himself for being so squeamish about his own.

He knew he had to make a splint of some kind to prevent his foot from moving around and worsening the injury. He discovered that his fall had knocked a small pile of rubble into the hole: stones, dirt, leaves, and a few short branches about as thick around as his thumb. He selected one of the branches and broke it to make two equal-sized pieces. Next, he went through his belongings in his bag and sacrificed an undershirt which he tore into strips so that he could tie the rough splint onto his foot and bind up his ankle. It all took a lot of energy to get his splint in place, and he was dripping with sweat by the time he had finished. He lay back to rest.

In his bag he had stowed a skin filled with water from the spring by Andreas's cottage. He sipped from it. He really wanted to drink the water to the bottom, but he knew that it might be a day or two before he was found. There was still rain falling outside, but not much water was coming through the hole, even if he had had something to collect it in.

Once all of that was attended to, Flavius sat with his back against the side of the cave and pondered his situation. Things did not look good. He knew that Aeditha would be expecting his return in another three days, at the most. If he was not back, then she would surely seek help. Perhaps then someone would ride from Canterbury to find him. But absolutely no one knew where he was, and he was uncertain that he would survive long enough to be rescued. He was in a grim situation.

He spent four damp, cold, lonely nights in the hole. He prayed, he thought about his family, and he prayed some more. He had heard it said on the battlefield that before you died your whole life flashed before your eyes. It was not quite the same thing to be dying slowly in a hole, but he found that he thought only of Aeditha and his children, Flavia, Synnove, and his baby son, Oswald. He remembered every detail of his courtship, baptism, marriage, the births and baptisms of his children. If he was to die in that hole, he was determined to be thinking of those that he loved when he did so.

On the morning of his fifth day, he awoke wondering if he could possibly survive the day. He had rationed his water, but immediately after he had woken, he consumed two mouthfuls to ease his parched mouth and throat and realized that the water skin was empty. He had survived four days on little more than a couple of cups of water and a rind of cheese that he had found in his bag. His broken foot was worse than ever. The gloom of his condition engulfed him.

And that was when a miracle happened. After four days and nights of hearing almost nothing from the world above him, he finally heard a sound. It was the yelping sound of dogs barking, and at that moment there was no more precious sound in all the world.

He heard two of them, and they sounded as if they were nearby, but they were not right at the opening to the hole. He listened hard and heard them bark again. That time they were closer. He wondered if they were Blaedswith's guard dogs, the ones that had wanted to tear him apart when he had been in her doorway.

Flavius's foot was in a bad state by then. He knew that it was becoming poisoned. He was definitely weaker than he had been the day before, probably because of lack of food and water and because his foot was swollen to the size of a small pumpkin, and bruised black and purple. He did not think he would have much strength to call out, but mustering all of his energy, he did so. His voice was hoarse. The dogs stopped barking as if they had heard him. He called out again and the dogs barked back in response. Flavius was overcome with a joy that was also tinged with panic. He was so close to being rescued after all, but if the dogs did not find him, he knew he would have to start praying for his own death.

Then, as if in answer to his prayer, even though he had never actually formed the words of the prayer, Flavius heard a man's voice. It was Eadric, Blaedswith's servant, and he was right near the hole, but apparently unaware of the opening in the ground.

"What did you find, Vesta? Oh, is it a hole? There is a hole, indeed! It looks like the ground has collapsed. Come on, Jupiter, you will fall in if you are not careful! Come home, Vesta! There is nothing here to get excited about."

But the dogs knew better. They recognized the smell of the man who had visited them a week ago and whom their mistress had disliked. Neither of them would leave. Both of them crouched by the hole and barked and growled until Eadric finally looked in to see what all the fuss was about.

Flavius's voice was weak as he called out, "It is I, Flavius. Lord have mercy. Thank the Lord for your dogs! I have been here four nights. Not much life left in me, I think. Can you get help to pull me out?" His tongue was dry in his mouth, making it hard for him to speak clearly.

Eadric was stunned. This man had been down in that hole for more than four whole days? He shuddered to think of what he must have experienced. He did not think he would have had the mental strength to last that long. There were too many ghosts in his life to have left him alone in the dark for four days.

"Four days? Have you had food and drink? Are you injured?"

"Water. Just a little. My foot is broken. Badly." Flavius was growing weaker in the attempt to call up to Eadric.

There was no doubt in Eadric's mind that he would do what he could to help a man in need, even this man. He knew that his mistress would not welcome another visit from the man who had stolen her niece away from her, but he also knew she would not want to let him die in a cave on her property. He called down, "Be strong! I will return as soon as I can."

He then disappeared and reappeared ten minutes later with Wigmaer, one of the farm hands, and some lengths of flax rope in a hand cart. They dropped a rope into the hole with the intention of Flavius wrapping the rope around his torso and allowing them to pull him out, but Flavius was so weak that he was unable to secure the rope around himself. Nor could he stand up. He was dead weight. After a short discussion between the two men at the top of the hole, Eadric lowered the farm hand down and he wrapped the rope under Flavius's armpits and tied it. With a tremendous effort, he managed to hoist him into a standing position. He was surprisingly strong for a young man, but Flavius was a much bigger man than he was, and he broke out in a sweat from the effort.

Once out of the hole, Flavius lay on the wet grass, just barely conscious, but deliriously gulping the fresh air as if it was the finest wine. Every time he opened his eyes and saw the blue Kent sky, he uttered a sigh and thanked the Lord for his rescue. If he had not been so dry from lack of water, he might have wept to think that God had been with him all the time he had been in the hole, and had finally drawn the dogs over the field to find him.

Then Eadric lowered the rope again and pulled Wigmaer out of the hole. The two of them loaded Flavius into the hand cart and wheeled him the half mile over the rough ground to the villa, jolting his injured foot every step of the way.

Blaedswith met them in the yard. Eadric had told her who they had found in the hole (which none of them knew about), and she was anxious to see the Roman she had banned from her property. It seemed superhuman to her that he had survived for so long. And then, too, she wondered about the hole he had fallen into. Perhaps it was another source of silver ore for them to mine. She would wait until he was stronger before she questioned him about what he had seen.

Blaedswith took over the care of Flavius. There was no doubt that Blaedswith was a skilled healer. She stopped the poison from rising further up his leg, set the bone properly in his foot – eliciting loud screams and groans from Flavius – gave him continuous sips of cold water and regular bowls of broth made from herbs and meat bones.

He rested, and soon he began to regain his health and his strength. He had much to thank Mistress Blaedswith for, and even more to thank her dogs and her servants for. When he got home, he would tell Aeditha how amusing and ironic it was that the hounds who had hated him a week or so ago, and had wanted to tear him limb from limb, had saved his life and now guarded his bed as if he were a prince. Even Blaedswith saw the amusing irony of that situation.

On the ninth day, to the surprise of everyone and to the tremendous relief of Flavius, a visitor arrived at the villa on horseback. It was Paulos. He had borrowed the horse from one of Father Oswald's richer parishioners and had ridden hard to get to Wingham to find out the fate of his new friend because everyone was worried sick about him. Paulos was as relieved to find Flavius still alive as Flavius was to see him. The reunion was raucous and filled with back slapping and manly hugging.

Paulos could not stay in Wingham for many days, as the longer he was away, the more Aeditha and Oswald would worry about Flavius. He knew he had to return promptly, but it had been Paulos's unrealistic fancy to hope that Aethelreda might be somewhere close to Wingham so that he could see her again. Unfortunately, she was not, and he was going to have to return to Canterbury without having reconnected with her. And so, despite the joy of finding Flavius alive, Paulos was downcast, and he made the return trip with a heavy heart. Thankfully, he could make a favorable report on Flavius and let Aeditha know that he would be joining them in a few weeks. The only bad news was that it was likely that Flavius would have a limp after his foot had healed. Nevertheless, everyone knew that the situation was so much better than it might have been.

By the eleventh day after his fall, Flavius had begun to take short walks with a crutch under his arm. By the fourteenth day, Blaedswith announced that he was well enough to be taken back to Canterbury. She provided a horse and a rider to accompany him. But before he left, she went with him to examine the hole into which he had fallen. To his surprise, Blaedswith took a rope with her, and asking Eadric to hold the end securely, she descended into the hole to see it up close.

It was something to see her trusty servant Eadric lowering her into the darkness in her elegant roman tunic and palla. He was as solicitous as a young man taking care of his grandmother. She was as intrepid as a desert explorer looking for an oasis.

Blaedswith returned with some small gray rocks in her belt and a big smile on her face. It was apparent that the rocks she had found contained silver ore. What the Christian God had allowed to happen when Flavius fell into the hole had aided the Druid gods of Blaedswith and her followers. It seemed that the hole that had almost ended the life of Flavius might be going to renew the life of the Wingham villa and its mistress.

Chapter Thirteen

Two Strong Women

Without delay, Blaedswith and her workers began toiling to get the new silver mine underway. It was a lot of heavy labor, opening the shaft with picks and shovels, providing access for the workers, keeping everyone safe, before even the first basket of ore could be removed. That was all the kind of thing that her beloved Godefridus had taken care of when he was alive, but Blaedswith found, to her surprise, that she was perfectly competent to do it herself. She also found that she enjoyed doing it.

The workers who had labored for them when the Romans were their overlords had long since gone on to do other things. Only a few of the faithful, like Eadric and Wigmaer, remained. But they had families in Wingham who needed work, too, and they joined the new endeavor, and gradually other people from Wingham began to provide help. And Blaedswith was a magnificent overseer. She was careful but decisive, making sure her workers were well cared for, but not putting up with any laziness or malingering. They soon learned that it was hard to get anything past Mistress Blaedswith.

Flavius and Aeditha arrived within a month. They came with the blessings of Father Oswald and the community of the Holy Trinity. Aeditha and the children moved immediately into one of the many spare rooms in the villa, while Blaedswith thought better of her ban on her niece's husband, and allowed him to live with the workers, for the time being. Flavius knew it was unwise to debate his living accommodation with Blaedswith after his conversations with her brothers Petros and Andreas. He thought that he would bide his time. At least he could still see Aeditha and the children.

And he did not have to wait very long.

Flavius did not have any specific role in Blaedswith's household, and so his days were filled with walking to Wingham and helping some of the villagers with repairs and assisting the farmers back at the villa. He had made himself familiar with the layout of the villa – house, fields, outbuildings, fences, and all – and made a mental note that some of the roofs had cracked and had broken tiles which were letting in the rain. He was preparing himself to make the repairs, having found a large supply of roof tiles in storage at the village church, when disaster almost struck the Wingham villa.

There had been a succession of rainy days, which was not at all unusual in that part of the world. The pouring rain had found its way into one of the buildings and had been dripping into an area that was being cleaned up to use again for storing the smelted ingots of silver once the new mine really got underway.

Flavius was poking around the building, looking to see if there was any work he could lay his hand to, when there was a sudden loud crashing noise and a rush of men to the corner of the building in front of him. Some tiles had been dislodged by the continuous rain and had fallen in. One of them had just missed the worker who had been sweeping the floor. It lay broken on the ground and the man lay beside it, stunned. It had not done more than glance off his shoulder, but that was enough to knock him sideways!

A servant was quickly dispatched to inform Mistress Blaedswith, which he did, but he also passed on the offer from Flavius that if she would allow, he would have the roof fixed within the day, in case any more tiles fell in and caused a serious injury. Mistress Blaedswith demurred, but did not make an appearance.

It was a master stroke of good fortune for Flavius. He made a quick trip to the church with an empty hand cart and brought back a supply of tiles. In the afternoon, he climbed up on the roof and checked it over, finding it in need of repair in several places. Back on the ground, he showed some men how to make a strong slurry of clay and enlisted them to help him pass up wooden buckets of the thick mud using ropes, to where he sat on the roof with his trowel. He worked hard, with one eye on the lowering clouds. He prayed that there would be no more rain until the tiles had set in place. He knew there was no way of predicting whether there would be more rain, but he had to mend the roof without delay. Prayer was his only recourse.

Blaedswith came to see what was going on just as he set the last tile in place. She thought that her indifference to the situation had gone on for long enough. She had given Flavius plenty of time to reflect on his status in her house. Her smile when she saw Flavius perched on the roof, having completed his repairs, was a smile of satisfaction. She had put the Roman in his place when he had asked to bring Aeditha back and join her household, and he had worked hard ever since to prove his worth to her. She supposed that after repairing the roof he had done that, quite undeniably. Now, if it did not rain and undo all of his work, she might begrudgingly have to concede that his god was at least as powerful as the one she prayed to when she was desperate. Not that she was going to admit that to Flavius.

It did not rain that night, and the next night Flavius moved into the villa with Aeditha and the children. It felt like a huge victory for him when he was able to join his family. Neither Flavius nor Aeditha could stop smiling at their many blessings. Blaedswith carried on as if nothing was different.

***

Midsummer was approaching, one of the times when Blaedswith made a habit of reconnecting with the old gods of her people.

About fifteen miles along Watling Street from Wingham, there were a number of crystal-clear springs which had been a gathering site for druids for many hundreds of years. The pool that was formed by the seven springs was believed to have healing properties. The Romans had added to the complex of buildings and shrines that had grown up over the years, offering rest and relaxation for travelers, and so it no longer needed to be a secret that one was going to Vagniacis. You might legitimately be going there for peace and rejuvenation, and to offer thanks to the Roman Gods.

But if what you were going for was a midsummer gathering of druids, and if you were intending to make an offering to the Druid gods, Blaedswith knew that it was best to be circumspect. She usually told her servants that she was going to Vagniacis to reconnect with other silver merchants. Accordingly, she took with her only Ionnia, her most trusted servant, and several small items of silver to advertise the quality of the metal that came out of the Wingham mine.

While part of that story was true, some of the silver items – small primitive figures – would actually be left at the shrine of Brigit as votive offerings. She prayed every year that Brigit, goddess of the hearth and the forge, would ensure a good yield from the mine. Blaedswith had been faithful in her offerings every year. Brigit was faithful, too, in the early years, but then, in the last ten years, the goddess had seriously let her down.

Under the influence of Flavius, Blaedswith had been thinking about the new god that he supported. Ever since his miraculous delivery from death after he had fallen into the hole, and followed by the cessation of the rain when he had prayed for it, so that the tiles could dry and stick to the roof, she had been wondering if she was following the wrong gods after all. Being a practical woman, she decided to test the gods.

Blaedswith would make her usual offering to Brigit, accompanied by her usual prayers for the success of her mining endeavor: a good yield of high-quality ore, and a healthy income to provide a comfortable living for her and for her family. Blaedswith thought for a long time about how she could get the gods to compete with each other. If she prayed for the same things from both gods, she would never know which one was responsible for the result. Besides, she had been told by both Father Oswald and Flavius that she had to turn her heart completely to the new god, or her prayers would not be effective. She was not ready for that. There was, however, a small church in Vagniacis that had been started by Father Oswald. She decided to go there and ask the priest to pray on her behalf, rather than praying herself.

But what to pray to the Christian God for was the question. Blaedswith was a very self-reliant woman. Her whole existence was evidence of how well she could take care of herself, using only what was in her natural surroundings to help her. Her allegiance to her druid ancestry was only tenuous. She relied on it when it suited her and ignored it when it did not. She did not spend much time in self-examination because she abhorred self-pity. But as she pondered what it would take for her life to be more fulfilling, she began to wonder if she should have the priest pray for something quite different from her usual prayer to Brigit.

Once she had started down that pathway, she found that there was something that she deeply desired, even more than having a successful business; something that would make her a better person, a happier, more loving person. One thought led to another, and very soon she found herself wondering if she should pray for a friend to join her at the villa. Since no one had dared to befriend her in more than fifteen years, she knew that was a huge request to make of a god she was not even sure of. But what good was a god if they could not answer your prayers?

Blaedswith and Ionnia made the trip to Vagniacis and left offerings at the shrine of Brigit. They immersed themselves in the holy water of the healing spring, put on their white robes, bedecked themselves with the blooms of columbine, day's eye, cornflower, and yarrow, and meditated under the branches of the sacred oak, whose lower boughs had been strung with a rainbow of midsummer flowers. They shared honey-sweetened cakes, and ale, and mead, with the other worshippers, and sang the ancient song of gratitude to the sun as they danced in a circle around the oak tree.

There would be more prayers and rituals at midnight, as they danced around a big fire, and lit a huge wheel of fire to roll down the hill to predict the next year's crops, and Blaedswith would participate in that ritual; but she had other things to do in the afternoon. While the others were gathered to tell stories, she stole away and walked to find the little church of Saint Paul. There, she planned to meet the priest and ask for prayers on her behalf.

The visit to St Paul's did not go quite as Blaedswith had planned. The door was opened by a priest she did not know, which was what she expected, and he invited her inside; but when she stepped into the room, who should be sitting at the big table, nursing a mug of ale, but Father Oswald.

Blaedswith was startled, and suddenly became conscious of her white robe and the flowers that were still in her hair. She had thrown a red palla over her head and shoulder, but she knew her midsummer solstice gown would still be quite evident to those who knew what they were looking for. Father Oswald would know she had come from the druid celebration, and no doubt he would be unhappy.

"Father Oswald!" The name burst out of her startled mouth.

"Mistress Blaedswith of Wingham, how wonderful to see you!" His smile was broad and genuine. It was almost impossible not to smile back at the congenial priest, and Blaedswith found the corners of her lips turning upward.

"You have been celebrating the Midsummer Solstice, I see!" Father Oswald pointed to the flowers that remained in her hair. But to Blaedswith's relief, he made it sound totally acceptable to have been doing so, even perhaps joyous. It encouraged Blaedswith that he did not sound at all judgemental.

"I have, indeed. It is, as you know, the custom of my people." There seemed to be no point in trying to hide something that was so obvious. "But I came here because I have a prayer request of the priest." She looked at the other cleric, who was older than Father Oswald by perhaps ten years, and Father Oswald realized that she was waiting to be introduced.

"This is Father Graeme. Yes. He is the leader of this congregation here in Vagniacis. Should I leave you? Do you require privacy?"

"No. There is no need. Perhaps I could simply tell him what I need and the two of you could both offer a prayer. Two is probably better than one, anyway, especially two holy men of God."

The two men looked at each other. Father Oswald knew that Blaedswith put a high value on commodities.

He fancied that she thought prayer and spirituality were just commodities. If that were the case, then two was definitely better than one. Inwardly, he wondered how long it would be before Blaedswith realized that spirituality and faith were not commodities to be bartered and traded, but were something altogether more precious than any worldly goods.

Father Graeme looked puzzled. He wanted to know more about the particular situation before he got involved, but he supposed no harm could come of hearing the woman's petition.

"Might you join us at table and share a little of why you came here today?"

Blaedswith suddenly felt reticent. She did not want to tell the men about her competing prayer requests. She knew the fact that she was setting one religion up against the other would not reflect well on her. Father Oswald was no fool. He knew she had come to Vagniacis to bring offerings to the old gods. But then, to her surprise, it was Father Oswald himself who helped her out of the sticky situation.

He interjected, "Before you get started, would you mind very much telling me how Flavius and Aeditha are doing? And Flavia, Synnove, and little Oswald, of course." His smile was even broader when he mentioned the infant who was his namesake. Seeing the cleric's pride in the young child caused Blaedswith to chuckle with genuine amusement.

"Your little namesake is growing like a weed. He is as adorable and chubby and good natured as any infant I have ever seen, and I have the privilege of watching him grow up under my own roof. Having Aeditha there at Wingham, and the girls, as well as little Oswald, has been pure pleasure. Even their father has made himself useful." She stopped. Her gain had been Father Oswald's loss. She did not want to gloat. "I am grateful that you allowed them to leave Canterbury."

Father Oswald pursed his lips. "It was not a case of 'allowing' them, mistress. Flavius is a free man. He can do what he likes and go where he wishes. We do miss his help at Holy Trinity, though."

"I am certain that you do. He has been helping Father Aelwyn on Sundays at the church there."

"Good Saint Martin's. I hoped he would find a place there. Flavius is a good evangelist, and he will be a blessing to them."

Blaedswith ignored his obvious love of the man she was still trying to figure out. Flavius was certainly a decent man. And he did love her niece more than the sun and the moon together. She supposed she would come to appreciate him as time went on. She looked at the two men at the opposite side of the table from her. How to introduce her prayer request was still troubling her. Why would they agree to pray for an avowed pagan who had so obviously been doing the rounds of her own religious resources?

Father Oswald noted her discomfort. He remembered her angry refusal to have anything to do with Christianity when he had first spoken to her about it, and he remembered her curses. Still, she must have noticed that they did not seem to have done him any harm. Perhaps she was coming to see the benefit to her land and to her family of believing in the Christian faith. He decided to go forward very carefully.

"Mistress Blaedswith, the last time I spoke to you about our Lord Jesus, you rejected him vigorously, and here you are asking us to pray to Him on your behalf. May I ask what has changed your mind? Are you ready to seek baptism?"

"No. I am not ready for that," she said flatly. In her head she was alarmed, but like her people, she was very adept at hiding her emotions.

"I hardly know why I am here really, except that Flavius seems so confident of his God's intervention in his life, and he was saved from death when he fell into the cave. And recently he prayed for the rain to stay away, and it did. I think your god may be better at answering prayers than mine."

Father Graeme spoke up then. "Mistress, we are glad that you are seeing how God works through His servant Flavius, but we do not offer an antidote to the troubles of this life. After all, our God was himself crucified and died."

Blaedswith sighed loudly. "So I have been told. And I do not understand at all how your religion works if your God suffered and died. But nevertheless, I felt that my prayer request was best brought to you, rather than to Brigit or Belenus.

Both of the clerics looked intrigued. Father Graeme spoke up. "You have me wondering what your prayer request might be. Not a request for a good year in the mine, because I am sure you have already asked that of Brigit; or the return of the sun for another year of life, which you probably already asked Belenus to provide. So, what, Mistress Blaedswith, is it that troubles you so much that you feel the One True God must be petitioned?"

"As you know, I am not greatly loved by the townsfolk, or even by my family, if it comes to that. But I am well aware that I have been the author of my own fate, and a self-exile.

"When Godefridus was with me, I did not feel the loss. But he is gone, and his death, along with seeing the little ones under my roof, has served to make me realize that life is often short.

"I have wasted a good many years living at the villa in a solitary state. Too many years. I have been a proud and stubborn woman. I still am. But as my old age advances, I have realized that I need to make some changes before I leave this earth. I need to reach out to the community. I need to be accepted by them. And, most important of all, I have realized what a precious thing it would be to have a friend."

"Is Aeditha not your friend?"

"She is like a daughter to me, but her connection is by blood. And her allegiance belongs to her husband and her children, not, in the end, to me."

Father Oswald continued, "You are right in realizing that a life cut off from community is a hollow existence. We were created to live with and for others. But I believe you have your own small community at the villa. I know you have faithful servants. Perhaps that is where you should start in developing friendships?"

"My house servants are faithful, that much is true. They have been with me for many years now, through good times and bad. I am grateful for the support of Eadric and Ionnia, especially. But a servant is bound by a kind of contract, not by mutual positive regard.

"What I am seeking is the friendship of someone who likes me for who I am, and sticks with me, through the good and the bad. That used to be true of my birth family; but, sadly, we have grown apart." Blaedswith did not mention that the cause of the waning of familial love had been her own fraternization with the Romans.

"If I should be able to reunite with my brothers Petros and Andreas, that would be more than I would dare to ask. But perhaps I will be bold and ask for prayers along those lines as well. My requests are in strictest confidence, of course."

"Of course." There was a long silence. Both clerics were considering the implications of what was being asked of them. Father Oswald, in particular, could not shake the feeling that this was some kind of a test of his own faith. If so, and if the results were not what Blaedswith was desirous of, what then? Although he no longer believed in the power of the old gods, he did not relish the thought of being the subject of Blaedswith's curses again.

The two priests were conflicted by Blaedswith's requests. Father Oswald, knowing as he did far more than his colleague about the older woman, felt that he was being manipulated somehow. But even if he was, he knew his Master's admonition that when you are slapped in the face you should turn the other cheek. Father Graeme, whose only knowledge of the woman was from gossip he had occasionally heard about the owners of the silver mine in Wingham and how they had sold out to the Romans, subjecting their workers to a punishing military regime, was also suspicious that her motives were not pure. He felt that he should at least offer her some instruction in the Christian faith and ask her what she would do if her prayers were answered.

But Father Oswald beat the less experienced priest to it.

"Mistress, I am sure you know that God promises to answer the prayers of the righteous, and whether you are righteous or not is known only to God. Whether or not I am righteous is a valid question, too, but I would be very happy to lift up a petition for you in evening prayer tonight. May I ask something of you in return?"

Blaedswith looked shocked for a swift second. She understood business and bartering and goods for services only too well, but she did not expect to be asked to provide some satisfaction for her prayer request, as if they were setting up a contract between two tradesmen. However, she recovered quickly, reasoning that his request would be benign and inexpensive. She could afford to spare some silver, or perhaps some of her Italian wine, although she was husbanding that commodity very carefully so that it did not run out too soon.

"What will you ask of me?"

"If God answers your prayers before the winter sets in, I would ask that you return to Father Graeme and inform him. I think that by that time you might be ready to accept the Christian faith, and be baptized.

It did not please Blaedswith to be asked to commit herself to the Christian faith. She would have rather paid in silver, or wine, or the labor of her servants. She hesitated. Both of the priests noticed her reaction.

"If my prayers are answered, I will certainly come back and let Father Graeme know."

When she left the two of them, the clerics made an informal wager that Blaedswith would not return, no matter the outcome of her prayer request.

***

Blaedswith and Ionnia attended the midsummer evening observances and returned to Wingham the next day.

On the afternoon of the following day, when the sun was warming the central courtyard of the villa so that the scent of the dog roses filled the air, Mistress Blaedswith sat with Aeditha, enjoying her company while they watched the little ones play with the water trickling in the fountain, a beautiful Roman addition to the courtyard. Eadric appeared and requested that the mistress go to her front door to greet a visitor. Blaedswith looked annoyed.

"Who is it, Eadric? You know I do not like to be disturbed at this time of the day."

Eadric was not deterred. "I think this is someone that you would like to at least greet, even if you do not invite her to stay."

"Her?" Blaedswith's attention was piqued. She had never, to her knowledge, had a visit from a woman, unless she was accompanied by a man.

"Is she alone, this woman?"

"Yes – well, no, Mistress. This woman is Aethelreda of the Cantii, and she is here with four of her men."

In the outer courtyard stood the tall, fair-headed woman, accompanied by two of her guards. The other two were tending to the horses. Aethelreda made an imposing figure. She was wearing a long leaf-green tunic under a delicately woven shorter tunic, dyed rose pink, and girdled with a plaited leather belt. Around her forehead was the thin gold coronet, inscribed with runes that declared her 'Queen of the Cantii'. Her bearing was, as always, regal.

Blaedswith found herself making a curtsey to the beautiful Queen on her doorstep. She seldom paid respect to others in such a way, but there was something about the younger woman that demanded acknowledgement.

"Welcome to my villa, Queen Aethelreda of the Cantii. To what do I owe this visit?"

"I am here to see Frater Paulos of Rome."

Blaedswith was surprised. "What makes you think that he is here at my villa?"

"I have heard that he returned here from Canterbury."

Obviously, there was more information traded between the two faraway villages than Blaedswith realized. Looking up to the younger woman she said, "He was here several weeks ago, but I am afraid he paid a very short visit and needed to return to Canterbury."

Aethelreda looked frustrated. "Then my informant was mistaken?"

"He was, my lady. I am very sorry for your inconvenience. Would you care to come in and have refreshment?"

One of the problems of living in Lower Combe was that it was still quite cut off from other communities. The news of Paulos's visit had taken a roundabout route to get to the Queen's ear, and then any trip to anywhere of consequence took several days. And so, she had missed Paulos by a mile. She was disappointed and angry, though who she was angry with, she could not have said.

She sat in Blaedswith's parlor and drank a cool cup of spring water with wild strawberries crushed into it, while she thought about what to do next. She was nearly halfway to Canterbury. She considered continuing on, but she was uncomfortable with the idea of leaving her people under the governance of Segovax and Lugotori for longer than a very few days. She wondered how much Mistress Blaedswith knew about Paulos and where he was and what he was doing.

The two of them soon struck up an amicable conversation, and although Aethelreda was at least thirty years Blaedswith's junior, they found they had a lot in common. Most of their commonality lay in their interest in native herbs and flowers, and their love for the people and traditions of Kent.

For Blaedswith's part, she found that she was attracted to the younger woman because of her loyalty to her own people. Even though one of the loudest complaints against Blaedswith and Godefridus had been that they were sympathizers with the Romans and that they had sold out to them, Blaedswith had always suffered in silence. Godefridus was the one who had led the charge on collaborating with them. They had had many conversations and Blaedswith had expressed her misgivings; but, in the end, she had thought that Godefridus was right, and she supported his decisions as if they were her own. But while she sat in the presence of a woman whose people had never sold out, she felt shame. It rose up in her conscious mind that it had been a very dishonorable thing that she and her husband had done. But, as was the way of her people, she hid her innermost thoughts from her visitor.

As it was, Aethelreda did not seem to hold it against her. She sat and talked with her as if they had been friends for ever. She seemed to understand that the community had gained a tremendous amount of wealth and comfort by being allied with the Romans, even if she did not agree with what Blaedswith had done. She could see for herself the quality of the buildings that the Romans had brought to Britain. She openly admired the lovely mosaics and painted plaster of the villa, and asked questions about the gods depicted in the artwork. For a young woman, she seemed to be amazingly wise. It appeared that she understood the value of the gray that lay between the black and the white of life.

But yet there was one thing in which Aethelreda did not seem to be very wise. She seemed to be much attached to Frater Paulos; almost, Blaedswith decided, enthralled by him. And, although Paulos was indeed a handsome man, he was not a man who was free to take a wife. That much Blaedswith understood. She found many of the ideas that the priests of the new faith taught difficult to understand, especially when it came to their bodies and sexuality. And although she no longer considered herself a faithful druid, she preferred the more natural attitudes toward sex that were taught by that religion.

"Why were you looking for Frater Paulos?"

"He is my dear friend." Like Blaedswith, Aethelreda had long perfected the art of closing off any emotion so that nothing showed on her face. You had to look into her eyes to see what she was feeling if she chose to keep her emotions to herself. Her face was blank. Her expression was neutral. She was giving nothing away.

"Just your friend?"

"Yes. Just my friend, unfortunately."

"So, you would like it to be otherwise? But, my dear, it cannot be so. His faith forbids it."

"I know." The blank expression remained on her face, but Blaedswith caught a momentary flash of something in her eyes. Clearly, there was more to the situation than Aethelreda wanted to disclose.

"But yet you live in the hope that he might give up that part of his faith?"

Blaedswith had a certain ability, some said it was given to her by the gods, of getting to the heart of an issue. Aethelreda turned her head so that the mistress could not see her face. She did not wish to expose her vulnerability, and she was upset that this woman had so easily seen through her carefully constructed outward appearance.

"You miss his presence in your life, I can tell."

Blaedswith found herself moved by the younger woman's attempt to remain composed. She had experienced something akin to what she imagined this extraordinary young woman was feeling, when she had been young. She had tried to be as calm and composed as Aethelreda when the desire of her heart had left her to return to his position as a soldier for Rome. But she had not been able to. Her older brother, Seanu, now known as Petros, had taken things into his own hands, sought out her lover and put him to death by slitting his throat with his dagger. It had taken Blaedswith years to get over her sense of loss and betrayal. But then Godefridus had come into the picture. And perhaps the ministrations of a druid herbalist had helped, too.

There was a growing silence in the room, but still Aethelreda kept her calm demeanor and revealed nothing. Finally, when she talked, her words were flat and spoke only of the facts.

"I miss him more than I can put into words, but there is nothing that can be done."

Blaedswith stood up. "I have something that might be of use to you." She left the room quickly, and Aethelreda waited, wondering what Blaedswith had in mind. Blaedswith went to the room in the back of the villa where she kept her dried herbs in a cupboard, and found the ones that she wanted. The smell of them reminded her of the sorrow and loss that she had experienced. She did not know if the herbs had helped, but it had only been a few weeks after using them that

Godefridus had arrived in Wingham, and they had met. Perhaps it had not been a coincidence.

She spooned out a healthy amount of the mixture – yarrow, meadowsweet, vervain, and berries and flowers of the elder tree, into a piece of linen which she tied with a thread of flax. She returned to the great room at the front of the villa and handed the small bundle to Aethelreda.

"Once, a long time ago, I suffered the loss of someone that I loved. I drank a tea made from this mixture first thing every morning. Within two full moons, I met the man who became my partner in life, Godefridus. Perhaps it will be the same for you, my dear."

Aethelreda looked at the linen bag with disdain. "I do not wish to meet anyone else, mistress. I only wish for Paulos to return to me."

Blaedswith shrugged. "As you wish. Sometimes what we desire is not possible. Perhaps this potion will help to heal your mind of your desire for what you cannot have."

Their meeting ended soon after that. Both of the women were disappointed. Blaedswith was saddened by Aethelreda's clear disdain for the herbal remedy that she had offered. Something had sparked inside her after spending time with the Queen of her neighboring kinfolk. She wondered if perhaps the Christian God had sent Aethelreda in answer to Father Graeme's prayer on her behalf. Only time would tell. At that particular moment, she did not seem to be a potential friend, but rather a truculent daughter.

Aethelreda was angered by Blaedswith's apparent inability to understand her feelings for Paulos. Something about the older woman's attitude which suggested that she knew more about relationships between men and women than Aethelreda did was intensely irritating, even in the face of the logic that it was probably the truth. Aethelreda felt belittled. She did not plan to return to the villa unless she was certain that Paulos was there. And why would he be there if he could travel another three days to Lower Combe and be with her?

Although she gave away nothing in her demeanor, she was inwardly seething with anger and frustration. The whole visit had been a waste of time, as far as she was concerned. And she had left Segovax and Lugotori in charge while she had gone on her wild-goose chase. She hoped that they had not overstepped their bounds in her absence.

Aethelreda's small party turned their horses into the woods and traveled a few miles in silence. Then, unexpectedly, Aethelreda stopped her horse. She removed the linen pouch of herbs that Blaedswith had given her from where she had tucked it in her belt, and hurled it as far as she could into the thicket, with a string of curse words.

Her younger brother, Toberon, who was one of her traveling companions, had never heard her utter such words before. When he got over the surprise of hearing his sister swear so fluently, he laughed quietly to himself. Something had gotten under her skin, that was certain. He hoped his older brother Wilfred, who had insisted on staying in Lower Combe to keep an eye on their cousins, would not add to her anger and frustration with his report on Segovax and Lugotori when they returned to the settlement.

Chapter Fourteen

While the Queen Was Away

There was a strained atmosphere in the settlement when Aethelreda rode in. Something had happened in her short absence that no one was eager to share with their Queen. Whereas there would have normally been cheery greetings to their ruler on her return, instead her people did not make eye contact, and scurried away about their business. The travelers noticed the change immediately.

Toberon quickly found his brother Wilfred and pried the information out of him. The chill in the air was, as Toberon had feared, because one of the Lords appointed to lead when their ruler was away had overstepped his boundaries and had not backed down when he was challenged.

It seemed that Lugotori, under the guise of watching over Aethelreda's quarters, had moved into her residence while she was away. He said it was necessary to be on the premises so that he could be assured that nothing happened to the building, but everyone knew that was nonsense. His brazenness had astounded even his own brother. Lugotori had long been envious of his cousin's quarters, which were much finer and more luxurious than his own, and within hours of her departure he had taken his personal belongings and his housekeeper and a friend and set up house in Aethelreda's quarters. He was participating in an ancient game of squatter's rights.

Tongues wagged at a furious pace, of course. Everybody knew that he would be ousted as soon as Aethelreda returned, and his companions with him. It was almost comical to many of the Cantii.

But the biggest scandal was that nobody knew the young man who accompanied Lugotori. Some said he had had a long friendship with him, and that Lugotori's frequent trips away from Lower Combe always involved a meeting with him. Some said that the man was of the Catuvellauni, their nearest neighbors, and that he was of noble birth. Others said that he was a druid priest, but that he had been exiled from his people. Still others said that he was Lugotori's lover, and that he was the reason that Lugotori had never been with a woman nor taken a wife. There was some truth in each of the tales, but none of them was exactly correct.

Segovax was furious with his brother when he discovered what he had done, but he assumed that he would move back to his own cottage when Aethelreda returned, and so he let it go. It was beneath his dignity to get involved in such a stupid action on his brother's part. He was sick of having to cover for his brother's misdeeds. He was also resentful that his brother had not introduced him to the friend from the Northwest who accompanied him. He knew that there was a significant relationship between the two men. He had long known that his brother preferred the company of men to that of women, despite the fact that his brother had never mentioned it to him.

On the second day of Aethelreda's absence, Segovax changed his mind and presented himself in Aethelreda's quarters to ask for an explanation from his brother.

He was met at the door, not by Aethelreda's servants, but by Lugotori's housekeeper.

"Hylldah." He bowed slightly. "I am here to see my brother."

"Yes, my Lord. He has not yet arisen."

The spark of Segovax's violent temper was dangerously close to lighting the flame. "Then get him out of bed, or I will turn him out myself, the lazy son of a putrefying sow!"

"Please, my Lord, sit beside the fire and I will tell him you are here." Hylldah was clearly flustered. She had witnessed dozens of fights between the brothers, and knew that little love was lost between them; and yet, ironically, they loved each other very much. She noted that the birthmark over Segovax's eyebrow was livid, a clear sign that he was in a fighting mood.

She returned from the sleeping quarters looking even more flustered.

"I have told him you are here, my Lord. He did not take kindly to my announcement."

Segovax did not wait to hear anything more. He barged past Hylldah like a ram trying to get through a gate to escape the butcher's cleaver.

In Aethelreda's bed lay Lugotori and his friend, as bold as brass. Neither one of them moved until Segovax yanked the covers off the two of them and kicked his brother in the ribs, yelling, "Get up, you useless piece of dung! Get out of your cousin's bed, and out of her house! I see what is happening here. You will not succeed if you think that you are moving in for good!"

Lugotori stood up with a linen sheet wrapped around his loins and gave his brother a look of hatred.

"You do not have a say in this. I am entitled to a grand house, now that I am a Lord, and now that I am married."

Segovax nearly choked. "Married! When were you married, and to whom?"

"I married Hylldah yesterday, in the Oak Grove, and Butu here was my witness."

"Butu, eh? Are you sure it was not the other way around? You married Butu and Hylldah was your witness?" Segovax's voice was dripping with sarcasm.

Butu had arisen also, but he did not bother to cover himself. He was proud of his own body and not in the least embarrassed at being naked in public. He spoke. His voice was quiet but authoritative.

"Would that it had been the other way around, but we have an arrangement between the three of us that suits all of us."

"Who in the name of all the gods are you?"

"I am Butu of the Catuvellauni. That is all you need to know. And I am your brother's friend."

"It would appear that you are far more than his friend, but no matter. I do not care one way or the other. What I do care about is that you three appear to think that you can move into Aethelreda's house. She is the leader of our people. She will not be moved."

Lugotori spoke next. "It is the custom of our people, is it not, that leaders who are married and have children are entitled to the larger residence?"

"Perhaps it is, or was in the past, but Aethelreda is our leader, and neither you nor I have any children."

"Ah, but it will not be long before I do. Perhaps a little less than six months."

Segovax swiveled to look at Hylldah. She did look a little rounder in the belly than when he had last looked at her.

His first reaction was to wonder who the real father was. It was hard for him to imagine that it could be either Lugotori or Butu. But Segovax did not ask. He decided it was not worth making a fuss over a detail which would be impossible to prove, in any case.

"That does not give you the right to throw out our cousin on her ear. If you do not remove yourselves before she returns, she will deal with you and Hylldah, AND Butu in the manner you deserve. My advice is to have vacated her dwelling well before she returns."

"Your advice is noted." Lugotori sounded unconcerned. And he did not take his older brother's advice.

Lugotori was not the brighter of the two brothers. His brain worked slowly, like the brain of a bear awakened too early from hibernation. As a consequence, he was easily led by others. Butu had been the one who had planted the idea of marriage in his head. When he heard that Aethelreda was to be away from the settlement for a week or so, he reminded Lugotori of the ancient law that said a married leader with children should be afforded the largest dwelling in a community. The problem that Lugotori did not have any children was very handily solved by the fact that Hylldah had fallen with child and was three months gone. She had not revealed the father, except to say that he was married already and could not marry her. It seemed to Lugotori like the perfect solution. He would marry Hylldah, claim parentage of her child, and demand a larger dwelling, more suited to his station in life as a leader, husband, and father.

Butu went one further than that. He suggested that they all move into Aethelreda's dwelling, and just assume their priority. He reasoned that Aethelreda would not want to make a fuss about something that was a Cantii tradition. She would not want to be viewed as someone who did not follow the old ways.

But Butu did not reckon on Aethelreda.

When she returned and found the three of them squatting in her quarters, instead of throwing them out, which was her first inclination, she simply threw back her head and laughed, loudly. It was impossible to tell if she was laughing at them, or if she was simply amused at the situation in general. With her face still creased in a big smile, she turned to Lugotori and said, "I cannot believe that you thought I would move out of my home! I was born here! I believe I will die here. But, Lugotori, I agree with you. Now that you have a wife and a child on the way, you are certainly entitled to a larger family home. We Cantii will need to get together and enlarge your cottage so that it is fitting for a man of your status. Come, let us discuss the matter."

And just like that the conversation turned from confrontation to planning for the future, and the four of them spent the next hour discussing how to enlarge Lugotori's modest cottage into a home large enough for a growing family and grand enough for a Lord of the Cantii.

It was a testament to Aethelreda's wisdom that she was able to negotiate the attempt to push her out of her home with as little conflict as she did. In truth, she thought of Lugotori as an overgrown ten-year-old, and treated him accordingly. It had always worked before, and she had been relieved to find that it still worked. She was concerned that Butu would change the dynamics in the future, however, and made a mental note to keep an eye on him.

As adept as she was with her own people, Aethelreda felt like a failure when it came to a certain Roman monk. She had given her heart to him. She would have done anything to join him, either in Lower Combe, or in Canterbury, or in Rome. And yet she knew that she could not leave her people. The conflict tore at her insides. She did not eat properly, nor did she sleep well. It had been several months since she had seen Paulos. She had his note safely hidden in a leather pouch among her private belongings. He had promised to come back to her when he could.

If he had said he was going back to Rome and would never see her again, she might have handled it better. She might have been able to set the matter aside and go on with her life; but as it was, she woke every morning wondering if it would be the day that he would return. She tried to pray with the prayers that Paulos had taught her, but she did not feel as if they were going anywhere above the roof of her cottage, or the branches of the trees, if she happened to be outside. The Christian God did not seem to be listening.

Each morning, she would take out the vellum that Paulos had given her and read the words, 'A, my beloved, I cannot come to you yet. Be patient. God is doing a work here that I must be part of. Peace and love to you, my dearest. I will see you again some day. P.'

And each day she wept, and then she became angry, and then she loved him all over again, and there was a physical ache in her chest, right where her heart was located.

Finally, she felt she could not sit and wait while there was still one source of aid that she had not examined. She took her most trusted servant, Mildreth, and they rode to the oak grove by the inlet. There she tethered her horse and the two of them gathered mint for faithfulness and borage for tranquility, and scattered them in a circle around the ancient oak. Then Aethelreda sang the song that she had been taught by her mother, who had been taught the song by the women elders of the Cantii, and she walked slowly around the oak with the ancient words on her lips. She asked for wisdom from the goddess Aine. She prayed for patience. She begged for the return of the one that she loved.

Then the two of them drank some mead, laced with a particular rare fungus, and lay on the moss while the strong beverage coursed through their blood and visions raced through their heads, until they fell asleep.

When they awoke, Aethelreda questioned Mildreth about her dreams.

"Mildreth, did you dream?"

"Yes, my Lady, I did have some dreams."

"What was it that you dreamed of?"

"I, I... do not want to say. They were not pleasant dreams."

"Did you dream of me, or of our people?"

"Yes."

"Then, Mildreth, you must tell me."

"My Lady, I dreamt there was a fierce battle and that wild men had taken over our settlement."

Aethelreda was silent. She, too, had dreamt of bloodshed and violence. And Paulos was nowhere in her dream at all.

***

Aethelreda had been pulled back into the old religion, but in Wingham, Blaedswith was trending in the opposite direction.

Each morning, she had observed that Flavius arose and knelt at his bed in prayer. Sometimes, Aeditha joined him, and sometimes she was busy tending to one of the children.

Every Sunday, he walked to Saint Martin's church for services, and took his whole family, and other days besides, if there was a feast day of some sort or other.

While she had greatly disliked the Roman soldier who had stolen away her niece, she had come to see that he was a man of unfailing good cheer, and that he cared about others around him, at least as much as he cared about himself. And the thing that she could not ignore was that he adored his wife and family.

Since he lived under her roof, Blaedswith was able to observe his life, up close, and there was something about it that was attractive to her. For one thing, he seemed to have a steady and constant connection to his God.

One evening, when Flavius was watching his children in the courtyard, while Aeditha was elsewhere, Blaedswith engaged him in conversation.

"I must say that I am favorably impressed by what a good father you are, Flavius."

"Thank you, Mistress Blaedswith. I do my best."

"You clearly love Aeditha and your children."

"I do, yes."

"And you also seem to be devoted to your God."

Flavius took his eyes off his toddler for a few seconds to see the expression on his hostess's face. He thought that she might have been baiting him, but she appeared to be serious.

"I do love God, yes. I have had the privilege of the good teaching of Father Oswald, which has given me a strong foundation to build on."

"When you came to Britain, what gods did you follow?"

"I was very confused when I came here. My brother embraced the Christian faith in his youth and became a priest. He rose up the ranks of the church. He is now the leader of the church, the Pope. But I was just thrashing around in a sea of discord. I did not know what to believe. The Roman gods were so numerous, and so, well, fallible. The Christian God was so singular and expected such a high standard of behavior that it seemed impossible to obtain. I was not much attracted to either faith."

"Quite so. What changed your mind?"

"Father Oswald changed my mind. He was not like any other Christian I had ever met. He was always so full of joy. He took life by both hands and wrung every second of pleasure out of it that he could. And yet he was a man of purity of life. I never saw him drunk. He never gambled, or bedded women, nor was he dishonest or unethical. But neither was he dour or judgemental. He introduced me to a God that has made this earth for its inhabitants to enjoy, as long as we love Him and take care of each other."

There was a period of silence. Blaedswith was remembering Father Oswald, who was indeed a joy-filled man. He had told her much the same things as Flavius had just expressed: that God wanted his people to enjoy the world he had given them. And yet she hesitated. She knew there had to be a catch. The cross and the crucifixion did not seem to her like much of a way to enjoy God's creation.

When Aeditha rejoined the little group, Blaedswith and Flavius were discussing the fact that Merewenne had just cut three new teeth at one time and had been crabby and inconsolable until they had broken through her gums. Flavius knew he would have to wait patiently for Mistress Blaedswith to give in to the tug of the spirit in her soul.

Chapter Fifteen

The Second Missionary Trip

In his later years at the monastery, Paulos had a hard time recalling what had happened on his second mission trip to Britain. That was mostly because his mind did not want to recall it, especially not as he lay dying. The memories kept trying to impinge on his consciousness and he pushed them away. He tried not to ever even touch on the nightmare that they had discovered when they had returned to Lower Combe. But the memories haunted him in blinding flashes like scenes illuminated from the darkness by lightning bolts. They came unbidden and he could only put his hands in front of his eyes and wait until the scenes had dissipated.

Fra Paulos and Fra Augustus had been asked to return to Canterbury a second time with a message for Father Oswald. The Pope ostensibly wanted to commend the cleric for his work among the people of Britain. Reports had arrived back to Rome of how many churches the saintly man had founded. It was astounding to the Pope how readily the Britons seemed to convert when they heard the Gospel from their own people. From what he heard in dribs and drabs from travelers, the numbers of the converted were steadily rising, year by year.

The Pope hoped Oswald could be persuaded to return to Rome to receive his thanks, in person. But his desires were not without self-interest. He also hoped he might persuade the cleric to be more closely associated with the church in Rome, which would bring the Briton more securely under his influence. He felt the need to regain some power and influence in a country where the Christian faith was apparently growing in leaps and bounds. It made him nervous to think that some bishop in Britain might rise to eminence and try to overshadow his own influence.

The mission from Rome made landing in Richborough, which the Romans had named Rutupiae, about sixty miles north of the Lower Combe inlet. It was not part of the Pope's instructions to visit Lower Combe (in fact, it was explicitly forbidden), but Paulos, who had worked his way back into the good graces of the Pope while he was in Ravenna, was bound and determined to do so, and to keep his visit a secret. He had left Aethelreda without a proper farewell, and with so many things unsaid, that, at the very least, he wanted to see her face to face and ask her for her forgiveness.

It was with stunned shock, then, that Paulos and Augustus discovered that Lower Combe had been subjected to a surprise raid by a band of Saxons who had landed in Lower Combe inlet, in the spring after Paulos had left Britain, and that Aethelreda had been taken prisoner by the Saxon leader, Garth. These things became evident to them before they even entered Lower Combe.

Paulos and Augustus, with a couple of Roman soldiers, had made their way, with difficulty, down the winding and overgrown trail to Lower Combe. The trip that would have normally taken three or four days, took five. They had expected to come to the entrance of the settlement of Lower Combe and to be invited in like old friends. But, instead, they had been intercepted about half a mile from the settlement by two lookout guards. One of those guards happened to have been in the settlement when the monks had last visited, although no one recognized him until later.

The hidden Lower Combe guards had let the Roman guards go past them and then had quickly and silently grabbed the two monks, stuffing cloth into their mouths and expertly tying their hands behind their backs, before whipping around and doing the same to their guards. One of the Lower Combe guards immediately recognized Fra Paulos, but could not say anything. Instead, he made a great show of apprehending the monks and facing down their Roman guard.

Paulos thought that he might have known the Briton who had looked him in the eyes and given him a slight nod of acknowledgement, but he realized that that did not mean he was a friend. He would have to work out if he was friend or foe before he engaged with him, if he wanted to stay alive, and that meant submission. The four of them were pushed to their knees by the side of the narrow track and interrogated. It had all happened so fast that both Paulos and Augustus were stunned into silence.

Paulos and Augustus and their two chaperones were marched into Lower Combe with their hands behind their backs and their mouths still gagged. The two monks tried in vain to communicate with each other, and with their guards. They had no plan for a meeting such as the one they had just experienced.

Inside the gate to the settlement, they were horrified to see the state of the village. When they had been there last, it had been primitive but orderly. In two years it had deteriorated into a filthy group of hovels without benefit of organization or order. The dye vats, colored yarns hung out to dry, baskets of herbs and flowers, all had disappeared. Here and there a sheep grazed on a patch of weeds without much enthusiasm.

There was no sign of Aethelreda. They were marched to the center of the settlement and tied to two posts at the edge of the square while the guards worked out what to do with them. The guards talked openly about the situation in front of Paulos and Augustus, and the other two men. It was almost as if they wanted them to know what would be happening. Again, Paulos wondered if one of the guards had recognized them and was informing them of their plans on purpose.

"I will tell Garth what we have found," one of them said.

The one whom Paulos thought he might have recognized said, "Garth will be out hunting. Hermanrich will be in charge. He and Thorsimund will be trying to persuade Aethelreda of their manhood. You know how that goes." He gave Paulos a look that was hard to interpret. Paulos was unsure if it was a look that said, 'It is what all men want to do to a woman like Aethelreda', or if he was saying, 'She is in danger'. But then he removed all doubt from Paulos's mind. He said in a flat, hard voice, "She will refuse them. They will force her and then they will beat her." The man glanced back at Paulos, and then said directly to him in a whisper, "Tonight they will all drink too much and fall down drunk. We will come back and attend to you and these men at that time. It will be better that way."

When they finally laid eyes on Aethelreda, they saw a tragedy that stunned them both. No longer the proud and beautiful leader of her people, a Kentish Queen, she had been reduced to the status of a slave. She was shackled and bound and being dragged into the village center, near where the Romans had been bound to posts. Her hair was matted and unkempt and her gown was torn and stained. Her posture was stooped, and her head was bowed. But yet there was still something of her old fire in her. As they tied her to the flogging post, she looked around at her captors with defiance and cried out at them, "Do what you will! I will never submit to your rule. I am the ruler here!"

And they flogged her publicly for her insolence until her back bled ribbons of blood.

Neither Paulos nor Augustus could look away. There was something in her pride and stubbornness that would not let them close their eyes to shut it out. It was as if they needed to keep looking at her, as if they needed to direct their own strength into her body, and their own prayers into her mind, to give her courage and strength, and so that was what they did.

When it was over, Paulos discovered that he had been weeping, profusely and unconsciously. He and Augustus were both still bound and gagged, and so he had nearly choked with the effort to keep breathing while Aethelreda suffered, and he wept.

When they untied her and dragged her back to her home, the two men were left with their own thoughts. What had happened to the Cantii seemed unreal. The proud people had been conquered. Their leader had been kept alive to suffer pain and humiliation. Paulos wondered what had happened to Aethelreda's family, her brothers and sisters, and her cousins. Surely, she had not been left alone in her family settlement to suffer the punishment of having been overthrown. But there was no sign of any of her supporters.

Their escape that evening happened as the guard Raedbora had said.

First, there was a loud upheaval as Garth and his men arrived back from their day of hunting. They had a boar on a pike, and they were jubilantly shouting and singing. No one even noticed the four men tied to the posts in the far corner of the village square, as intent as they were on getting to the ale and celebrating the success of their hunt.

Shortly before sundown, while the boar was slowly being turned on the spit and the settlement was filled with the delicious smell of roasting pork, Raedbora quietly returned to his prisoners.

"Fra Paulos," he whispered, "it is I, Raedbora. I recognized you from when you were here two summers ago." He removed the gags from the men's mouths with a warning to be silent or they would all be killed. "Fra Paulos, I apologize for taking you captive, but I did not immediately recognize you, and by the time I did, I did not want to raise my partner's suspicions of my own loyalty to Lower Combe. So, I had to think on my feet, take you captive, and worry about your release on another occasion. But it seems that fortune is smiling on us by providing a boar and a feast. I can get you out of here tonight. I will encourage my partner to overindulge in ale and meat at the feast tonight. That will not be hard at all." He smiled ruefully.

"Then, when everyone is staggering, I will come back and set you all free. Since Garth does not even know you are here, it should not be difficult to do.

Unless my partner talks. But I know some things about him that I can use to keep him quiet."

The two monks looked at each other. Augustus knew what Paulos was going to say before he even opened his mouth.

"What about Aethelreda? We cannot leave her here. She must come with us."

Raedbora looked unhappy. "You perhaps are unaware that Aethelreda has a child? A girl?" He knew that the presence of a child would complicate any escape. They were, of course, not aware, but as far as both monks were concerned, that did not change anything. The solution was obvious to both of them.

Paulos said, "Then the child must come with us, too. And we must get out and be well on our way before anyone realizes we have gone. And you, too, Raedbora. Your life will be on the line if you stay here."

And so, that night, after dark, when not a man was left standing and sober, except Raedbora, who pretended to be as drunk as the rest of them, he arrived at the square, untied the four men and set them free. They hastily made their way to the entrance of the settlement, where they found Aethelreda waiting with a small child strapped over her bandaged wounds on her back, and Raedbora led them all into the woods.

If she recognized Paulos and Augustus, Aethelreda showed no sign of it. They all simply turned their backs on the settlement of Lower Combe and, using the light of the moon, they retreated as fast as they could, back up the rough trail toward Watling Street, where they would turn toward the coast, board the ship and make haste for Gaul.

At least, that was the new plan. But there was a small problem. Both Augustus and Paulos knew that they had a task to complete for the Pope, who had funded their voyage and provided all the crew. If they arrived back in Rome barely six months after they had left, having not even met up with Father Oswald, or Flavius, the Pope would be most unimpressed, even if their early departure had been to save lives. They well knew that Aethelreda was nothing to the Pope. She was a convert, certainly, but not a very important one. Her influence was quite limited. If they had been saving the life of Father Oswald, that would have been a different thing entirely.

Paulos and Augustus had made themselves known to Aethelreda once they were far enough away from the settlement to be sure that they were not being followed. Her reaction was an odd one. They expected some sign of joyful remembrance, but instead she turned from the two of them. It was as if she did not want to know either of them.

In fact, the situation was complicated for her. She hated that she had been a maiden in despair, in need of being saved. She was humiliated by being in such a destitute situation when they had found her. She had brought her woes upon herself by refusing to give in to Garth and his men, but she was not sorry. She might have appeared to have been conquered, but her heart and mind had never given up on being the Queen of the Cantii.

The two monks looked at each other in dismay. Neither of them knew how to react to her silence. Paulos spoke first.

"Aethelreda, beloved of God! I came back for you as soon as I could. Please believe me. Certainly, it was by no means soon enough, and I cannot comprehend the suffering you have endured. Had I known this would happen, I would never have left this island. Please forgive me for the delay in our return. It must have seemed like an eternity of waiting."

She turned to him then with her eyes blazing. "You deserted me when you went to Canterbury. I do not think I can forgive you for that. You were not to know that Lower Combe would be raided by the Saxons, that much I will allow, but you had given us up long before that, and it seems that your God had deserted us, too." She turned her back on them again and slogged on, with her child swaying on her back.

Paulos was cut to the quick. It was one thing to be lashed by her tongue for having left her. He deserved that. It was quite another to have the God he believed in, and loved, excoriated as well. But what was there to say? He hiked silently on, behind her. After another half a mile of hard going, he tried again.

"Aethelreda, please let me assist you in carrying your little one. Your back must be painful, and you must be very tired." Paulos had noticed the slight swelling of her abdomen and he suspected that she was again with child. That, and the malnourishment and physical mistreatment she had received, all contributed to the once strong and hardy woman looking weak and delicate. It was her fear of being caught that had kept her going in the first few miles, and then her anger and resentment fueled her legs and drove her on after that.

But at his offer to help her, she stopped. His kindness was always so unexpected to her. In the days when she reigned as queen of her people, men deferred to her, and were respectful, at least to her face, but very few had ever been kind, save Paulos and Augustus. They said they were following the example of the Lord Jesus, who was always kind. It was the one thing that interested her in Paulos's religion. It was the thing that had pulled her in. And it was very true that she was not going to be able to carry Merewenne for much longer. There was hardly any strength left in her. And her back was bleeding again. She could feel that the bandages were wet against her skin.

She untied the cloth sling that had held her daughter to her back and let the little tow-haired girl down. The child looked uncertain about what she was to do until, without looking at Paulos, Aethelreda whispered in her daughter's ear. Whatever she said, it did the trick, and when Paulos opened his arms to her, she scrambled up and clung to his hip. Between the two of them, he and Aethelreda shifted her to his back and tied the sling to enclose and support her. She was not heavy, and did not add much to Paulos's burden, but Aethelreda was glad to be able to straighten her back and walk without stooping. She said not a word to Paulos. She did not even look at him. They turned and resumed their journey.

Much of the trek to the ship was made in silence. The six adults and one small child ate sparingly, drank whenever water was available, slept under the trees, and all were glad to finally arrive at Richborough, where they boarded the ship and could rest and regroup.

Augustus had tried to talk to Aethelreda in lieu of Paulos, but she did not warm to him, either. In his less charitable moments, Augustus wondered why they had bothered to rescue her at all. Surely it was just a way of life for the people of that island that they were overtaken by one tribe, or another, including his own 'tribe', the Roman army. He wondered if they were not just delaying the inevitable by taking Aethelreda with them. What good would that do for her people in the long run? But he did not share any of those thoughts with Paulos.

In the evening of their first night aboard the ship, the captain, the second in command, and the two monks met to discuss how to fulfill their mission with their new responsibilities on board. Paulos wanted to sail immediately for Gaul and make haste for Rome. Augustus did not see why they could not delay a week or so and get a message to Flavius, and speak to Father Oswald, in person. The captain did not care one way or the other, as long as he did not have to take the responsibility for having already diverged from their planned mission. The monks might not be punished for failing to fulfill their mission, but he would be.

And so, it was decided to delay a few days, or as long as it would take to get a message to Flavius and to Oswald. Aethelreda and her child would remain on board the ship, under heavy guard, until the emissaries returned. They would leave for Canterbury at daybreak.

To Paulos's surprise, when he rose in the morning to pray, he found Aethelreda waiting for him. Without any pleasantries, Aethelreda said, "I feel I ought to say that I am grateful for being rescued from Garth's clutches, even though I feel shame in not being able to fight him off myself."

Paulos was shocked. He could not imagine why a woman, even one as strong and motivated as Aethelreda, would ever think they could fight off a lump of a man like Garth. But, apparently, she had been suffering because she had failed to get free of him, as well as suffering all the physical abuse she had endured.

"You do not need to feel shame about anything that has happened to you. How could you be expected to free yourself from that monster?"

"Segovax and Lugotori did their best to help me. They managed to get my brothers and sisters away. They are somewhere in northern Kent now. I hope they are safe."

"That is very good to hear. But where are Segovax and Lugotori now? Are they in northern Kent, too?"

Her answer saddened him, even more.

"No. Alas. They were both killed. They were publicly and slowly executed for attempting to free me."

Paulos muttered a quiet prayer for the souls of the two men who in their last hours had behaved bravely and with honor.

"I am so sorry to hear that they died."

A derisive snort escaped from Aethelreda. "The one time in their miserable lives that they acted with honor, and they were not rewarded for it, but rather punished with a cruel death!"

Paulos caught the inference in her words. The gods had not seemed to be there for her or for her cousins, and neither had the God that he believed in. He said the only thing he could think of.

"That is a terrible injustice. It is the hope of every Christian that all the injustices of this world will be made right in the next world."

"My cousins were not Christians. They followed the old gods," she retorted.

Again, Paulos could only say what he hoped would be true. "It is my belief that God will judge them according to what was in their hearts. Their attempt to save you speaks of men who were brave, men who loved their queen, men who were faithful to their family and their tribe. God will see that, Aethelreda."

"I hope you are right. I am terribly confused by your God. I have tried to understand, but I do not know what good there can be in worshipping a God who died a horrible death himself."

"The good is found in that our God knows what it feels like to have been tortured, beaten, and killed. And our God stands with all others who suffer the same. And in the life beyond this one, there will be rewards for enduring."

At those words, Aethelreda made a choking sound. Paulos looked at her with concern. He did not know if she was still being derisive, or if she was trying not to weep. She turned toward him, and he saw there were tears pouring down her contorted face. She, who had been so brave for so long while she was being tortured, beaten, and raped, and had rarely wept, had finally let go. He took her into his arms, and she wept for what seemed like a very long time. Paulos simply held her.

The others were getting ready to leave for the mission, but Augustus quietly told them that they would not go until Aethelreda had composed herself again.

When she was calm, Aethelreda stood and moved away from Paulos. She turned to him and said, "I can never thank you enough for caring about me."

There was open love in his eyes when he replied, "And I can never thank you enough for being the inspiring, brave woman that you are. You are worthy of the title 'Queen of the Cantii'. I hope I can help you to live a good life in Rome, even if it is only for a little while, until you are recovered enough from the injuries to your body, and spirit, and soul."

She turned away again and said with surprisingly little bitterness, "I hope you will not go to Canterbury and leave me again."

It was Paulos's turn to admit the thing that had troubled him for so long. "I know it was a terrible thing to leave you with only a small note of farewell. I realize that was not anywhere near sufficient after what we had been to each other. I promise you that unless something untoward happens, I will be back here in less than a week, and perhaps I will have Father Oswald with me. And then we will go to Rome and be together."

This time, he was as good as his word.

The mission to connect with Father Oswald would have been a resounding success if Father Oswald had agreed to return to Rome with them. But Father Oswald had no use for Rome. He hated the groveling of some local clerics who, in his estimation, were trying desperately to grab hold of the hem of Rome. He did not need the Pope to tell him what to do. He resented the whole notion of the need for papal oversight, as if he could not be trusted to teach the right things to his people, and to shepherd them as a faithful leader. There was only need for one overseer, as far as he was concerned, and that was the Lord God Almighty. He had founded church after church in the Canterbury area, and his own church of the Holy Trinity was bursting at the seams with faithful Christians who had given up the old ways and were following Christ. The only accolades Father Oswald sought were the words of his Savior, which he longed to hear when he finally crossed over to the greater life – "Well done, Thou good and faithful servant!"

And so, armed with facts and figures of souls saved, members baptized, churches founded, but not accompanied by Father Oswald, Paulos and Augustus returned to the ship.

Neither did they physically meet with Flavius, but they received a report of him from Father Oswald that Flavius was doing good work in Wingham. He was now the father of four children, and he was making a good living mending roofs, walls, and even building small dwellings for the people of Wingham. Best of all, from the Pope's point of view, Flavius was assisting Father Aelwyn at St Martin's church in Wingham. All in all, it made a very positive report to present to His Eminence on their return.

Chapter Sixteen

The Voyage

The crossing back to Gaul was a rough one. The sea was choppy, and an unseasonably strong wind did its best to capsize them, even though their ship had a good draft and was built to withstand such storms.

It was hardest of all for Aethelreda, who was feeling most unwell due to the fact that another new life was developing within her womb, the result of being systematically raped. In general, her health was fragile due to months of sustained beatings and violations of her person. She stood in the bow of the ship for most of the journey, where the salt spray lashed at her, but she felt less nauseous there in the open air than when she was down below. Her little daughter was always close beside her, and either Paulos or Augustus was always near to the two of them after one of the sailors had attempted to assault Aethelreda in the first few hours of the voyage.

At the start of the journey, she had been down below where the hammocks were, attending to her little girl, when one of the sailors came upon her. He approached her stealthily, but she saw him and turned quickly to face him.

"So, you are a Queen, are you?" he leered. She ignored the insult. She hoped he would be rebuffed and go away without violence. But he did not go away. He went right up to her and said, "You do not look much like a queen to me. You are filthy. You need a bath, and your hair disgusts me." But then he leaned toward Aethelreda, stretching out his hand to touch her face as he added, "But I would love to help you bathe."

That was the moment that Paulos came down the hatch. He did not hear their conversation, but he saw the sailor reach out to touch Aethelreda and he heard her proclaim in a strident voice, "Do not dare to touch me!" and in her hand, as if by magic, appeared a dagger which she pressed against the sailor's throat, drawing blood.

He stepped back rapidly with an exclamation, "Stercus!" – just as Paulos grabbed his arms and held them roughly behind the man's back. The blood from the wound in his neck dripped on the man's shirt, and on the floor.

"If you as much as look at the Queen of the Cantii again, your head will be removed from your shoulders by the Queen herself." The anger in Paulos's voice nearly choked him. After all she had suffered, to be set upon by a man on the ship, where she was supposed to have been under his protection, was almost too much.

The sailor left with as much dignity as he could manage, to find a rag to press against the cut on his neck. Aethelreda had only scratched him, but she left no doubt that she could, indeed, cut his whole head off if she was angered. Paulos had forgotten how strong and wild and free the Queen of the Cantii really was.

That was the only attempt to take advantage of Aethelreda for the rest of the journey.

Paulos was puzzled as to how Aethelreda had come by the dagger she had used on the sailor. He knew that she had not been armed when she had left Lower Combe.

Although Aethelreda clearly still had not forgiven Paulos for deserting her, and might refuse to speak to him, he decided to simply ask her where the dagger had come from. Her answer surprised him and brought a whole new emotion up from the hidden depths of his soul.

"Augustus gave me his own dagger for my protection. He at least thinks ahead and plans for what might happen."

Augustus! He had given her his own dagger, which he kept on his person for his own physical safety. Paulos had never suspected that his brother in the faith might be subject to Aethelreda's charms, but that was what immediately sprang to mind when he heard that Augustus had thought to protect her.

Paulos had never before experienced the gut-twisting feeling that came over him when he considered the possibility that Aethelreda might begin to love Augustus more than she loved him. He did not at first even recognize the jealousy that made him feel the bile rise from his stomach, and he pushed the feeling speedily aside with a prayer for his salvation from all evil thoughts.

Because of the weather, the crossing took more than one day. As they prepared to bed down for the night, Aethelreda found herself watching Paulos and Augustus praying the evening office together. She listened to the melodious sounds of the Latin as they chanted the psalm in unison. Something moved in her soul as she observed the men of God, on their knees, in a world of their own where time seemed to stand still for them. She knelt down next to them and bowed her head. She hoped that their calm would fill her heart also. She needed it because although she knew she was in a safe place, she did not know what was ahead of her, and she was apprehensive for the future.

The sea had calmed down considerably by then, but the ship still rocked, and Paulos put out his hand to hold her arm and steady her as she knelt in prayer beside them. She acknowledged his help with a short nod.

When the prayers were over, the men stood, but Aethelreda made no move to go and lie down in the space allotted to her. She remained there on her knees. Paulos was puzzled. Clearly, Aethelreda had something else on her mind.

"Is there something that I can do for you, my dear?"

"I do not think so. Not beyond what you have already done for Merewenne and for me. I can never repay you for that. But I was just thinking of how you must have been shocked when you returned to Kent and discovered our settlement had been overrun by the Saxons."

"Of course we were, but the worst thing was finding out that you had been held captive all that time. How you must have suffered."

Aethelreda was still on her knees. She did not look at Paulos as she spoke, but she focused on the hammock where her child lay, attached to the side of the ship. She spoke as if she was remembering a dream.

"I was taken on the first day that the Saxons breached our fences. When I heard the fighting, I came out of my house with my dagger and was immediately overtaken by Thorsimund. It was a stupid move on my part. I should have known better. I should have stayed in hiding and then stolen away to safety. But all I could think of was that I was the leader and that I needed to save my people. How foolish I was to think that I could have done so."

"You were trying to put your people first."

Aethelreda gave a slight grimace. She knew that Paulos was trying to make her feel better, but she had bottled up her guilt and shame for a long time and she felt an intense need to admit her own culpability to someone who would understand her. She turned to

Paulos and with characteristically brutal honesty she said what was on her mind.

"But I ended up leaving them to fight a battle they were not prepared for, and without military leadership. If I had just been more careful. If I had not thought I was invincible..." Her voice petered out.

Paulos continued, "But Segovax and Lugotori were there, and your house guards. They must have put up a good fight, did they not?"

"Truly the guards did, but my cousins were occupied with the struggle to get Wilfred and Toberon and the others out of the settlement and away to safety. I sometimes wonder if they should have stayed and fought, but because of what they did, my brothers and sisters are safe somewhere and did not have to suffer like so many of my people.

"And then Segovax and Lugotori were discovered in Lower Combe a few days later when they crept back in to try to regroup. I believe they were going to try to free me. But they were, as I have already told you, captured, tortured, and killed. The Saxons made me watch while they did it, as a warning of what would happen to me if I tried to escape. It surprised me how brave they were. I am so sorry for the years that I thought they were useless excuses for human beings."

Paulos felt a pang of deep remorse himself. He, too, had thought they were spineless and unethical.

"Yes. Sometimes you see remarkable heroism from the people you would least expect to show it. I think we can pray for God's mercy to receive the two of them. How horrifying it must have been for you."

"It was nothing compared to the days, weeks, and months that followed. If it had not been for the fact that I never lost the hope that I might get free and kill Garth and his henchmen, I would have rather died with my cousins."

"But now you are free."

"I am free, and for that I am in debt to you, and the Pope, but my people still are not."

"Perhaps we will be able to raise a fighting force and return to Kent to overturn these evil usurpers."

"Perhaps. But I cannot allow myself to hope for so much."

***

The journey across Gaul was painfully slow for the group. What normally would have taken three months took four, because Paulos insisted that they rest often for Aethelreda and Merewenne's sake.

As they crossed the Alps, the sky darkened into the color of a bluish bruise, and there was a late-season snow fall. It made them miserable as they slogged on through the icy wetness. The worst was when they made camp for the night. There was no shelter except what they put together from a few branches and some loose stones and erected on the lee side of the wind. The small fire that they made to warm themselves was inadequate.

They needed to lie bundled together to share what body warmth they had. Paulos organized them so that Aethelreda and Merewenne were in the middle of the group, with he and Augustus on each side of them, and the four soldiers who accompanied them were gathered around their perimeter.

Aethelreda's face was white as she lay down. She did not do well with men being so close to her. It brought back far too many ugly and recent memories. Paulos could feel the tension in her body when he lay down beside her. She wrapped the rough blanket more tightly around her so that her body was separated from his, but the tension did not go away. After a few minutes of lying rigidly still, a low moan forced its way out of her clenched teeth.

Paulos sat up on his elbow. "What is wrong, Aethelreda?"

"I cannot breathe," she choked. "I need to be by myself without people touching me." She was almost weeping with agitation and fear.

Paulos understood quickly the source of her feelings after what she had been through in her own house, being forced to lie with men who raped her, but she could not leave the warmth of the group when it was so cold.

"I am so sorry, but we all need to be bundled together or you will get frostbite in the cold!"

Another moan escaped her lips. "I cannot do this. I am used to the cold. I will be protected by my clothing and blankets, and by Almighty God."

Paulos was too agitated to be upset by the immaturity of Aethelreda's faith. The inadvisability of testing God in such a way was a conversation they would have to have, but he knew that was not the right time. Her breathing was ragged, and she struggled to get up from her place in the middle of the group. She scooped up Merewenne and stepped carefully over Augustus, who was already soundly asleep. The soldier next to Augustus muttered angrily when she accidentally stepped on his foot.

She moved to a place just out of sight and under a bush, where she brushed the snow off the leaves on the ground and made a place to lie, with her little girl bundled inside the blankets and next to her chest. Paulos let her go. When he thought she was asleep, he joined them, wrapping his blankets securely around all three of them, and praying for the protection of the whole group from wolves, bandits, and all other things that might be a threat in the night.

In the morning, as Aethelreda was waking, she became aware of the warm body beside her. She knew who it was, and instead of fear she was surprised to feel a moment of contentment.

"Paulos?"

He sat up quickly. He had intended to move back to the other group before she awoke, so that she would not be alarmed.

"Please forgive me. I only wished to help you and Merewenne keep warm. I was afraid you would not survive."

To his surprise, she smiled. "But we did survive. All three of us. Thanks be to God."

She said no more about the incident, and bundling together in such close proximity was not necessary on any other night. Paulos remembered how she had reacted and wondered how it would be if they had to share a bed in Rome.

It was summer by the time they reached home.

Chapter Seventeen

In Rome

On his monastery deathbed, the aged Paulos's mind turned to brighter things. He had glossed over what had happened to Aethelreda at the hands of the Saxon, Garth, because there was no longer any point in recalling the pain. He preferred to think of the times when they had been happy together, like the time when they were living in the small villa on the outskirts of the city of Rome, where no questions were asked about who they were, and where nothing was expected of them. They were simply a couple with a small child and another baby on the way, who, for reasons best known to themselves, chose to live outside the city. It was assumed that their history involved some scandal about a well-born Roman man taking a barbarian wife.

Many of their neighbors were outcasts, too. They included people who had been accused of crimes and had served their sentences, but who were no longer accepted by the citizens of Rome. He did not mind living among the outcasts. His Lord had done the same.

Paulos had taken up the work of a potter again, remembering his family occupation, and found that he enjoyed the feeling of the clay in his hands as he made rough pots for themselves and for the market. As the clay was formed into bowls and pots, he was reminded that God was the Great Potter, and it pleased him to be involved in the art of creation in his own small way. Life, then, was simple and fulfilling. It was one of the happiest periods in his long life, and despite what his abbot might have thought, it was also a time when he felt very close to God.

Aethelreda had been kept busy caring for her young daughter, cooking and cleaning their small cottage. It was a new life for a woman who had been cared for by servants ever since she had been born, even if her physical surroundings had been so much more primitive back in Kent; but Aethelreda was adaptable. She never complained about her lower status as the life of a Roman commoner. And she had been happy in her new life and new home, at first. She had been amazed to discover that Paulos knew how to cook, because each monk had to help in the kitchen of the monastery. It made her love him all the more to see him stirring the lentils over the fire, with his dark hair damp from the heat and his cheeks ruddy. What other man in the whole world would care so much for her that he would rise early and light the fire and warm the water for the broth while she awakened slowly to take care of her little girl? What other man in the whole world would love her and ask so little of her body as he did, but whose eyes would brighten with an inner light when he saw her standing in the doorway?

Each day she set aside some time to walk in the nearby countryside with her little daughter at her side, where she would gather interesting herbs and flowers from the fields and roadsides. There were so many colorful and fragrant plants to be found that she was amazed. And she was delighted to find that the Roman plants were tasty, too. There was peppery oregano, savory parsley, and spicy rosemary to begin with. They all had such delightful names and such delicious aromas when they were crushed or cut up for cooking.

She had befriended an elderly neighbor, Octavia, who told her the names of the plants she had gathered, and their uses in cooking, medicine, and some more questionable practices such as making people ill, or rendering them unconscious. Octavia reminded Aethelreda of the older women among her own people who knew their herbs and their uses, and she quickly discovered that she had made a good friend.

Octavia had accepted Aethelreda quite readily. At first, she had thought her new neighbor was a barbarian, but she was soon put right by Aethelreda, who had told her that she was from the island of Britain, which explained why she spoke Latin with such a strange accent. Octavia was delighted to have Aethelreda and her little daughter living near her, even though the man she thought was her husband seemed much too interested in religion. He had already talked with her about her faith, and encouraged her to speak about hers, which she had declined to do. She had shaken off all the old gods when she had been cast out of the city, and was not interested in the new God that Paulos spoke of so passionately.

But Octavia had no family of her own, and she was often lonely in her exile. The only visitor she ever had was a cured meat seller who occasionally came by on his sales route, and she suspected that even he had an ulterior motive. She suspected that he was a spy for someone in Rome. Octavia could also see that the new family needed someone for support, which meant that their need for community was mutual.

And then there was the fact that Aethelreda was with child. She would soon need someone to help her at the birth. Octavia had brought many children into the world. She had also stopped many of them from being born. It was because of a failed pregnancy termination, resulting in the death of a highly born Roman woman, that she had ended up living on the outskirts of the city. It was a disaster for Octavia at first, because she loved the comforts of Roman life, and the community that was found there. But as it turned out, she came to enjoy the country life as much, if not better, than the life she had previously lived as the wife of a senator who did not appreciate her.

In due course, Aethelreda's child was born. Octavia had assisted at the birth. Paulos remembered with a shudder how shocked Octavia had been when she saw Aethelreda's brutalized body. He was thankful that Aethelreda was so busy with the process of birthing her baby that she did not see the expression on her midwife's face.

Despite the injuries that Aethelreda had suffered, she gave birth to a healthy boy, and the memories of those days after his birth seemed to be lit with the suffused golden light of a late summer afternoon for Paulos. He remembered only the harmony and the happiness. He thought about that period of his life often, and with joy and gratitude. It had been easy for him to imagine during that time that Aethelreda was his wife, and that the newborn boy was his own, which was an altogether much more pleasant fantasy than the reality of the situation.

An outsider would have looked at the couple and seen that the two of them were deeply bonded and loved each other completely. Aethelreda's love was grounded in gratitude and respect. She found it easy to love a man who treated her like a queen and loved her children as if they were his own. And as inexperienced as Paulos was, he knew how to love someone.

But the outsider would have been surprised to discover that their love was platonic. They did not live fully as man and wife. After what had happened to her, Aethelreda would never again be willing to allow a man to enter her. She had suffered beatings and torture, and had been repeatedly raped by the man who called her 'wife', as if the word was an epithet. She had been damaged beyond repair.

Paulos knew most of what had happened to her and how she was still badly affected by the trauma, but some things she had kept to herself, like how, even now, she found it hard to bear being touched by anyone, and how much hate she harbored for the man who had held her captive.

Instead of dwelling on the horror that he had discovered on his second trip to Britain, Paulos brought to mind the events of the night in the first week after the birth of the boy that Aethelreda called Aedisonne. She had wanted to call the baby Paulos, but he persuaded her that using his name would not be seemly. He was not the father of the child, and he was a monk, after all. Monks were not supposed to father sons. Instead, she named him Adam's son, knowing that Adam was the first man that God had created. She refused to even speak of the man who had planted his seed in her, against her will. In fact, she could not be sure if it had been Garth or Hermanrich, or Thorsimund.

Her secret fear was that she might see one of those beasts in the face of her baby and be unable to love the child. But it had not been so. The infant was beautiful and more like its mother than anyone else, and she loved him as much as she loved Merewenne. They were innocent of the crimes that had planted them in her womb. She believed that if she loved them, they would grow into good people, without the mark of their violent beginnings causing harm in their lives.

After Aedisonne's birth, Paulos once more found himself admiring Aethelreda's incredible resolve. He knew that she would survive the terrible treatment that she had received and that eventually she would thrive. She was like the oaks of her native land – strong, resilient – and despite all the darkness that she had been surrounded with, she was filled with the desire to spread her arms up to the sun, like the branches of the noble tree, and to live.

He remembered a particular night that had changed everything. That night when the little girl, Merewenne, named after her grandmother, was asleep in her small bed – the one that he had made himself out of olive wood – and so, too, at last, was Aedisonne. Aethelreda was preparing herself for the bed that they shared because of lack of space in the small cottage. After the episode on the road through the Alps, they slept with space between them, neither one touching the other.

As she washed, her linen nightgown had slipped over her shoulder and exposed part of her back. Paulos winced at the sight of the many ridged and purplish scars which were evidence of the beatings she had endured at the hands of her captors.

His emotions were tender that night. The mortification of her body was something that he could hardly bear to think of, and he usually turned away from the sight. But that night was different. He had never approached her before in such a way, and although he expected her to push him away, he went to her, and holding her gently, he kissed the scars on her back, as if with his love he could erase them from her flesh. For the first time, she let him touch her.

"I am so sorry for your suffering, Aethelreda," he murmured. His voice was uneven from emotion.

"Do not be sorry," she said almost roughly, steeling herself to allow the man that she loved to get so close to her bare flesh. Her voice caught in her throat as she continued, "He could do whatever he wanted to my body, and he did. But he could not take from me my heart, or my soul." Still with her back to him, she said, "My heart belongs to you, Paulos, and my soul belongs to God."

He had never heard such precious words in all his life, and he found himself holding his breath, for fear of breaking the spell of the moment. He wanted to respond, but he was reduced to silence. What could he say that would let her know how tender he felt? What could he say that would not sound conflicted by his love for her and his love for God?

She pulled away from him and lay down on the bed with her face turned to the wall. After a moment of uncertainty as to whether he had hurt her by his silence, Paulos lay down beside her and held her close to him. They lay cradled together, and both of them wept for the sadness and cruelty of the world, and for the beauty of the love that they knew could overcome it all.

In the morning, Aethelreda was up before Paulos, even though she had been up twice through the night to nurse Aedisonne. Her demeanor was the same as it usually was, and she seemed to have forgotten the events of the previous night, when she had allowed Paulos to get physically close to her. But Paulos knew she had not forgotten. She was just an expert at living life without letting the events of the day before overcome her spirit. He had not forgotten, either. He would never, ever, forget the night that he had held her and prayed for her to be healed of all the pain that she had suffered. It was one of the most sorrowful days, and at the same time one of the most joyful days in his life.

The day after she had allowed Paulos to hold her was also a significant day for Aethelreda. It was the day that she discovered the opium poppy and its uses. Octavia smiled when Aethelreda took the beautiful scarlet poppy flower to her house, showed it to her, and asked her to identify it.

"This, my dear, is the perfect poison," Octavia said, her smile covering her mixed emotions.

"What do you mean by 'perfect' poison?" Blaedswith had told her about nightshade, and belladonna, and yew, but she had never described them as a perfect poison. There were always risks to their uses. Aethelreda was intrigued.

"Opium in small amounts helps digestion and helps a person to sleep. In larger doses, it kills a person without a trace. This is perfect for killing violent husbands." Octavia was no longer smiling. What had occurred to her was no joke. Aethelreda looked at her uncertainly. She thought that the only 'husband' Octavia knew about was Paulos.

"Surely you do not think I want to kill Paulos?"

Octavia gave her a sharp look. "No. Not Paulos. Your husband in Britain."

"Garth!" The name burst from Aethelreda's lips with explosive hatred. "He was not my husband! I was his prisoner! Did Paulos tell you about him?"

Octavia was not surprised at her young friend's outburst. Octavia had been mistreated by her husband decades ago, and she hated him still. If only she had known then what she now knew about herbs, she might have freed herself much sooner. She sighed and took Aethelreda's hand.

"My dear, when I came to assist you with the birth of Aedisonne, it could hardly escape my notice that you had been repeatedly raped and violated. You were scarred from the tears and cuts you had received. But even before that, when he asked me if I might assist at the birth of your little one, Paulos told me that you had been taken prisoner back in Britain and subjected to these terrible things that had damaged your body and your mind. That was why he had brought you here to Rome. To seek peace and a calm place for you to recover from your injuries."

Aethelreda gently withdrew her hand. There was a silence while she contemplated the fact that Paulos had spoken about the horrors she had endured, to their neighbor, without telling her. He was usually so protective of her privacy. She reasoned that he must have been feeling desperation over the impending birth of her child. After all, he had had no experience in birthing babies. But he must have sensed the same things in Octavia as she did when he went to seek her help. She had an inner strength that showed in her bearing and a kindness that showed in her face. She was someone that could be trusted.

Then Octavia took Aethelreda firmly by the shoulders and said with passion in her voice, "My dear girl, the man who did these things to you deserves to die!"

Aethelreda drew in her breath, sharply. Garth's death was something that she had fantasized about almost every night that she had been held captive. She had wanted to plunge a knife deeply into his chest and watch him die slowly, and in pain, if possible. She had wanted to see the bloodstained bubbles of his last breath bursting slowly on his lips while his eyes glazed over as his life left him. She was sure that she would hold those memories in her mind forever and take pleasure from them.

But to get near him to do the deed had been the problem back then. A brutal man like Garth had many enemies and always surrounded himself with guards, night and day. She had also contemplated poisoning him, but Garth had never eaten a bite of food without it being tasted first by a servant. Sometimes he even forced her to be his food taster. It made him laugh to see the fear in her eyes as she tried the mushrooms before he ate them, never sure if they would be her last bite on earth.

That was back then, and now there was the added problem of her new-found faith. You were supposed to love your enemies, not murder them, according to Paulos. But one of the tenets of the Christian faith that Aethelreda had problems with was that of forgiveness. She and Blaedswith had both agreed that the whole idea of forgiving someone seventy times seven times, as Jesus had taught, did not make any sense. They talked endlessly about it and wondered how anyone could forgive someone who had badly harmed another person, especially someone that you loved. At that time, Blaedswith was the only one of the two who had suffered a devastating personal loss.

But Aethelreda had been raised with the same principles as Blaedswith. Revenge was strong within their culture. Above all, neither of them could understand how the loving, kind, and perfectly good Jesus Christ had forgiven those who crucified him. Paulos tried to explain that forgiveness was one of the central tenets of the faith, and why. He said that if you held on to grudges, you really only harmed yourself. But when she exclaimed that some wrongs resulted in more than just grudges, some wrongs were too awful to forgive, and that made the whole idea preposterous, he ended up by saying that he hoped she would one day come to understand the importance of forgiveness. She knew then that he had never suffered such wrongdoing, and also that he had given up on trying to persuade her, for the time being.

Aethelreda began to collect the seedpods of the opium plants that she found in the fields. She slit them open, collected the precious milky juice, dried it, and stored the gummy resin in a pretty clay pot that Paulos had made for her. It was the first pot he had fashioned when he began to work at making pottery again. He had etched a simple pattern of crosses around the rim and she had carved a stopper from a piece of olive wood that fitted the jar precisely.

She kept the jar of potential bane on a high shelf above the bed so that little Merewenne could not get at it. Paulos thought she put it there because she treasured his first piece of pottery. She did treasure it for that reason, too, but even more so for its secret contents. The lovely pot, a gift of a man who loved her, contained the poison that would free her from her hatred of the man who had abused her. The irony made it even more precious to Aethelreda.

From the day that she discovered the perfect poison, she began to plan her return to Britain, with the sole purpose of seeking revenge on the man who had brutalized her.

Paulos did not know about the opium, nor did he know of her murderous plan, until it was all over and done with.

Chapter Eighteen

It All Goes Wrong Again

Aethelreda began to register her desire to go back to Britain by making steady complaints about the Roman summer weather and suggesting that the climate was bad for her health and for that of the children. It was true that she was having difficulties adjusting to the comparatively intense heat difference between Kent and Rome. She had suffered sunburn on her face and hands, more than once, and her beautiful pale complexion had darkened to a light golden tan. Paulos thought it was a pleasing color and served to heighten the blueness of her eyes, but she did have to be careful that she did not stay in the sun too long, to avoid being painfully burnt.

And then one extremely hot day she had suffered a severe heat stroke after staying out in the field too long collecting wild arugula, which she loved to eat raw. She arrived back at the cottage with a white face, and beads of sweat on her brow. She had swooned at the doorstep when Paulos opened the door to her.

Paulos never suspected anything other than what he saw before his eyes, and when he bent to place his fingers on the tender spot in her neck, the faintness and feebleness of her pulse frightened him half to death. In fact, Aethelreda had taken a tiny dose of the opium to create her symptoms. She hoped to push Paulos toward helping her to return to Britain. She confessed her misdeed to Paulos only twenty years later.

With Aethelreda on the stone flags in front of him, Merewenne clinging to her skirts and Aedisonne wailing from the sling she carried him in on her back, Paulos realized his time in Eden was not going to last for very much longer. He had hoped for a year or two. He had really, in the secret places of his heart, hoped for forever with Aethelreda and his family, but he also suspected that was only wishful thinking. He thought that someone, soon, would find out where he was, and they would have to leave.

After that day when she had swooned in the heat, he realized that he would have to work out how to get Aethelreda and the children – who he was now bonded to as if they were his own – back to her native country.

That meant he would have to go and seek an audience with the Pope to explain the truth about his absence from Ravenna these last few months, and to get permission to go back to Britain. He did not relish the idea.

Augustus had shouldered the burden of explaining his disappearance to His Eminence when they had first returned. Although the Pope's official residence was still in Rome, for safety's sake the Pope had relocated himself temporarily to Ravenna, since the city of Rome had been overrun by the barbarians. That meant Augustus had gone to Ravenna to give the Pope his report about Flavius, but Paulos had not gone with him. In order to avoid the likely refusal from the Pope, Paulos had not gone to his monastery, but he had gone directly to Rome with Aethelreda and found the cottage that would shelter them for as long as would be needed. He could not risk the Pope denying him permission to care for her and to keep her safe.

In truth, she probably would have been just as safe living in or near the papal residence, but Paulos could not give her up to the care of others. The potential for mistreatment of her was far too great. He had witnessed how men treated her on the voyage to Gaul.

And there were other, more personal reasons as well. He wanted to be with Aethelreda, not separated and confined in a nearby monastery, which is what he knew would happen if he passed her care over to the Pope. He struggled anew with his vocation as a monk, and his desire to be a husband and father. He poured out his heart to God in his prayers, but could not hear an answer. Looking back, he realized that he already knew the answer, but he did not want to hear it.

In retrospect, the decision to skip the audience with the Pope and travel straight to Rome might have been his first and greatest act of disobedience to his superior, but at the time he was too confused to see it.

Paulos was unsure of the excuse Augustus had offered to the Pope for his absence. They had not really discussed it much, except to agree that the Pope was to be told as little as possible. Knowing Augustus, Paulos thought that he would have probably stuck close to the truth. (He was like a guileless dog that could not prevent the wagging of his tail even when he had just done something of which his master disapproved, and so he seldom tried to deceive anyone. His blushing was legendary.) Paulos felt sure that Augustus would have explained that his brother was accompanying the young woman they had rescued, and her family, to a safe place, and that he would return when he had found it.

Paulos hoped and prayed that the Pope would be so pleased by the good news about Flavius, and the wonderful news of the ongoing growth of the church, mostly due to Flavius's outreach under Father Oswald's guidance, that it would be enough to make his absence hardly noticeable.

But because he knew his community would be worried about him, he directed Augustus to send a secret message to the monastery to let the monks know that he was safe, and that he would return when he could.

Augustus was reliable, and Paulos was sure that he would have passed on the message to his abbot; but the truth was that he could have returned to Ravenna within a week or two after they had arrived, and he had not done so. He had stayed in his little cottage with his beloved family and would have stayed forever if Almighty God had allowed it. Paulos had found that he enjoyed his new role as caregiver, provider, and father to his little adopted family in a way that filled his heart with wellbeing and overflowed into his life as joy. He had never expected to be so fulfilled by becoming a family man. His previous family had been the men that he had been surrounded by at the monastery, and he had been satisfied with their companionship, until then.

But there on the outskirts of Rome with the rejects of Roman society, he had discovered something deeper in his life. His mind was changed by a small child who climbed on his knee and put her hand on his newly bearded chin to pull his face over for a kiss. His heart was softened by an infant who smiled his gummy smile at him every time he caught his gaze, and wiggled his whole body, and kicked his little legs in sheer pleasure at his presence. And most powerfully of all, he was persuaded by a woman whose loving gaze turned his legs to jelly and made him reach out to hold her in his arms. The idea of disrupting their peace and tranquility so soon, or ever, was abhorrent to him.

Aethelreda had blossomed under the golden Mediterranean sun in her first few months in Rome. Her broken body had healed of its bruises and lash marks, but her mind was still troubled. She had dreams at night that she was struggling with Garth, and woke with her cries strangled in her throat. Paulos would hold her close and whisper soothing prayers for her, until she slept again. The gentleness of her life in Rome was restorative, and she quickly grew stronger. She soon seemed to be returned to the proud and graceful woman that Paulos had met in Lower Combe. Her daily walks helped, as did her friendship with Octavia.

And then all of the progress that she had made began to fade. Paulos saw it happening in front of his eyes, and he was heartbroken. She did not divulge to him the cause of her malady, which was simply the drive for revenge that was eating away at her. She felt in her bones the truth of what Paulos had told her – that holding on to resentment caused damage to your own soul – but she was unable to shake the sickness. It seemed to be a part of her lineage, as deeply embedded in her as it was. Neither Paulos's prayers, nor her own, made even a dent in the hard exterior of hate that she felt, and the poison of the need for revenge that rose up in her throat like the sour contents of her stomach when she had eaten too much.

Paulos had no recourse but to leave her, go to Ravenna to see Pope Innocent, and to request papal permission to take her back to Britain. He had never thought he would have to be back in Ravenna so soon. The heartbreaking turn of events was something that he had not bargained for, because he had forgotten how vulnerable some people were to having their minds changed. Life in the monastery had no such ups and downs. The daily routine was as steady as a heartbeat, and once a man relaxed into it, there was little to cause mental anguish. Friendships were made and broken, of course, but all were subsidiary to their relationships with their abbot and with their Lord and Master, Jesus Christ. It seemed to him that no one was left to be heartbroken for very long.

He made the journey to Ravenna, carefully skirting the troubled areas. It had only been a few years since the barbarian hordes had overthrown Rome, and there was still the occasional skirmish between the new rulers and the Roman citizens. But Paulos had become skilled at remaining unseen, and he disappeared into the shadows whenever it looked as if trouble might lie ahead.

Coming into Ravenna for the first time in nearly three years was a complex emotional experience for Paulos, as he knew it would be. He fell in love again with the sight of the hills curving in layered scallops of varying greens on the horizon, and he savored the particular spicy smell of the atmosphere, perfumed with cypress and olive leaves and the hot salt air. But mixed with the warm memories of contentment and happiness that he had experienced in Ravenna was an unwelcome feeling of guilt. He had broken at least two of his monastic vows – chastity (in his heart, if not with his body) and obedience – and worse than that, he was not repentant. He found he had no desire to stay in that place, as beautiful as it was. His only home in Ravenna had been the monastery, and he was not sure he would be welcome back among the brothers after his period of apostasy; or, indeed, if he would want to stay.

He made his way to the papal residence near the center of the town and asked for entry to see His Eminence.

He found Pope Innocent seated in a throne-like chair in a grand receiving room. He was robed in a simple tunic of purple fabric, edged in gold, and was wearing a white cap that partially covered his silvered hair. His face was kindly.

Paulos knew that this Father of the Church had faced immense challenges. There were at least two major heresies of the faith that had arisen since he had been elected, and he was desirous of stamping them out. Then there was the constant threat to life and limb that was posed by marauding barbarians. All of that had taken a toll on a peace-loving man like Innocent. The Pope arose and opened his arms in welcome.

"Frater Paulos, welcome! It is so good to see you at last. May God be thanked for your safety, and for the success of your mission in Britain."

Paulos bowed in reverence. It was a good start.

"Thank you, Holy Father. I am also grateful to God for my safe deliverance from the voyage, and for the conversion of so many souls in Britain. And, of course, I am more than grateful for the health and safety of your brother Flavius, who has remained in Kent."

"Yes, Augustus gave a full report that made me leap for joy!"

Paulos smiled inwardly, imagining the holy man in front of him doing anything as undignified as leaping for joy. But the smile on Pope Innocent's face was genuine, and it encouraged Paulos to continue.

"Holy Father, your brother Flavius is a devout man. And a family man, too. His wife and children are faithful, and all have been baptized."

The Pope bowed his head and made the sign of the cross on his chest in gratitude. "That is another reason to give thanks to God."

"Indeed. But, Holy Father, I have come not just to tell you about Flavius; I have come to ask for your forgiveness for a private matter, and then, if I may be so bold, to also ask you for a favor."

The Pope did not react. Paulos heard his own heart beating loudly in his chest. What he was about to ask was very bold.

"Proceed."

"Holy Father, I went to Rome rather than stopping in Ravenna as my brother Augustus did, because I was accompanying a Kentish Queen and her daughter to a safe place where she could recover from injuries she had sustained at the hands of her Saxon captors." There was no change to the expression on the Pope's face. Paulos hesitated. He feared his request might not be going to get a favorable reception, after all. His reception had been so warm until that moment. But even though he felt that something had changed in the Pope's demeanor, he rushed on with his apology. "Please forgive me for assuming that I would be better able to care for her than you would have been. Forgive me for not realizing that you, too, would have felt pity for her and found shelter for her family, and that I did not need to overstep my boundaries. And please forgive me for not returning to my community here in Ravenna much sooner."

The Pope realized that Paulos was a clever man. By appealing to the Pope's own Christian sensibilities of compassion for others, he thought he would make it difficult for him to refuse his request. A pope should be a representative of Christ himself: loving and forgiving. Of course he would have sheltered the woman, who by all reports was beautiful and intelligent. But as certain as he was of Paulos's intelligence, he was equally certain that Paulos was not divulging all of the truth.

"Fra Paulos, for your doubt of my charity you are forgiven." The Pope made the sign of the cross over Paulos. "But, my brother, you have been away from your community for nigh on three years now. Will you ever come back, or have you strayed too far from your vows?"

Paulos was startled, and he was immediately stricken with guilt and fear. It appeared that Pope Innocent was no fool. He realized that he was the one who had been a fool to think that he would get away with his behavior and not suffer some consequences from his superiors. He wondered what his punishment might be.

"Holy Father, I have not broken the cords of my vows, but perhaps I have stretched them very tightly. I took Aethelreda into hiding on the outskirts of Rome and lived with her there until she had regained her health and vigor."

The Pope gave him a hard look. "Paulos, I know where you have been."

Paulos looked shocked for the second time. "How is it that you know? Even Augustus does not know where we are!"

The Pope's smile was weary. "I have people who keep an eye on things for me, in every winding pathway of the city, and far outside it. There is a purveyor of meat who visits the outskirts of Rome, at my request. A pope has to know where and who his enemies are."

Paulos rapidly put the pieces of the puzzle together. They had been visited by the cured meat seller. He had come to their door to offer his wares. Aethelreda had even bought some of his delicious home-cured sausage.

"So you knew where we were all along?"

"Yes, my son, I did."

"But you did not send for me? Why was that?" Paulos sounded incredulous.

"My son, I think you and Augustus did a brave thing by rescuing the young woman. But, by your avoidance of me when you first returned, I realized that you were having a spiritual struggle. I decided it would be wise to let you find out for yourself whether you wanted to be a monk or a husband. As it is, I think you are still torn between the two."

Paulos found himself quite suddenly short of breath and in need of a seat. He thought he perhaps had not breathed the whole time he had been in the presence of the Pope, who, appearing to have just noticed the whiteness of his face, gestured quickly toward a seat.

That the Pope had seen right through his subterfuge was bad enough, but he suddenly found that he was not as sure of his feelings for Aethelreda as he had been before coming face to face with the Holy Father. As it had just been put to him, Paulos discovered that he was unsure of what he wanted in the long term. He felt as if the Pope had plunged a dagger into his chest and twisted it. The pain was real. He knew he loved Aethelreda, but he also knew that she would never be completely happy in Rome for ever, and he was not sure that he could be happy in Britain forever. She was drawn back to her own country, and culture, and family. There were things that she needed to do back there in Lower Combe. He did not know exactly what she had in mind, but he was fairly certain that it was not anything that either the Pope or he himself would approve of. He was fairly certain that it involved death – and, more specifically, murder.

Gathering himself up, Paulos stood again.

"Holy Father, you are a wonderfully wise man. I am going to be brutally honest with you at the risk of being excommunicated. I fear you would know, somehow, if I was not honest.

"As I stand here before you, I do not know what I want. I love Aethelreda, and when I am with her, I want to be with her for the rest of my life. But now that I am here, I see more clearly the problems that would present. She is suffering from the intensity of the heat in Rome.

"There are cooler places to live, perhaps even here in Ravenna, but I think that it is more than just the heat that is affecting her. I think that Aethelreda is homesick, and for her, that is no small thing. She will continue to suffer if I do not take her back to Britain. But what it will mean for her, or for me, when we get there, I do not know.

"Her village is in the hands of a cruel Saxon. He is the ruler now. Aethelreda cannot go back to him, and all I can see is that there must be a battle to rid the people of the Saxons, so that we can hand back control to the Britons."

The Pope had listened patiently while Paulos told his tale. Then he spoke, thoughtfully.

"Perhaps we could send a small raiding party, of about thirty or forty men, back to Britain. Do you think that forty trained Roman soldiers would be able to overcome the Saxons, with the help of whatever local warriors you could gather?"

Paulos looked at the Pope with a puzzled expression on his face.

"I regret, Holy Father, but I do not know. I am not a soldier and I do not know or understand the ways of warfare."

The Pope replied in a voice so mild that it totally belied the content of his words. "What you have said is indeed true, Frater Paulos. You are not a soldier. And for that reason you are not to go on this mission. I will send Frater Augustus as my envoy to accompany the troops when Aethelreda returns to Britain. He is skilled at warfare of the physical and of the spiritual kind. You will remain in Ravenna."

Paulos was stunned. He felt like he had been hit by a bolt of lightning. He had not even considered the possibility of Aethelreda returning to Kent without him. And to be accompanied by Augustus was rubbing salt in the wound. Though Augustus had not shown any signs of being in love with Aethelreda, Paulos still could not forget his actions in giving her his own dagger, nor Aethelreda's taunting words to him about the incident.

The Pope had been so congenial until that point, so understanding, that he had imagined he was on his side. But, apparently, his spiritual leader meant to punish him for his shortcomings after all. It hurt twice as much as it would have if he had not been led to think that the Pope had understood his needs and desires. He felt manipulated, like a horse realizing the bit in his mouth was for the man to control him. He burst out, "But, Aethelreda will not go back if I am not with her!"

The Pope gave him a sardonic smile and nodded slowly. To Paulos, he had begun to look like a politician rather than a man of God. The voice of the man of God was tinged with something like scorn when he replied,

"We shall see, will we not? If she will **not** go back to Britain without you, then I have a greater problem to solve than that of returning a homesick Kentish Queen to her people." He gave Paulos a piercingly sharp look as if to say, "And you are the biggest part of that problem."

"For now, Frater Paulos, you shall shave your beard and your hair, and return immediately to your community at Pomposa Abbey. I will send a message to the abbot to receive you, and to ensure that you spend your days praying and meditating and doing penance for the vows that you have broken."

So he was to be a prisoner of the Pope in his former community and would not even be allowed to say farewell to his family! He had gone to Ravenna to get help, and would never return to collect Aethelreda and take her to safety! It was so punitive and so wrong as far as Paulos was concerned, and he could only imagine what Aethelreda would think. But he did not have a say in what was to happen. He was a small pawn in the game of chess that the church was playing. That sardonic smile of Pope Innocent's had said it all.

He did have a choice, of course. He could have given up his vows, publicly, and taken up the life of a working man, with Aethelreda at his side. It was the possibility that Paulos had been mulling over ever since he took up residence with Aethelreda. But something held him back. He found that he was no longer certain that was what he wanted to do, after all. He was no longer certain that God would approve of his choice to give up his vows. He needed time to consider what it would mean to turn his back on God. That, after all, was how he saw his choice. He chose either God or Aethelreda, and it made him feel physically sick to think about it.

How had it ever come to this? He was a careful man, a thoughtful man. He always looked for the logic and the reason of the situation before he made decisions. But where Aethelreda was concerned, it was difficult to be thoughtful and reasonable. The truth was even more complicated than his conflicted emotions would allow. Aethelreda had her whole life ahead of her, and he was uncertain that she would choose him over returning to her people. In her place, he did not know that he would find it a clear-cut choice, either.

Meanwhile, he was accompanied by two of the Pope's guards to ensure that he went to the monastery, and not back to Rome, and Aethelreda. They were well armed and did not even try to pass themselves off as merry traveling companions. The thought that the Pope did not trust him made Paulos want to choke someone. Was it not enough that he had been forced to make a choice between an earthly love and a spiritual one, without humiliating him as well?

On his way to the monastery, his mind was humming like a hive of agitated bees. He could not find the peace of God anywhere in the events of the last twenty-four hours. He tried to pray, but his mind was muddled and confused. And then God gave him a small miracle.

He had finally become exhausted by the mental turmoil of trying to work out why things had gone the way they had, and he had turned his attention away from the two muscular guards and from his anger and frustration, to observe the ethereal sky above him. The heavenly dome of Ravenna was a deeper, clearer blue than the slightly hazy skies of Rome. He noted that the clouds were high and wispy that day, like the vaporized breath of angels, and he felt that he was being observed by someone who occupied the heavenly realm. As he let the anger go and breathed more easily, a new thought hit him as sharply as the blade that had felled Martialis back on Watling Street when they were on their way to Canterbury. He realized that if all he had done for Aethelreda was to secure troops to fight off the Saxons, perhaps that was enough. Perhaps that was what God had intended for him to do. Perhaps their relationship was not the main thing, after all. Perhaps he would get back to Lower Combe some other time. And perhaps Aethelreda would be able to see that he had done the best that he could.

He fervently hoped so, because he was fully aware that, for the second time, he had seemingly abandoned the one person on this earth that he loved more than any other earthly thing, and, if he was honest, the one person he loved as much as he loved God.

Chapter Nineteen

The Overthrow

And so Paulos did not go back to Britain with Aethelreda when she left two weeks later, to make the long journey back to her homeland. Instead, it was Augustus who went with her, and another monk from his monastery, Frater Theophilus, because the monks were always sent out two by two. Paulos was confined to his cell in the monastery, spending most of his days in prayer and meditation, making his confession to the Abbot daily, and forbidden from speaking with the other brothers. That was to be his life for the foreseeable future, and although Paulos was plunged into a morass of jealousy and depression for the first few months, he eventually came to terms with it all, and forgave God for the wreck of his life. There was nothing for him to do but to accept his circumstances and to love God in spite of them. But he always lived with the hope that one day he would see Aethelreda again.

Aethelreda never divulged her feelings about the absence of Paulos to either of the monks who accompanied her, nor to anyone else. She was absolutely stoical in her manner. She simply did not want anyone to know how hurt she felt and how lost she was without Paulos. She felt that was undignified for a woman in her position, and that it made her seem weak if she vented her feelings with their odd mixture of anger and love. She was single-mindedly focused on returning to Britain and overthrowing the Saxons. That was enough to concentrate on.

Her apparent stoicism was a trait that Augustus did not know whether to admire or to despise. On the one hand, he found it admirable because it allowed her to stay focused on what was happening next, rather than dwelling on the past. She was able to direct all of her attention toward getting back to Britain and retaking her village. On the other hand, it made her seem cold and distant, even rather callous. Augustus knew that Paulos had loved her to the point of almost giving up his vows, and he had been led to believe that she had shared his feelings. But in all the time they spent together traveling the hard roads up through Gaul, she never mentioned his name even once.

What Augustus did not know was that it was far too painful for Aethelreda to think about Paulos, let alone to mention his name. Sometimes at night, she would wake with his name on her lips and a longing so deep in her heart that she almost did not want to see another day. But when the sun rose, she would remember that there were others who depended on her – two little children, right in her bed, and a whole tribe of Kentish people who would lay down their lives for her. She had to return for their sakes.

The little army sailed across the channel from Gaul to Britain when autumn was at its peak, landing at Richborough, the terminus of Watling Street. All of those aboard admired the stunning yellow and gold of the elm and lime tree leaves, and the burnished coppery brown of the oaks as they displayed their autumn glory on the surrounding hills. There were far fewer deciduous trees in Rome, and Augustus had been amazed by the brilliant colors of the trees in Britain. He saw deciduous trees as symbols of acceptance and hope, as each year they let go of their leaves and trusted that new leaves would sprout in the spring. As the group gathered before disembarking, he offered their mission up to God with the same sense of trust as he imagined was displayed by the trees. They would be bare of leaves for a long, cold winter, but they trusted that spring would bring new growth. Their mission might go through a time of intense need, too, like the dark of winter, but he prayed that their faith and trust would be rewarded, and bud anew in the spring.

The crew members who had not seen the glory of the Roman Empire in Britain before also marveled at the triumphal arch that stood at the entry to the port. As a sign of the magnificence of Roman engineering and the hope of continuing expansion, however, now that the garrison no longer guarded it, it was an ambiguous one.

Aethelreda's spirit rose within her at the sight of her homeland. She thought she had been happy in Rome, with Paulos and her two darling children, but that had been before she became obsessed with the idea of ridding her people of the Saxon lord who ruled them. When it came down to it, the land of Rome did not feed the part of her soul that had been birthed in her by her parents and grandparents, and that had been nurtured by the rich heritage of the soil and plants and animals of the island she called home. The nature of her connection to her homeland was elemental, built into every organ and limb, and deeply seated in her brain.

As she stepped back on to British soil, she felt almost a thrill of electricity, as if her homeland welcomed her return. She picked up a handful of the golden leaves carpeting the ground and murmured a prayer of thanksgiving. But if you had asked her which god she had addressed, she would not have been able to say.

She led the group of forty with the aid of Augustus, whose phenomenal memory of places and trails and roads was a great advantage, until they were close to Lower Combe. There, they camped and laid out their final strategy.

The next day, Aethelreda took a small group of soldiers and went closer to the village at about the time she thought Garth, her former captor, would have been eating his supper. He had enjoyed his food and drink with what Aethelreda felt was a primitive, animal-like gusto, and he made sure that he and his men were not disturbed during that time. She had been kept shackled so that she could not escape while the men were drinking, eating, and carousing. It was after dinner that they turned their attention to her.

She had a hunch that she would recognize one of the guards to the village enclosure, if they were still the same as when she had left just over a year earlier. While she had been held captive by the Saxons, several of the guards had become sympathetic toward her because they had seen how badly she had been treated. They could not be open about their sympathy, but she knew they had been instrumental in getting Paulos and Augustus into the settlement to rescue her, and had helped them to escape, risking their own lives to do so. She knew it was entirely possible that they had been implicated in her disappearance – in which case, they would have been executed – but Aethelreda felt in her bones that they would have been clever enough to have escaped notice. She hoped that she could catch the attention of one of the guards and let him know they were back in Britain. Perhaps she would even get information about how many were currently living in the settlement, and how well armed they were.

As she had hoped, she recognized one of the guards instantly. His red beard was his fiery identification, even in the dying light of the autumn evening. She stood up cautiously from where she had been hiding under cover.

"Roderic!" Her voice was just a hoarse whisper, but it reached the keen ears of the vigilant warrior, twenty feet away from her. He spun in her direction with his spear at the ready. Aethelreda continued in hushed tones.

"Hush! I am Aethelreda. Do not give me away!"

"Saints be praised! It is you, back from the dead!" His whisper reached her ears with difficulty. He was trying not to attract the attention of the other guard. Aethelreda had to be brief so that suspicion was not aroused.

"Let us meet tomorrow at dawn, by the waterfalls at the river. If you heard me, give me a sign." Roderic raised his arm and scratched his head rather theatrically.

"Good. Farewell." Then she melted back into the woods and returned to the camp for the night.

It was in the morning, at the river's edge, that she passed the opium to Roderic.

The falls had been a place of delight for Aethelreda. She remembered the day that Paulos had accompanied her and had stared at her with his mouth agape when he saw her half-naked body. She recalled the satisfaction that she had felt at being able to arouse the Roman monk, against his will. But all that was in the distant past. She was a different woman now.

She gave Roderic strict instructions for how to administer the poison. It was to be stirred into a strong mead drink and given to Garth toward the end of his usual gargantuan meal, when he would already be drunk from the ale he had consumed. He would not be likely to notice the strange taste, if there was any. Roderic looked at his Queen with a mixture of admiration and fear.

"Will it kill him?"

Aethelreda tried to tell from Roderic's expression whether the idea pleased him, or not. She guessed from the strangely eager light in his eyes that the idea did please him. And because she had been planning the murder for so long, she replied without emotion, "I certainly hope so."

And that was how it was done. On the same morning that she had given the poison to Roderic, she divulged to him that there were men waiting in the woods to overthrow the Saxons so that Aethelreda could return to her people and begin to rule, as was her birthright.

Roderic knew of at least ten men who would be eager to join in the battle on her behalf. He himself, although he was a Saxon, would also join the uprising. He hated what Garth had turned the settlement into. The Saxon rulers cared only for hunting and not at all for farming or weaving or dyeing. When they were not off in the woods searching for wild boars, they were lying around the village, drinking, and telling bawdy jokes and tall tales.

In the evening, Garth drank the mead down to the bottom of the cup and minutes later was slumped in his chair in a dreamless sleep.

At dawn of the next morning, the Romans attacked. With twelve of the local men joining them, they easily overcame the sluggish Saxons. It was a slaughter. A bloodbath.

Aethelreda herself killed as many as three Saxon men as they arose in confusion from their beds to find out what all the clamor was about. She stood behind their front doors and slit their throats as they stepped out of their doorways. They dropped at her feet. There was no intention of leaving any of the Saxons alive to flee and tell the tale of what had happened that day, when Aethelreda took back Lower Combe for the Cantii people.

When it was all over, Aethelreda sat in the doorway of her former house and wept. The smell of the blood that had been shed hung over the settlement like a cloud of swamp gas, putrid with the memory of dead things.

She had not expected to feel so depleted by the battle. In all of her captivity and in all of her recovery time in Rome, she had imagined the exultation she would feel in their victory over the Saxons. She had savored the idea of being overcome with the relief and satisfaction of revenge. But instead, she felt nothing but a swirling mixture of anger and sorrow.

Except for Garth and a few of his closest henchmen, she knew that the Saxons were people just like her own. She and Paulos had discussed it many times. The Saxons had escaped their own countries, where their prospects were dim, and they were just trying to find a better life for themselves. Her own people had probably done the same thing generations before, to whoever was living there then. The anger rose within her as she wondered why it had to be the way it was. Why could they not have lived peaceably together instead of having to kill or be killed?

And for her own part in the slaughter, she had an odd kind of feeling that she had not felt before. She wondered if what she felt was shame. Paulos would have known. But he was not there to ask. Aethelreda was both saddened and angered by that fact. Paulos should have been there. She was furious with the Pope and with Paulos for his obedience to a man who would prevent his return to her.

She forced herself to stop weeping, stood up and slowly entered the house that had been her father's before it was hers, and then it had been occupied by Garth and his two most faithful and brutal servants, Hermanrich and Thorsimund. Their bodies lay where they had fallen by the door, each in an individual pool of blood.

Garth lay where he had fallen, near the dead coals of the fire. But as Aethelreda approached him, he moved and groaned. He had not died after all, but was semi-conscious from the effects of the opium. Aethelreda could detect an odorous smell that rose above the stink of the blood of the two guards. It was the odor of vomit. Apparently, Garth had spewed out at least some of the contents of his stomach after consuming the opium-laced mead, and he had survived.

As she planned the massacre, Aethelreda had wanted to make her mark on Garth by plunging a dagger into his dead chest, just so that she could exalt in the pleasure of it. She had fantasized how she would carve her initial into his forehead; the initial that Paulos had taught her to write. Garth and his men had hurt her so many times; surely, she would be forgiven that small act of revenge. Besides, he was supposed to be already dead. But he was not dead.

She stood next to him as if she were made of stone. The choice was hers. She could actually plunge the knife into his chest and finish off the man who had caused her so much suffering, or she could get someone else to do it. As she stood there, immobilized by the change in circumstances she had found herself in, she realized that she was being given the chance to wreak the vengeance on her former captor that she had longed for.

Garth tried to raise his head, but he was still too groggy from the effects of the drug. Aethelreda was unsure that he was aware of who was in the room with him, and so she stepped forward, right into his view. He was still only partly conscious. She pulled his beard until he was face to face with her. When she spoke, it was with a voice filled with wrath.

"I am Aethelreda of the Cantii, and I am the ruler here. You will die at my hand because of your cruelty to me and to my people." And so saying, she slit his throat from ear to ear, and watched as he gurgled and died.

After the events of the morning, she had no more desire for blood or pain, or mutilation, or death. She was filled with revulsion for what had been done by her, and in her name. She fled the house, with its odor of death, and went to find Augustus. She needed to talk with him about what to do next. There were so many bodies lying around the village. They would have to be removed from the settlement or disease would follow.

Paulos had said that many of the Saxons were Christian. She had not seen one act of Garth's that would have implied he was, but if any of them were, they had to at least be buried, rather than left on the dung heap. And there were a few of her own people who had died, too. They would need proper funeral rites.

When she finally tracked down Augustus, she was surprised to find him in the company of Sigeburg. Augustus had intended to make himself useful before the battle by secretly visiting the cottages of the remaining Britons, under cover of darkness, to alert them to the mayhem to come. He had visited several cottages when he came face to face with a woman that he knew. He was startled, and so was she. Had he known she was going to be there, he would have avoided that particular door, but Sigeburg had moved since he had slept with her that night four years ago. It threw him quite off balance. He was sure that he blushed redder than he had ever blushed before. His cheeks felt red hot and sweat broke out on his top lip and in his armpits.

Sigeburg recovered more quickly than Augustus. She drew him into the cottage and led him to the bed of a sleeping child. There on the animal skins lay a boy, about four years old, with sandy hair. He looked like an angel, blissfully sleeping. His lashes were long, and his cheeks were plump and pink. Sigeburg said nothing. It was not necessary for her to explain what she was showing him. Augustus looked at the boy and he felt as if he was looking at his own self.

He looked from the boy to his mother and back again, several times. Whatever had happened to Sigeburg since that night, after the feasting, when he had had too much ale to drink, and whoever she had slept with since, there was no doubt that this child in Sigeburg's bed was his boy. There was a surge of joy in Augustus that made him want to dance. He turned to Sigeburg with a huge smile and said, "He is my son?" He did not know why he asked the question. The boy was obviously his. He laughed, and before she said anything in reply, he added, "He **is** my **son**!", and Sigeburg had to put her finger to her lips to warn him not to be so loud, in case he woke the child.

The battle began within minutes. At first, there were just the noises of men moving around and being as quiet as they could be. You would not have paid any attention to it unless you had known what was planned. But soon, the sounds of yells and shrieks, of metal blades striking each other, of thuds, and of women loudly wailing filled the air. Augustus remained with Sigeburg and his son throughout it all. His role as father and protector had just begun.

When Aethelreda found him, he was at table with the two of them, as if nothing unusual had happened that morning. He had not even ventured out to witness the carnage, and he found that he had no stomach for it. He knew he would be called upon to help in the aftermath, but for the time being he had four years of absence to make up for. He and Sigeburg had talked and shared their hopes and dreams for the future, and there beside his young son, he had made a life-changing decision. But he stood up to acknowledge Aethelreda and bowed respectfully. Aethelreda spoke first. Her voice was breathless with urgency.

"Fra Augustus, I must speak with you."

"Certainly, my Queen." It was the first time he had addressed her in that way. He had habitually called her 'my sister' before that morning. Aethelreda recognized that a change had taken place.

"What is it, Fra Augustus? Am I your Queen now and not your sister?"

"You are indeed my sister in Christ, but now you are also my Queen."

Aethelreda looked at him questioningly. "What has happened here?"

"This little lad, Wregan, is my son!" He could not hide the joy that was in his voice. "I have decided to make Sigeburg my lawful wife, and to stay in this village to help you rebuild your lives. I can be your priest."

At that news, Aethelreda almost forgot the urgency of her need to speak to Augustus. She took Sigeburg's hand and said with a smile, "Sigeburg, this will be a good thing for you and for the village. Fra Augustus is an honorable man. And he is wise and strong. He will make a wonderful father and a fine spiritual leader."

Sigeburg curtseyed. "But, my Lady, you wished to speak with Augustus?"

"Yes." Aethelreda turned to Augustus. "I need some urgent spiritual advice about today. Please come and walk with me, Augustus. I trust you to be my companion so that I can be honest before you and before God. I need to think and plan for the future, but I also need to confess and be forgiven for the past."

And so the two of them walked together, out of the settlement, and into the woods, and Aethelreda talked to Augustus without reservation.

Her gait sped up when she spoke about her anger with the Pope and with Paulos, so that Augustus could barely keep up with her. She was taller than he was, and her legs were longer. She confessed her bitter resentment at what the Pope had done when he refused to allow Paulos to return to Britain. She angrily declared that Paulos had been weak in not standing up to his spiritual leader. She thought one of her own people would have been more steadfast and resolute.

Then her pace slowed down when she spoke about what was to be done to mend the damage that Garth had brought to her people. It would take years to repair the harm he had caused. She spat out her bitter hatred of Garth, who had tried to make her serve him as wife and as slave, and of his two guards, who had tortured and abused her more than Garth ever had.

The words flowed out of her like a river that was swollen by flood waters. The broken pieces of her life went with it, as if they were flotsam rushing with the current to the sea. She wanted to be done with it all. She wanted to be washed clean from the bloodshed, and from the disappointment, resentment, and bitterness. She wanted to start afresh.

And Augustus, adding nothing to the conversation, because he knew it was best that way, exercised his priestly duty to absolve her from her sins so that she could start again, symbolically washed clean of all her guilt. She knelt down with her head bowed, and he made the sign of the cross over her. Then he joined her on her knees, and they prayed in silence together until the dampness of the earth seeped through his leggings and her skirt, and they struggled up and walked back to the settlement arm in arm.

***

Frater Theophilus performed the marriage of Augustus and Sigeburg, but he had to be talked into it. He was not happy about being left on his own to fulfill the Pope's mission, and he dreaded having to report to the Pope that Augustus had abandoned ship and stayed in Britain. He thought Augustus had made a hasty decision to give up his vocation and stay in what was to him a very foreign land. He did not realize that it had been a decision that was four years in the making. Augustus had wanted to be a husband and father ever since he had seen Flavius and his wife and children in Canterbury, although he had pushed his desires aside. He had been on his knees in a passion of jealousy, which he could only confess to God, when Paulos had disappeared into the countryside near Rome with Aethelreda and her children. The discovery that he had a son, Wregan, growing up in Lower Combe, had only pushed him to step into the sunlight that he had been avoiding for a very long time.

The marriage was the first celebration in the village after the overthrow of the Saxons, and it was a riotous affair. The dead had all been buried, the village had been cleaned and repaired as much as possible, and all signs of Saxon occupation removed. The whole village labored together in the tasks. Aethelreda mused that if they worked as hard together to move their community forward into the future, as they had worked to remove the signs of the past, they would be assured of success.

A small building, no more than a hut, in truth, was quickly constructed to be used as their church. There was much serious discussion about what name they should give to the church and to the Christian congregation, which they trusted would grow and thrive there. Many wanted to simply call the community The Church of the Savior, because they wanted to honor the one who was at the center of the faith. Others wanted to honor someone who had given themselves to that faith, like Saint Stephen, the first martyr. In the end, Mary the mother of the Savior was chosen as the honoree. It seemed appropriate for a church located in a community that was led by a woman.

St Mary's was consecrated by Theophilus to shelter the new congregation when they gathered for worship, until such time as a stone church could be built. Augustus knew just the man who might be persuaded to spend some time in Lower Combe, overseeing the construction. He gave Theophilus special instructions to speak to Flavius about the project when he saw him next, as he assumed he would when he passed through Wingham on the way to Canterbury.

Chapter Twenty

The Queen Reigns

When Aethelreda again took leadership of her people, she had changed. She was no longer the young girl who presented a face of confidence and leadership to her people, despite the fact that the only leadership she had witnessed was that of her father, and, for a brief unofficial period, her mother. Back then, her bravado had all been an act, designed to give her people confidence in her leadership. It was a game of mind control, as if she, their leader, was trying to lead their way through a thick fen fog where she could see nothing, and her people could see nothing, either. They had to trust each other and follow the sound of their leader's voice. Back then, she had tried to do things the way she thought her father would have. But that was no longer the case. She had learned that in order to be the best leader for her people, she had to be herself.

Still only in her twenties, Aethelreda had experienced more than most people did in their whole lives. She had been raised a princess, seen the deaths of both parents, become the Queen of a stout-hearted people, fallen in love, been deserted by the one she loved, been conquered by a brutal enemy, suffered imprisonment, been regularly beaten and raped, had a child, and then she had been rescued by the hand of God, and Paulos and Augustus, and taken to Rome.

In that vastly different, dry, and golden country, where olives grew on trees for the picking, and wine was rich and red, her singular experiences continued. She had lived with a monk who had loved her and birthed her second child, a son, recovered her health and sanity, returned to fight off their conquerors, and, finally, she had settled down to quiet and peaceful leadership while her two children grew up. She had already lived a hundred different lives and she had internalized all of her experiences so that the sum total of them informed all of her decisions. Her people loved and trusted her as much as they had loved her father.

One of the first things that Aethelreda took care of was to find her brothers and sisters and return them to the settlement.

Segovax and Lugotori had gone to Butu's people, the Catuvellauni, and bartered for a safe haven for them when the Saxons came crashing into their lives. It had not been an easy task. Butu was not popular among his own people. In his youth, his father, King Caradeg, with whom he had a troubled relationship, had suggested that he train as a druid priest, presumably so that he had something useful to do and would stay out of the way.

Butu had begun the training, but had not been a devoted student after he met Lugotori when he was scouring for herbs in the woods. And then he had disappeared altogether. Catuvellauni scouts believed he had joined the Cantii.

But, despite the difficulties between Butu and his people, the two Cantii brothers had been able to impress Butu's father of the urgency of the situation when they appeared in the Catuvellauni village with nine children ranging in age from eight to seventeen, huddled in a frightened group.

The Catuvellauni king had struck a bargain with Segovax and Lugotori that they would shelter Aethelreda's family if the two tribes would join together in war to drive out the Saxons, should the time ever come when that was necessary. It seemed like a good bargain to the cousins, since their own people were not likely to be of any help as long as Garth and his men ruled them. Segovax vaguely hoped that by making the treaty, Caradeg might come to the aid of the Cantii before any more Saxons arrived in their midst. In any case, the cousins did not live long enough to have to make good on the agreement.

Aethelreda was greeted with respect when she rode into the Catuvellauni village. Caradeg received her as a Queen. She relayed the sad news of Segovax and Lugotori's brutal end, and Butu's disappearance. Catuvellauni scouts, who had their finger on the pulse of what was going on in the area, had relayed the news to Caradeg that Butu had returned to the druid training camp just a few days after the Saxons had attacked their neighbors to the south. It was old news. Caradeg had not heard from his son, in person, since his disappearance from their village, and considered him dead, also.

The king returned the family to the arms of their sister in an emotional reunion, and after a night of farewell feasting, the whole group left and returned to their own village. Aethelreda had not been at all fazed by the terms of the treaty that her cousins had struck with Caradeg. She reasoned that she herself would have made that bargain had she been the one seeking refuge. She was glad to reaffirm her tribe's allegiance to any form of resistance to invasion.

Aethelreda had once been wholly concerned with her people staying separate from those around her. Her people had lived in obscurity and steadfastly resisted any progress. Their lives were spent resisting the future and maintaining the past, and in order to do that, they had to close themselves off from the outside world. But in her maturity, she sought to move forward. She well knew that meant they would have to make allegiances. Consequently, she had made an agreement with the Catuvellauni to resume joint market days with them and with other nearby settlements. In Lower Combe, weaving and dyeing resumed as the center of the tribe's economic life.

The biggest new endeavor that Aethelreda undertook, however, was to build a road to the inlet. She insisted that her men use Roman techniques to do so. Amidst much grumbling, the men dug trenches, built an agger of the material from the trenches to raise up the road, and then carefully fitted together stone for the surface of the road. Their workmanship was not as precise as that of the Romans, since they lacked some of the stone-cutting tools, and most of the desire to build a superior product that had been the case with the Roman builders. But the end result was a serviceable road that stayed dry and provided a smoother surface to get carts down to the ocean and back again, quickly, loaded with kelp, shellfish, and other gifts of the sea.

But perhaps dearest to her own heart, Aethelreda had overseen the widening of the trail between their village and Wingham so that there could be connections forged between them and the much larger town to the north. Flavius had begun a road-building project, too. He was building a road south from Wingham, working back towards Lower Combe. There were wagers as to how long it would take for the trails to meet, and how close to the middle they would be.

There were the expected problems. Some of Aethelreda's people resisted the progress she wanted to make. Some thought she was not moving fast enough. But Aethelreda was a patient and tolerant leader. She listened carefully to all of her people, consulted with others, then did what she thought was best.

The beauty about constructing a road between Lower Combe and Wingham was that both Aethelreda and Augustus could ride to Wingham in half the time it used to take. Augustus took the opportunity to ride over to visit Flavius regularly to talk about the mission church of St Martin and to share the progress he was making at St Mary's. They also shared notes about raising children. Flavius's brood seemed to increase every year. Aeditha had the benefit of the servants who lived at the villa to help her out, but she was still extremely busy.

Sigeburg was less fertile than Aeditha. She and Augustus had two more children, spaced out by three years each. Then two more, but those precious babies had died at birth. The grief was deep and lasting for Augustus and Sigeburg. They decided that the three children given to them by God were enough for the two of them to cope with, living in a small cottage in Lower Combe.

Flavius, at the invitation of Aethelreda, spent a summer in Lower Combe, helping to construct a pretty stone church, which Augustus dedicated to the Blessed Virgin Mary. The former Roman soldier's excellence in Roman building techniques had become widely known in Kent.

Aethelreda discovered the personal pleasure of riding with Augustus over to Wingham and calling on Blaedswith. Her brother, Wilfred, having reached his adulthood, was able – in fact, he was keen – to lead the community while she was away. And he had proved a competent leader, so that Aethelreda no longer spent her time away worrying about what was taking place in Lower Combe in her absence.

Blaedswith and Aethelreda had become fast friends. Aethelreda found the older woman was always interesting to spend time with. She had so much knowledge of the past and loved to share what she knew with Aethelreda. Much of what she knew was druid lore. Once the Romans had left, there was no longer such a stigma about practicing the old religion, but Flavius and Aeditha did not like Blaedswith to be involved with it. They hoped that she would become a baptized Christian before she died. She was proving to be a reluctant convert. Always weighing the one against the other, her nature was to go with the religion that gave better results. Sometimes, it seemed to her as though the two religions were neck and neck. Being a practical woman, Blaedswith was content to sit on the fence until she was certain of the advantages of jumping to one side or the other.

Aethelreda called herself a Christian, although she was not baptized. She, too, had been sitting on the fence for a very long time. Augustus had been unable to persuade her to make a public profession of her faith. She was attracted to the God that Paulos had taught her about, but she was still haunted by certain aspects of the old religion. She told Blaedswith about the vision that both she and Mildreth had experienced in the sacred oak grove. Blaedswith agreed that the fact that what they had dreamed about while they prayed to Aine and drank the sacred mead had come to be was very difficult to argue against if you were weighing up the validity of the Gods.

Blaedswith had wandered through life without needing to make a commitment to any religion, but then she had suddenly found herself needing to be assured one way or the other. It was not for herself that she needed the assurance, but it was for someone she loved deeply who needed prayer, and it had to be the strongest, most potent prayer available.

Aeditha's tenth pregnancy had not progressed in the way that it should have. Even when she was large enough to have felt the child move, there had been no movements. Her abdomen had grown, and she had suffered from nausea, as she had in her other pregnancies, but she still bled each month. The women gathered around her in consternation, to offer her support, encouragement, and advice. Blaedswith, experienced in the ways of women, even though she had not borne a child of her own, could feel no movement, either. Flavius was scared into silence. No one wanted to state the obvious that despite the fact that Aeditha's belly had grown, she was not with child. Something else was growing in her womb.

When it could no longer be denied that Aeditha was seriously ill, the whole community of St Martin's, including all those who lived and worked at the villa, got together to hold a prayer vigil in the church. Candles were lit and Fra Augustus led them in prayer, while

Aeditha knelt at the altar rail, and those who were close enough to reach laid their hands on her.

They stayed together praying and meditating all night, and when morning arrived, Aeditha went back to the villa, physically spent but spiritually comforted. She felt supported by those who loved her, no matter what lay in her future. She knew that whatever happened, she was in the hands of a God who loved her. She knew that if she died, Flavius would be supported by the congregation, and their children would be raised by the community. She did not want to die, but she no longer feared death.

The Autumnal Equinox was approaching, and Blaedswith began to feel the pull of her old faith. She saw no reduction in the size of Aeditha's belly after the prayer vigil. There had been no contractions, no bloody flux to signify the end of a bad pregnancy. As far as she could see, nothing had changed after the Christians had prayed for her, except that Aeditha had stopped worrying and was calm and tranquil, accepting her future, whatever it might hold.

Blaedswith was not tranquil. She had seen other women die from growths in their womb, and she was desperate not to see that happen to her beloved niece.

Her servant, Ionnia, still made an annual pilgrimage to Vagniacis to make offerings to Brigit, although she herself no longer did. Blaedswith decided that she would accompany Ionnia to Vagniacis that autumn to honor Mabon, the son of the Mother of the Earth, and the God of Light. As the autumn light was dying, it was deemed the appropriate time to honor Mabon each year. A deer would be killed, and its organs offered as a sacrifice to ensure a good hunting season in the following year. There would be the usual big fire, and dancing, and feasting on the venison that would last well into the night. Men would dress in deer antlers and act out a deer hunt. Other offerings of the autumn harvest would be made in hopes of a good harvest in the following year. Blaedswith took a bag each of barley and rye, and root vegetables from the villa farm. Ionnia took fruit from the kitchen garden. And they both took desperate prayers for Aeditha in their hearts.

Vagniacis was filled with pilgrims who were there to honor the god Mabon. There were also people who were going to St Paul's Church for the Harvest Festival, which would be held the next day. To Blaedswith's amusement, the two groups of pilgrims were indistinguishable.

After the revels of the feast of Mabon, Blaedswith and Ionnia sought out a former mansio to stay the night. The next day, Blaedswith went to St Paul's for the Harvest Festival service. She was surprised to see quite a few of the same worshippers as she had seen the night before. Apparently, there were others like her who were unsure of the efficacy of the gods, and were playing both ends against the middle.

The little church was filled with gifts of the harvest. Vegetables, grains, and fruits were piled in slightly haphazard profusion around the altar. It had been a good year, and the seeds on the corncobs were plump and golden. Even the little wildling apples were larger than usual, and their red skins seemed to glow from where they were stacked, in the dim light of the church. Father Graeme preached an excellent sermon on being thankful for the harvest, and encouraged the congregation to live lives that were fruitful for God. Blaedswith gave close attention to what he said. Against all of her best intentions, she found that his words were inspiring. After the service, Father Graeme met his congregation in the narthex of the church. He was openly delighted to see Blaedswith there.

"Mistress Blaedswith, welcome to St Paul's! I believe this is your first time of worshipping with us. Am I right?"

"Yes, indeed you are right, Father Graeme. It was a lovely service and you gave a good address."

"Thank you. I am glad that you thought so." He looked at her enquiringly and asked, "Vagniacis is a good distance from Wingham. Are you staying with a friend?"

She did not know why he was interested in her accommodations, but she sensed no prurient intent. She thought he was simply keeping the conversation going. He seemed a kind and gentle soul.

"I often do when I come to Vagniacis, but not this time. I am at the mansio."

He nodded. "A comfortable place to get a bed, I have been told."

Blaedswith looked Father Graeme right in the face, and with his gentle hazel eyes seemingly seeing right into her soul, she felt courageous enough to be honest about why she had come to Vagniacis, even though he had not asked why she was there. She said, "I came to the grove to make offerings to Mabon."

He looked faintly amused. "I see. But you are hoping for the support of both gods, and came here to pray today as well?"

"Something like that. I hope you are not offended. My niece is desperately ill. I am praying for her healing."

"Oh!" Father Graeme looked distressed. "I am so very sorry to hear this news. May I say some special prayers for your niece?" He had looked past her apology and homed in on the heart of the matter, and for that act of sensitivity Blaedswith was grateful.

"You may. Of course, her own community of St Martin's has been praying for her, night and day."

"I am glad to hear that she has support from her church. Supporting those in need is the meaning of loving your neighbor, in my opinion, and it is a principle that our Lord taught." Father Graeme looked at Blaedswith with renewed interest. He had had a good idea. "Mistress Blaedswith, would you perhaps dine with me this noon? My servant will be there and the church staff, and would you bring your servant, too?"

Blaedswith hesitated. She was not sure that she wanted to put herself in a situation where she might be pressured to do or say anything that she did not at that moment feel. But with the encouragement of his reassuring smile, she agreed to join him. He had a most agreeable face, with laughter lines around his eyes. She wondered how old he was. His hair was graying, and his back was a little stooped. There was something about him that reminded her of Godefridus, or at least of how she thought Godefridus would have looked if he had been granted the grace of another fifteen years.

At the midday meal she met some of the other members of the church – the sexton who cared for the building, the sacristan who helped Father Graeme in the services, and the warden who was the intermediary between Father Graeme and his congregation. They were pleasant people, and they made her feel very welcome. She was sure that they could not have known about her questionable background, otherwise why would they have been so accepting of her presence?

As she went to take her leave of her host, Father Graeme asked her a discrete question.

"I remember the time you came to ask for prayers that you might find a friend. I was wondering, Mistress Blaedswith, if our prayers for you have been answered?"

Blaedswith found herself smiling. She did not really know how to answer that question because while she thought she had developed a new friend, she was not sure about the other woman's affections. But she found that she wanted to say something that would be pleasant for Father Graeme to hear. She turned her smile toward him.

"Father Graeme, I am not sure if it was Brigit or the God you call your Heavenly Father who answered my prayers, but I think they may have been answered in the person of Aethelreda of the Cantii. She has visited me, and we have become friends, I think. I very much enjoy her company and I think she enjoys mine. We have several things in common, despite our age difference. For one thing, we have both loved and lost a partner in life. My husband died, as you may know, and she was deserted, and so we have no man in our lives to be our provider. Nor do we need one, either."

She was surprised at the haste with which she had qualified her statement. She did not want the priest to think she was on the hunt for a husband. She looked to see how Father Graeme had reacted. His face registered nothing beyond benign interest, and so she went on. "And both of us, it must be admitted, are closely connected to the faith of our forbearers. We share a knowledge of plants, medicines, and healing, and she also knows about the herbs of Rome, because she has been there, too!" She stopped. She was suddenly embarrassed at her girlish chatter. She felt that she probably sounded like a young girl who was trying to impress a young man, and that was most unlike her. She was a matron of long standing, with no plans to change her marital status.

Father Graeme interrupted. "Mistress, that is very good news! I am glad that you have found a kindred spirit. I am glad that our Lord saw your need and fulfilled it."

Blaedswith's smile did not reveal her doubt that Father Graeme's Lord had anything to do with the situation, even though she had originally set up the prayer request as a kind of test. She found that regardless of the end result of her testing of the gods, she really did not want to believe in the Christian God, despite the fact that Father Graeme's prayers seemed to have been answered.

Father Graeme looked at his guest in a kindly fashion. He was intrigued by the woman who stood before him. He knew that she had run a successful mining operation, along with her husband, but that she was widely known to be the brain behind the business. He knew that she had resisted several attempts to convert her to Christianity. He thought that her strength was admirable, and he decided to try and forge a connection with her, because, although she did not know it, they were quite similar in some ways. He felt that they could be friends. He maintained his gaze with his warm eyes under their bushy brows.

"You may have heard that I, too, studied the ways of our druid ancestors before I became a Christian priest."

Blaedswith had not heard, but she looked interested, and so he went on. "I have always been very drawn to things of the spirit, ever since I was a little boy. When I lived with the druids, I learned about herbs and plants and their uses, as everyone does. I was astonished at how all of our human needs had been provided for by fruits of the earth. Of course, I have put aside the practices of the druids now, because I have found a better way. But yet, there is much to be said for the way in which our ancestors honored the gifts of the earth. I am seeking ways to connect that spirit to the Spirit of the Lord God whom I now worship."

And at that, the two of them talked for another half an hour, like a couple of best friends sharing recipes for pheasant stew, while Ionnia waited outside.

Chapter Twenty-One

The Funeral

It was the evening of the Sabbath that Aeditha died. She was surrounded by those who loved her most: Blaedswith, Flavius, Eadric, Ionnia, her own three older children (the little ones were all asleep in bed), and Father Aelwyn.

Her passing was the most gentle that Blaedswith had ever seen, and she had seen a lot of deaths in her nearly sixty years of living.

As Aeditha's disease progressed, it became apparent that no amount of prayer to any number of gods was going to restore her to health. Even though no one wanted it to be so, and few mentioned the hard truth, they had to accept the facts. She stopped eating and the pain eased some, but there was no hope there, only the realization that her body no longer responded to the normal requirements of life. After slowly becoming less and less communicative in the last two days of her life, on that Sabbath eve Aeditha unexpectedly raised herself up from the bed, looked around at her assembled and grieving family, and said, "I love you all. Look after my children." Then she lay back down and was silent, as everyone murmured how much they loved her, in response, and tears were brushed away from eyes.

Flavius was kneeling at her side. Flavia, Synnove, and Oswald were arranged around her bed. Father Aelwyn was at the foot of the bed with Blaedswith. There was a silence of such depth that the air seemed to be charged with holy electricity. They were waiting in the sacred space between life and death.

Finally, Aeditha held up her arms to something or someone that she was seeing and said, "Lord, I am coming," and took her last breath.

Blaedswith left the room abruptly and went to her own bed chamber, where she wept, quietly and privately. The others stayed with Aeditha as Father Aelwyn prayed for her departing soul. No one else said a word, not even the children.

Flavius and Father Aelwyn had tried as best they could to tell the children, gently, that their mother was dying. They had seen death before in farm animals, and a pet dog that was old, but they did not understand why their mother was leaving them so soon. Neither did any of the adults. But right there, in the presence of her cooling body, as odd as it was in retrospect, everything seemed to be the way it was meant to be. There was a serenity that came from the realization that nothing further could be done. At least Aeditha was not suffering any more.

They buried her the next day in the graveyard behind Saint Martin's church.

The death was easy, but the funeral was hard. Even in the church there was a lot of open weeping and calling out to God. The death of a beautiful woman in the bloom of her life, leaving nine children behind her, was a terrible thing to grasp.

Many of the townsfolk came to the graveside because they had grown to know and love Flavius. To Blaedswith's surprise, both of her brothers were there, too, for the same reason, not because they loved their sister. She felt a pang of sadness about her estrangement from them. But they did not seek her out for comfort, nor to offer comfort to her, and Blaedswith felt her heart hardening even more toward them. It seemed that they did not understand the importance of forgiveness any more than she did, and they had been baptized into the new religion and supposedly made new.

She wished it had been otherwise. She mostly wished that she had had the courage to go to them and say she forgave them for what they had done to her. Perhaps that was what they were waiting for, after all. And yet she could not shake the resentment from her heart at the treatment she had received from them, and the childish desire to point out that they had started it all by refusing to accept the man she had loved, and then by killing him because he was leaving to go to Rome. They had intended to keep the family together, but they had only brought the opposite upon themselves. It was a long-ago tragedy, but it was still disrupting their lives. And they were family. They should have still been there for each other.

Feeling her estrangement from everyone at the graveside, Blaedswith had moved to the side, away from the group that surrounded the damp, brown earth of the burial pit where Aeditha's enshrouded body lay. She kept her eyes shut tightly and her head bowed so that no tears would fall in public.

But as the mourners left, Blaedswith felt a presence at her side. Someone had moved to be with her. Looking up, she found that it was Flavius. He tentatively put his arm around her shoulders. He had never dared to touch her before, but she did not flinch or pull away. He acted out of compassion for her and out of need for his own spirit to be comforted by the warmth of another human being. It was, in fact, exactly what Blaedswith needed in that moment as well. Sighing deeply, she took his hand in her own and said quietly, "Oh, Flavius, I shall miss her so badly." He hugged her harder. Blaedswith leaned into the support of Flavius's strong body. "How will we manage without her?"

He was silent for a while, wondering the same thing. Then he said, "We will never forget her, but we will learn to live without her. We must, for the sake of the children. They will need me, and they will need you, Blaedswith, more than ever."

"And we will need them, too, I think."

The priest and the sexton were filling in the grave, raising large shovels full of soil and throwing them into the hole with heavy thuds. Flavius moved to help them and held out a smaller shovel for Blaedswith. He said, "This is the last earthly thing we can do for a beautiful wife, mother, and daughter. Will you join me, Mother?"

Blaedswith heard what he had said, and, with a silent but grateful nod, she accepted both the shovel and the loving title that Flavius had bestowed upon her.

As she poured small shovels full of earth over the gradually increasing mound of dirt in the grave, she considered her future. She had lost a woman she thought of as her daughter, but perhaps now she had gained a man who would be to her as a 'son'. There was hope in the future, after all. And there were nine children to raise, which would take much time and energy; but they were family, and they would do it together.

And perhaps she did have the courage to go to her brothers to see if they could be reconciled and become family again, too. After what she had lost, it seemed harder to hang on to the resentment and anger of things that had happened so long ago than it did to swallow her pride and give it all up. Only time would tell.

Chapter Twenty-Two

Fourth Mission Trip

Paulos had discovered the tragedy of what had happened in Lower Combe and returned to Rome with Aethelreda in the year of our Lord four hundred and fourteen, when Innocent I was the Pope.

Augustus took her back to Kent with the small army to retake Lower Combe from the Saxon invaders in the following year and stayed there for the rest of his life.

Word of his defection from the monastic life in Rome was received with resignation by his Abbot. It was the kind of thing that happened, occasionally, to men who were drawn off the monastic pathway by love of a woman, and by the modest pleasures and contentment of family life. Unfortunately, it often happened to monks, like Augustus, who had the greatest promise as spiritual leaders. But in the case of Augustus, he hardly missed a beat. He moved from being a promising monastic leader in a community of men to becoming a promising leader of a congregation of believers, with a wife and family. He kept his vows to serve God with all his heart and soul and mind. He simply moved the focus from doing so within the closed walls of the monastery to the openness of a small town.

Paulos was confined to his cell in Pomposa Abbey in order to help him to remember the vows he had made. He did what he was supposed to do, examining his soul each and every day as the years of his life ticked by, measured in the daily office of prayers, in the regular, simple meals, and in periods of reading and reflection. He spent several years repenting for the way in which he had broken his oath to his Lord, his church, and his Abbot. Finally, because he could see no way out of his situation, he came to terms with his failures and tried to move on from his self-recrimination. He came to see that God had forgiven him, even if the church had not. All that remained was for him to forgive himself.

Popes came and went: Innocent, Zozimus, Eulalius, Boniface, Celestine, Sixtus, and finally Leo, who would be called 'Great'.

In the early years of Pope Leo's reign, Leo was determined to consolidate the influence of Christianity over the known world. He felt that he might have been called by God for just such a purpose. He did not think that it was arrogant to believe such a thing, just that it was a possibility that God was calling him for the task, and that he was up to the challenge.

He was particularly interested in what was happening in the island of Britain, where bishops and priests were gathering in new converts to the faith without the guidance of the church in Rome. That situation, outside of the influence of Rome, seemed like a liability to Leo. Bishop Pelagius had come from Britain and was stirring up passion in his own country to follow the wrong pathway. Pelagius was a thorn in the side of an ambitious pope like Leo. If Britain was filled with bishops like him, the church was in for a lot of unrest, and he knew he had better do something to stem the tide of apostasy before it infected the wider church like a bad case of the pox.

It came to Leo's attention that there was a monk still living in the monastery at Ravenna who had spent time in Britain. He was told that the monk knew the people of Britain and that he had been part of a short mission set in place by his long-ago predecessor, Pope Innocent. The monk was getting older now, and he had been in some sort of trouble for insubordination, but he had more than made up for his past sins by his quiet submission to authority. Leo had tagged him for a mission to Britain to assess the willingness of the local Christians to come under the cloak of the church in Rome.

He called the monk to Rome for an audience.

Paulos was first dumbfounded, and then exceedingly annoyed to be recalled to Rome by the new Pope. He was not given any reason for his audience, but Paulos was known for only one thing, and that was his mission trip to Britain, and his subsequent punishment for straying from his monastic orders while he was there. It had been nearly thirty years since he had set foot on the island occupied by the Britons, and although he thought of Aethelreda every day, he had almost given up the idea of ever seeing her again. He was nearly sixty years old, for one thing. Long journeys across land and sea were the purview of young men.

He probably seemed testy when he was shown in to see the Pope. He certainly felt bad tempered, and he was not inclined to hide the fact. Leo was no Innocent as far as his reputation allowed.

Whereas Innocent had been a modest man, Leo had grand ideas. He wanted the whole world to turn toward Rome as the center of the church. His biblical mandate was found in his reading of the Gospel of Matthew, where Jesus had said to the apostle Peter, "You are Peter, and on this rock I will build my church." Peter, according to tradition, had gone to Rome, and had died there. Therefore, Rome was the hereditary center of the church, and whoever led the church in Rome, led the church in the world. Bishops in Constantinople, Alexandria, Gaul, and other dioceses in the known world did not agree with him, but he gradually won them over by his powerful churchmanship. In time, every other bishop came to see himself as the assistant of the Pope of Rome.

Leo looked very grand in his ornate vestments, heavily embroidered with gold thread, and luminous with other bright silken colors. Paulos was glad to see that the Pope had chosen not to wear his triple crown for the occasion, and instead wore a simple white cap. Apparently, Paulos's humble presence did not demand such imposing regalia as the crown. But the Pope was wearing the large papal ring, and the staff of his office, decorated with three crosses, was in clear view, being held up nearby by a servant.

Paulos tried to control his annoyance at the major disturbance in his life a papal audience had caused. He knew he did not stand to gain anything by being rude to the most holy and politically powerful man in the world, but even the comparatively short trip from Ravenna to Rome had been a huge inconvenience to him. He had arrived in Rome, dusty, tired, and completely out of sorts.

And then, when the Pope told him what he wanted him to do – to go back to Britain and find out how amenable the bishops of that region were to the supremacy of Rome – he was aghast. Why him? He was nearly sixty years old. His knees creaked from long hours of kneeling, and his back could no longer stay straight when he had to stand for any length of time. For certain, he was older than his chronological age due to the long voyages he had already made, but that being so, there was a strong possibility that another trip would finish him off.

He said nothing. There was no need. The Pope had requested that he do this thing, and so he would have to do it. And the sooner, the better.

***

After three months of traveling across Gaul, Paulos was not in any better frame of mind. He did not know the other two monks the Pope had sent with him, neither did he care to. He kept his distance. They prayed together and he prayed alone. A report would go back to the Pope that he had been uncooperative, but he did not care. What could the church do to him that it had not already done? He had been essentially kept captive for decades. Now that he was being set free, he no longer wished to spread his wings and fly. They were crippled by lack of use. If he could have, he would have stayed on board the ship and sent the other monks on to Canterbury.

After Canterbury, they were supposed to go on to Londinium. He thought he might head in the opposite direction.

The more he thought about it, the more cheerful he became. Why could he not go in the opposite direction to Lower Combe? Why could he not stop off in Wingham and see who was still there? Blaedswith would be very old, if she was even still alive, but perhaps Flavius and Aeditha would still be at the villa. And if he got that far, he would certainly get himself down to see his dear brother, Augustus.

And finally, he knew what it was that he was going to do, and he understood why he had been so aggravated by the Pope's request. He was back in Britain with a task to complete, and there would again be no time to see the one person he had never forgotten. If he did nothing else, he was going to find out if Aethelreda was still alive and still reigning over the Cantii. And if she was, maybe he would do what Augustus had done, and stay in Britain with her, for the rest of his life.

Of course, Paulos realized that there were many unknowns. First of all, he had no idea if any of the people he wanted to see were still alive, or if their circumstances were in any way similar to the way they had been when he last heard about them. It was a distinct possibility that other Saxons had come to the coast and raided the towns in the years between his visits. Britain was still a frontier, and life on the frontier was often uncertain, hard, and short.

The two monks, Fra Marcos and Fra Julius, who accompanied Paulos, were unaware of all that was seething below the surface of his quiet attitude. He did not show his feelings, except for a faint air of annoyance which leaked out of him whenever they tried to engage him. They were therefore dumbfounded when they arose one morning to find that Paulos had disappeared.

He had found a horse from somewhere and headed off toward Lower Combe. He hoped to get back to Wingham, and perhaps even to Canterbury, to see for himself how the church was doing there; but he had other things that he wished to do first. Marcos and Julius were well trained. They could handle the religious part of the mission themselves. They would get all the glory, and that was the way it should be. He had never cared for any of the accolades.

Paulos rode into Lower Combe in the early evening. He could smell the cooking fires and the warm, homely scent of stew simmering on various hearths in various cottages. He was surprised to find that there was a little part of him that felt like he was coming home.

When he told the guards who he was, they let him pass without comment. He wondered if Aethelreda had informed them of a monk called Paulos who had visited long ago and might one day be back. But he realized it was more likely that security was much more relaxed in the village than it used to be. He went straight to her dwelling and knocked at her door.

The door was opened by a young servant woman. Paulos noticed that she was wearing a simple wooden cross on a leather thong around her neck. She looked at Paulos with interest, but said nothing. She appeared to be sizing him up. Paulos took the initiative.

"Good evening to you. I am Frater Paulos. I would like to visit with the Queen of the Cantii, if that be possible."

"Frater Paulos. I believe I have heard your name mentioned in this house." Paulos thought he saw a sparkle in the young woman's eye, but he could not be certain. "Let me tell her you are here." She turned and left him standing in the open doorway.

After all the times Paulos had disappointed Aethelreda, he was by no means sure of receiving a favorable reception from her. She was just as likely to lunge at him with a dagger as she was to throw her arms around him, and he did not blame her in the least. The two of them had both been caught between their life responsibilities and the desire of their hearts. And yet, even as he pondered that thought, he realized that his heart's desire had always been a multifaceted thing, like a prism of light. Looked at from one perspective, it was a rainbow of color, and from another, it was nothing but the pure brightness of white light. He had made his vow to God and his oath to the Abbot at Pomposa Abbey, and that promise had taken precedence over any other. If he had met Aethelreda before he had made the oath, it may have been different, but it was impossible now to guess.

It had been the same for Aethelreda. She had been wed to her people by an accident of birth. If her father had not died when he had, and if she had met Paulos before she was made Queen, the outcome may have been different. But, in the end, she had chosen her people. And she would do so again.

Aethelreda appeared. Her face was alight with joy. She ran to the doorway and embraced Paulos with a cry of delight and happiness. They hugged for a long time. Docillina, the maidservant, and Harold, another house servant, looked on, bemused. What they were observing was highly unusual behavior. Aethelreda had never shown any interest in men. She had no use for them as partners, nor for women, either. She was a single woman who had raised her two children to be independent, strong adults, the same as she was. And yet there she was in the arms of a stranger, and after they had embraced, the monk kissed their mistress on the lips, like a husband.

Aethelreda exclaimed, "Paulos, I dreamed that you had come back, just last night!"

"You did? That is amazing. It must have been God speaking to you. I have dreamed about you almost every night of my life."

"**That** is amazing," she replied with an amused smile.

The truth was that Aethelreda had frequent dreams about Paulos, too, but the dream she had had the night before was one of those that was marked as different by its intensity. She had prayed before sleeping that Paulos would be safe, wherever he was. Only as she drifted off to sleep did she wonder why she had prayed such a prayer. Paulos was in the monastery in Ravenna, where he had been kept as if in prison since he had visited the Pope, all those years ago.

In the morning, she remembered her dream and its intensity. Paulos had been with her in her house. He had looked into her eyes and said, "Aethelreda, you are my beloved," and then he had walked out the door into the darkness. In the light of day, she wondered about the meaning of the dream. It crossed her mind that Paulos might have passed on into the greater life with the saints, and that her dream was a message from God. All day she had been oppressed by the idea that Paulos might have died. And then, there he was, in her house and very much alive!

Aethelreda pulled Paulos into the room and over to the benches that surrounded the fire. She turned to her servant with her face still beaming with an interior light that came from the joy of seeing a long-lost friend.

"Docillina, bring a jug of ale, and bake a honey cake. Tonight, we will celebrate!"

The servant looked startled. Cook a cake? It was already nearly dark. But whatever her mistress required would be attended to, even if she did not feel like doing it. Paulos, whose stomach had rumbled at the savory smells of dinners cooking as he rode into the settlement, needed more immediate nourishment than a cake that would be two hours in the making. He asked carefully, "Aethelreda, the cake sounds delicious, but do you have any soup or stew? I have not eaten all day, and I am weak with hunger."

"Of course! Harold, bring Fra Paulos some stew! He is my dearest friend from such a long time ago. He has traveled a very long way to be here, and he shall have whatever he needs."

When Harold arrived with the bowl of steaming meat and vegetables, Paulos immediately dug in with the wooden spoon he was given. Aethelreda, Docillina, and Harold watched with amusement. Then, ever the helpful servant, Harold asked, "My Lady, would you like me to run out and let Merewenne and Aedisonne know that Fra Paulos is here?"

His mistress gave him a big smile and replied, "Not tonight, Harold. We will let them know tomorrow, and Augustus and Siggie, too. We will invite them to eat with us at midday. But tonight, I want Fra Paulos all to myself."

Chapter Twenty-Three

The Power of Forgiveness

Aethelreda and Paulos sat by the fire and talked for hours. While they were awake, Docillina was supposed to remain awake also. She sat at the far end of the room, with a deer-skin blanket covering her, and dozed as the two talked and laughed and talked some more. After a while, she lost interest in trying to hear what they were saying to each other and nodded off. Most of what Aethelreda shared with Paulos about the community in Lower Combe was not news to Docillina. They were things that everyone in the village knew: Augustus and Sigeburg remained a happily married couple; Augustus had baptized most of the village of Lower Combe; Blaedswith had taken on a new servant, Vrocata, who was a cousin to her faithful servant Ionnia. She had been wonderful as a caretaker of Aeditha's children. Flavius had slowly fallen in love with her, and they had married. They had raised the children together. Blaedswith was still alive, and she, too, had married. Paulos was glad to hear that Blaedswith had found another husband, but when he heard who she had wed, he was astonished.

"The ways of God are truly mysterious," he exclaimed. "Blaedswith married to Father Graeme! However did that happen?"

Aethelreda laughed out loud. She supposed that the person Blaedswith had been when Paulos had met her was not a natural fit for the wife of a cleric, but he had not had the privilege of the long acquaintanceship with Blaedswith that she had enjoyed.

"The two of them struck up a friendship when she went to Father Graeme's church to ask for prayers for Aeditha. They were both lonely and they found they had much in common. I think they have been very happy together."

"Does that mean that Blaedswith was finally converted to the Christian faith?"

"Indeed she was. In fact, she and I were baptized on the same day."

Paulos felt a pang of guilt on hearing that news, because he realized that he had not inquired after the status of Aethelreda's faith. To a Christian monk, her spiritual status should have been one of the first things that he had inquired after. But it was a touchy subject for him. He knew that Aethelreda found much of the Christian faith attractive, but that she had held back from full commitment in the time when they were together. She had discouraged him from asking about it too often, saying that her faith was a private thing, and he had demurred. After all those years, he had been half afraid that she had reverted completely to the faith of her people.

"Oh, my dear one, forgive me. I should have asked you if you had taken that final step. I am glad and relieved to hear that you have, and that we will join together around the throne of God in the life hereafter. Tell me about the day of your baptism! It must have been a big celebration for everyone."

"It was a day I shall remember forever. Blaedswith was baptized at Saint Martin's by Father Aelwyn, and Father Graeme was her sponsor. Blaedswith and I had talked about the upcoming event for months. We shared many confidences. She took a long time to make the decision of publicly professing the Christian faith. Blaedswith is no fool. She knew it would require her to make major changes to her life. She decided to convert mostly because she loved Father Graeme, though I believe that she was sincere by the time her baptismal day came around. We talked much about the faith together, and she shared with me the things that Father Aelwyn taught her in catechism.

"By the time we were halfway through Lent of the year of her baptism, I had learned much of the catechism material with her, and I decided that I was ready to commit, too. And so, on the Eve of Easter Sunday, we both went to St Martin's church, to pray through the night with the other baptismal candidates."

Paulos, wanting to experience the events as if he had been there, put up his hand to interrupt her narrative. "Tell me, step by step, the events of the evening," he begged.

Aethelreda obliged. "Just before dawn, Father Aelwyn kindled a new flame in the courtyard of the church and lit a torch. We dressed in white baptismal robes and walked behind the priest, who was carrying the torch into the church. The people were chanting and singing. It sounded so holy and mystical that it brought tears to my eyes. The church was decorated with flowers for the Easter service, and it smelled wonderful. And there was incense, too, smoky, and reminding all of us of sacred things. We heard the scriptures being read, and Father Aelwyn prayed for us each by name. He had a large cauldron of water that he had drawn from the river, and he ladled the water over each one of us, 'in the name of the Father, and the Son, and the Holy Spirit'.

"It was cold, so cold, in that church, and with water that was almost freezing poured over me, it took my breath away. But as we were received into the church and wrapped in woolen shawls (made by the weavers of Lower Combe!) by our sponsors, we felt the warmth of everyone's love. I will never forget that day. The only thing that would have made it more perfect would have been if you had been there, Paulos." Her eyes were shining as she relived the events of that glorious day. Paulos felt again the sadness of the years they had spent apart.

"I wish I had been."

There was a long silence as Aethelreda laid her head on Paulos's shoulder. He was thinking about what she had said and reliving the event in his imagination, when he realized she had left out an important detail.

"Who was your sponsor? Augustus?"

"Yes, he was. How did you guess?"

"It seemed appropriate for the Queen of the Cantii to be sponsored by her own priest, though I wonder why you were not baptized in your own church at Saint Mary's?"

"That would have been the natural way of things, and as such it presented a problem which had to be worked out. In the end, Augustus recognized my need to be there at Saint Martin's for Blaedswith, and the primacy of that need. We all agreed that because Saint Martin's was a larger space, we could accommodate more people if we held the service there. And so we made it a kind of joint celebration between Saint Mary's and Saint Martin's.

"With the road between the two towns mostly finished, it did not take very long for folks to travel from one town to the other. And there were a lot of folks who walked from Lower Combe to Wingham for the service. The people of Wingham made us very welcome, and we had quite a feast after the service."

"I am sure that you did. One thing I remember about the Cantii was your ability to have a wonderful feast." He chuckled and hugged her warmly around the shoulders. "I am so very glad that you have been baptized. And I am glad that Augustus is your priest. He is a good man, faithful and devout. You know, I was jealous of his being so near to you for many years."

Aethelreda turned to him in surprise. "You were? Why?"

Paulos did not entirely believe her innocence. "I believe you may have manipulated my jealousy of him when you were still angry with me for leaving you in Lower Combe. Do you remember when we were sailing to Gaul, and you told me that Augustus had given you his dagger and you implied that he cared more about your physical safety than I did?"

Aethelreda gave a short laugh. "I remember. And I may still be angry at you for leaving me in Lower Combe."

"Oh, Aethelreda, you have every right to be. I regretted what I did for so many years."

"And then, it seems, you forgot about me?" Her voice was teasing, but Paulos took her seriously.

"Oh no, I did not! It may have seemed that way to you, over here in Britain, but I never, ever, forgot about you. What happened was that after being sick with regret for so many years, I realized that God had forgiven me. And then I had to work to forgive myself. I do better at that some days than I do on others. Do you forgive me, Aethelreda?"

She turned and kissed him on the cheek. "Forgiveness is a hard thing for me, Paulos. It was my sticking point for years. Neither Blaedswith nor I could come to terms with it. We thought Christianity would be far more palatable if it was a more militant religion, with less emphasis on the weak idea of forgiveness. Our heritage is one of conquest and fighting, rather than of discussing and forgiving. I do not necessarily think that is a good thing, but it is the way I was brought up. But then something happened that made me see things in a new light." She paused to give Paulos a chance to prepare for what she had to say. "Of all the people that I might have gone to for a lesson on forgiveness, it was the person I would have least expected who taught me about it, and that was Blaedswith and her brothers."

Ignoring for the moment the fact that she had not answered his question about whether she had forgiven him, Paulos asked, "What happened between Blaedswith and her brothers?"

"They were estranged for decades. I thought you knew that."

"I do know. I met them in the alehouse in Wingham, and they told me as much."

"They came to Aeditha's funeral because they were close to Flavius, but they did not say a word to Blaedswith. On top of her grief over losing Aeditha, she was upset that her brothers had not ever reconciled with her. That was when she realized that she was going to have to be the one to reach out to them for reconciliation, even though they were supposedly Christians and she was not, and even though, in the beginning, it was she who was the most grievously wronged."

Paulos sighed. "What a shame her brothers could not let bygones be bygones. But I know from experience how hard it is to forgive and be forgiven. I also know how central and powerful the idea of forgiveness is in my Christian faith. How did she manage to bring about reconciliation with her brothers?"

"Not long after Aeditha's death, Petros took a bad fall. Word got back to Blaedswith and she decided that she had better go and see him, in case it was the last opportunity she had to reconcile with him. She went the next day, but was barred from entering the house by Andreas.

She stood outside the cottage for the rest of the day, knocking on the door and asking, begging, to be allowed to see her brother each time someone else came by and was admitted to the bedside, but she was always refused. It rained for a while and still she waited, while the shower soaked her through. Finally, it grew dark, and still she waited outside. Blaedswith is a strong and stubborn woman. I believe she would still be there now if Andreas had not finally relented."

Paulos snorted. He wondered if Aethelreda knew how strong and stubborn she was herself. He ventured an interruption. "Not unlike someone else that I know."

Aethelreda ignored Paulos's comment. She knew he was right, but she was not going to dignify his retort with an answer. She continued with the story which she had heard from the lips of Blaedswith, many times.

"Eventually, Andreas opened the door and asked her what she wanted. He was deeply irritated by her persistence. Blaedswith took all her courage into her two hands, squeezed them together as if she was praying, and said words that surprised even her. She said that she wanted to ask forgiveness of her brother.

"There was no logic in Blaedswith asking her brother for forgiveness, since he had committed the far greater wrong in killing the man she loved; but those words must have opened up a space in Andreas's heart, and he looked at his sister, wet from the rain, and nearly falling over from her day-long vigil, with a newfound respect. He invited her into the house.

"When she was at Petros's bedside, she took her brother's hand and said again the words that she had not thought she would ever say, 'brother, forgive me.'

"He was dying, but he heard her words and grasped her hand and asked for her forgiveness, too.

"It turned out that there was much to confess and forgive on all sides. Andreas joined them and added his own. And there, at the side of the dying man, they reconciled.

"I realized then the power of forgiveness. I realized that it sets a person free, and most often the person that is freed is you, yourself." There was a pause as she looked directly at Paulos. "And yes, Paulos, I do forgive you. And I ask you to forgive me."

The power of forgiveness. Aethelreda had used those words, but Paulos wondered if even he really knew what that meant. He had come back to Britain aching with the desire to see Aethelreda again and to hear her say the words that he had just heard. And yet now that he had heard them, he felt that they had come too easily. The problem was not Aethelreda; the problem – which he had not yet admitted – was that he had yet to forgive himself completely for choosing to obey his vows to God, rather than following his heart.

He held her tightly. He was in danger of losing control and weeping in a very unmanly way. In that moment, he wished for the stoicism of the Britons. But he was not of the Britons. He was Roman. The hot climate seemed to raise hot-blooded, emotional people in his land.

Aethelreda saw his tears and she wiped them gently away with her fingertips. She kissed his wet eyelids and laughed softly. "You are so tender, Fra Paulos. What shall I do with you?"

"Nothing, my beloved, nothing. I am soft and easily moved, and it has become more evident as I have aged. But that is just the way it is."

"Ah, yes. You are not at all like your Roman brothers who were soldiers, and that is one of the things that I have always loved about you."

Nothing more was said.

***

In the morning, when Docillina roused herself to stir up the fire and begin the day, she found the two of them still curled up in each other's arms beside the embers. She was moved by the tenderness of the scene, even though she had lived for years hearing about how badly Fra Paulos had let her Queen down. He was the reason that she had never married, Aethelreda had often claimed.

It was true that Paulos had also done some wonderful things for Aethelreda, such as rescuing her from the hands of the Saxons, and providing an army to overrun the interlopers, but Docillina had heard all the other tales of sadness from Aethelreda herself. She knew that for more than twenty years her Queen had lived with the grief and disappointment of being deserted by the man that was now in her house and in her arms.

The night before, Docillina's husband had sought her out as she emptied the scraps from the evening meal into the pile at the edge of the vegetable garden. He had heard that a Roman was back in the house of Aethelreda, and he wanted to know who it was. Docillina's husband, Chad, was fiercely protective of his Queen.

"It is Fra Paulos, the Roman monk."

"What is he doing here?"

Docillina shrugged. "I do not know, but he was well received."

Chad seemed agitated by the whole idea of any kind of Roman under the same roof as his Queen. He went away with a troubled look on his face.

Docillina went about her morning duties as if it was a normal day, heating up the water for Aethelreda and her guest to wash in, preparing the oats for the breaking of the fast, and boiling water for the herbal tincture that Aethelreda drank every day.

And just as Aethelreda and Paulos were waking to the golden streaked morning, there was a loud shouting and banging of pots and sticks outside the door. Someone was yelling, "Romans get out! There is no place for you here!"

Someone else was screaming, "Leave our Queen alone!"

And as one they began to chant, "Aethelreda stands alone!"

Neither Docillina nor Wilfred were bold enough to open the door to the throng, but Aethelreda, still in the blue gown she had been wearing the day before, and with her hair unbound and tumbling around her face and down her back like ropes silvered by moonbeams, flung the door open and faced her people.

"What is the meaning of this?" Her voice was harsh, authoritative.

Someone shouted, "Send the Roman home!"

Aethelreda was incredulous. She shouted back, "This is Paulos! He is the one who rescued me from the Saxons. He is the one who asked the Pope to intervene and sent soldiers to fight off the Saxons! He saved us all!"

Someone under cover of the dimness of the morning light yelled, "We still do not want him here. Send him home!"

The rabble began their banging and shouting again. "If you do not hand him over, we will take him!"

That voice sounded familiar to both Docillina and to Aethelreda. She drew herself to her full height, and in her angriest voice she cried out, "You will not dare to do such a thing. Paulos is a guest in my house!"

As the men milled around, Aethelreda began to regret that she had long ago given up her house guards, believing that she was safe enough with her servants to protect her. Wilfred was right in the doorway with her, and he had a cudgel in his hand, but she knew that would be useless against the ten or more men who were at her door. She noted that all of the men were young, perhaps under twenty-five. That meant they had not met Paulos when he had first come to Lower Combe. They did not know the role he had played in their future. She was stunned at how quickly the history of a village was lost if it was not constantly, intentionally brought to the attention of the people. She would be sure from now on that they all knew their recent history as well as their more distant narrative.

Paulos stepped forward. His grizzled hair and beard were clear signs of his age. He did not look like a threat to anybody. He stood beside Aethelreda, and just as he did so, a stone whizzed by his ear and another one hit him on the shoulder. Aethelreda let go a string of curses.

"You drooling curs! You jealous sons of Abarta! May he strike you down in your damned stupidity! Put your weapons away!" she shouted, "otherwise some of you will be severely punished!"

Paulos raised his hands in surrender and stepped forward in front of her. If anyone wanted to kill him, he had given them an unobstructed opportunity, but no more stones were thrown. With Aethelreda's curses ringing in their ears, the mob was momentarily silent and waiting to hear what he had to say for himself. He cleared his throat and spoke clearly and loudly in his best Britonic.

"Good people of Lower Combe, how glad I am that you love and protect your Queen. She is worthy of your protection. She is worthy of your lives, should you have to give them up for her. She is a Queen above queens, except for the Queen of Heaven!" The silence continued. No one could argue with a word of what he had said. Paulos continued, "But I am not the enemy. I am only an old man who has made many mistakes in his life. I hope it was not a mistake to come back here to see your Queen and to renew my friendship, and to renew my friendship with Fra Augustus, my monastic brother. I hope you will forgive me for my past misdemeanors and allow me to visit with you for a while. I promise you no harm."

From the back of the mob came a voice. Augustus had just caught up with the fact that something was going on in the village outside Aethelreda's residence and had run to see. He was stunned to hear a voice that he never thought to hear again.

"Fra Paulos? Fra Paulos! My long-lost brother!" And Augustus pushed his way with difficulty to the front of the group of men. He ran forward and threw his arms around Paulos, while the crowd of rabble-rousers watched. "I thought never to see you again, my friend."

The two of them laughed and embraced, and when they finally drew apart, half of the rabble had disappeared, slinking off to their cottages. Aethelreda spoke sternly to those who remained.

"The rest of you can head off to your homes as well. But let me tell you this, I will remember this day. I will remember who was here in this little group. You attacked a visitor right under my roof. Do not think that what you have done will be ignored."

Augustus, Paulos, Aethelreda and the two servants went back inside, leaving two servants to guard the door, and closing it carefully behind them. It had been a rough start to the day.

As he walked to the fireside and took a seat with his dear friend Augustus, Paulos noticed for the first time that the floor of Aethelreda's house had been paved with stone. He missed the pleasant scent of dried herbs that he remembered and associated with his time in Britain, but he saw the renovation as a sign of progress. To

Augustus he said, "It looks like my friend Flavius has had a hand in improving the quality of life here in Lower Combe."

Augustus laughed. "Good guess, brother Paulos. We have much to thank him for. Almost as much as we have to thank you for."

"You are kind. But as for what I have done that is due gratitude, there is as much in need of mending in my association with Lower Combe and its people."

Augustus looked carefully at him for elucidation. "Are you referring to your 'association' with our queen?"

"Of course. I dealt poorly with her. Thankfully, she has not remained in the place in which I left her, but she has moved on, forging a pathway that is for the betterment of her people."

Paulos had heard many hints in what Aethelreda had told him the night before that indicated she had moved from the isolationist position of her father. He felt that was a very good thing for the people of Britain. Change was coming to them all, even in Rome, and it was best to be flexible and accommodating.

Docillina got to work to prepare more breakfast for their unexpected guest, and tried to stay out of the way of her mistress. She felt guilty about what had happened, even though she had no idea what her husband would do with the information she had provided. Aethelreda retired to her room to properly prepare for the day. She called Docillina to attend her. It had not escaped her attention that Docillina's husband had been at the front of the clamoring crowd in her entrance yard.

"Docillina, how did your husband know about Fra Paulos?"

Docillina looked shamefaced. "My husband asked me who was at your house, and I told him, my Lady. I did not know it would lead to anything like this."

"I do not find any blame in you, Docillina, but why is Chad so sensitive to my safety? Is there something going on that I do not know about? Is there an uprising being planned?"

"Oh, my Lady, I pray not! If there was, I am sure that my husband would have informed you."

"Are you sure? Perhaps he is not as loyal to me as he wants you to believe."

Docillina looked suddenly ill. Her pert young face had paled to the color of unbleached linen cloth. Sweat had broken out and beaded on her upper lip. She had suddenly put a few previously random acts of her husband's together in her mind, and she realized that Aethelreda might have been right. Her own loyalty to husband and to Queen was about to be tested to its limits.

There was the time that Chad had gone to the coast with a few of the same young men he had gathered with that morning. He said they were going to check the tides to see when the best time to gather kelp would be. They had stayed away for three days, and she had never found out why. She suspected they had held a meeting on the beach, perhaps with another tribe, but for what reason, she could not imagine. In retrospect, she wondered if they had been planning an insurrection.

There was another time she had found a cache of spears, pikes, and clubs, hidden in the straw of the byre beside their cottage. When she had questioned Chad, he was vague. He told her they were his own personal supply to protect them against Saxon raids. Docillina believed him because she wanted to believe her husband. She still did.

"My Lady, he is loyal. I swear."

But the truth all came out when Aethelreda called a council later that morning to examine the uprising that had taken place. Neither Paulos nor Augustus was admitted to the meeting, but her brothers were there, and some of the older men in the settlement.

After being prompted repeatedly and finally being threatened, the men explained the meaning of the morning's demonstration. Chad spoke for the dissenters. He was nervous and showed it by being surly. He told the council that he and a group of the younger men had grown concerned about what they perceived as the slackness of government in Lower Combe. He did not mention that they considered Aethelreda had become unfit to rule now that she was older, and that she seemed weak and permissive to them. But Aethelreda seemed unsurprised when one of the men of the council, who was at least fifteen years older than she was, forced the truth out of Chad.

"Are you saying that you think we, the elders of the tribe, are too old to do our duty? Are you saying that our Queen is unfit to reign?" The old man's voice was strained with hostility.

"I am saying that our Queen, as wise as she is, appears to have forgotten how vulnerable we are to invasion and how easily we were overcome by the Saxons, those many years ago. We feel that the threat of Saxon invasion is an ever-growing concern."

"Do you not think that we, too, are aware of the threat from across the sea? Do you not know of the treaty we have with the Catuvellauni to come to our aid, and for us to give them aid, should there be an attack?"

Chad looked embarrassed. He knew, of course, but he did not trust the leadership of the elders to protect them in the event of a Saxon raid. They had gathered weapons themselves and made plans for the eventuality of an attack. They thought that there should be daily practices so that they would be fit and ready to combat an enemy.

They also never believed that the Romans had gone forever. The longer they were away, the greater the likelihood of another invasion, in their opinion. They were concerned for the future of Lower Combe. And then a Roman had arrived out of nowhere.

Aethelreda listened carefully to what the men had to say. She offered no rebuttal to the accusations that her leadership was weak. She simply let the men speak. She knew that no good could come from young men having to drive their suspicions and ambitions underground. But she was biding her time.

Eventually, they stopped, and all eyes turned on their queen, regal in her purple gown with a heavy silver chain around her neck, a gift from Blaedswith, and the gold circlet of her royal status across her brow. She let the silence sit for a moment or two. Then she spoke in measured tones.

"You have had your say. Now I will have mine, without interruption. You think because my hair is gray that I am old and weak. You think because my menses have long since ceased that I am useless to our tribe." The young men looked startled. No one had said anything so radical to their Queen. But Aethelreda was adept at reading between the lines. She continued.

"You think that because I do not wage war or start petty fights of ownership and control with our neighbors that I am blind and deaf to our differences and lacking in ambition. You are wrong on all counts. I pick my battles, and when you are older you will discover the wisdom of what I have chosen to do, and what I have chosen to ignore.

"My hair is gray because of the shocking things that I have seen and done, right here in this village. Seeing the streaks of silver each day reminds me of the past and fills me with ferocity to prevent such evil from happening again. Each day I vow anew that such atrocities as I saw and lived through will never be repeated in this village. Nor have they been.

"I may be old by your estimation, but I have used the accumulation of years to obtain wisdom. Women are not only useful while we can produce new life, but in the years we live beyond child rearing, we grow shrewd and wise. The fact that I have lived many years beyond my ability to bear a child has freed me to produce a new kind of life – a life that is far broader than that of a single individual and his or her brothers and sisters and offspring. I have been free to think about the future of our people, not just the next year, or the decade after that, but in the next hundred years, and to plan for that future, without conflict or warfare." She looked around at the young men, fixing them with her gaze, still piercingly blue.

"The years that our God has given me are a blessing, every one of them. I would not trade one second of my life for different experiences, because each second has taught me something about the past, the present, and the future. I hope you all are given the grace to reach my age and beyond.

"But what you do not understand in your youth is that it is useless to spend your days worrying about what might happen in the future. You must take what happened in the past, learn from it, live fully in the present, and walk confidently each day, trusting that the future will take care of itself. You do this by preparing for the future, by working with your neighbor in this village and your neighbor in the next village, and you must try to live lives of decency and goodness, such that you have nothing to be ashamed of, before God.

"I fear the events of this morning might be a source of shame for some of you. But it does not need to be so. If you will apologize for your rash behavior, and swear new fealty to me, we will go on from here."

The young men were showing a mixture of shame and confusion. They had expected to be severely punished for what they had done. But from what Aethelreda had said, it appeared they might get off more lightly.

Aethelreda turned to the older men who accompanied her. They were her council of elders. They clustered together to discuss what to do next. After several minutes of murmured conversation, Aethelreda turned back to the young men.

"It has been decided by the council that each of you will serve a sentence for your unseemly behavior this morning. First, you will have your cottages searched for items that should not be there. Anything we find will be removed and added to the supplies available to every townsman. Then your punishment will begin. You will be tied to a post in the square for a full day and night as an example to others never to behave so foolishly. You will also be required to serve the village by cleaning and maintaining our public spaces for the cycle of six moons. After you have served your sentence, you will take a public vow of fealty to me. We will then consider the events of this day forgiven."

There was visible relief in the room, and a newfound respect for Aethelreda and her council.

Fra Paulos and Fra Augustus had been banned from the proceedings, but that did not mean they were shut out entirely. The two of them had listened from Aethelreda's private chambers. Paulos had never been prouder of Aethelreda than he was when he heard her decision. She was a wise ruler indeed.

***

In the afternoon, Sigeburg and Aethelreda's brothers and sisters joined them for a time of celebration over Paulos's return, which lasted into the evening. The news of the council decision had been passed around the village. Most were glad that the air had been cleared and that Aethelreda and her council had remained strong but merciful.

The family and friends of Aethelreda and Paulos sat and shared stories, eating and drinking, and renewing their acquaintance with each other. It felt as if the years between the last time they had seen each other, and that day, had melted away to nothing.

Finally, the guests left, and Paulos and Aethelreda were alone together. Paulos complimented her on the way she had handled the situation as they reclined beside the fire in Aethelreda's private quarters.

"You have always said that you found the idea of forgiveness a difficult one. I think that the events of today showed that you do understand the power of forgiveness, after all."

Aethelreda sighed. "If you only knew how I struggle with forgiveness and reconciliation."

"It does not show. Your actions are full of grace."

"You are so kind. It is what I have always loved about you." There was another silence while the fire crackled beside them. In that moment, both of them were content in each other's company, and nothing else existed beyond the two of them. But moments such as that cannot last forever. Sooner or later, life intervenes. Aethelreda was the one who broke the spell.

"Paulos, what is next for you?"

Paulos answered carefully. "I had planned to join my colleagues and then return to Rome with them."

Aethelreda noted that his comment was in the past tense. She felt sure she knew what he would say next, and her heart was sore, knowing what she would have to say. Then, acting on the longing that he was feeling, Paulos said, "It would not take very much to persuade me to stay here with you, my beloved, for whatever is left of my life."

Aethelreda drew closer to Paulos, hugging him, then she slipped onto her knees on the stone floor that Flavius had put in for her, which reminded her always of those peaceful days in Rome when Paulos had been her husband and she had been his wife. She laid her head on his lap and he stroked her beautiful hair.

He wanted to hear her ask him to stay, but he also knew that Aethelreda was far wiser than he, and he had a feeling that she would turn him away. She did not look at him. Her voice was tender.

"My dearest Paulos, for some reason I do not think that our lives were ever destined to be entwined as one. We have met and loved, and parted, but except for the precious time we spent in Rome, we have lived separate lives. And I think that is the way it was meant to be.

"You saw today what unrest there was over your presence here in Lower Combe. But even more important than that is the plain fact that I owe my people my wholehearted service in my final years." She stood up and kissed him tenderly on the cheek, and then she went to prepare herself for bed.

Chapter Twenty-Four

A New Journey

In the space of one night, Frater Paulos had relived the major events of his long and interesting life. Like Aethelreda, he did not regret one minute of the time that God had given him. The good and the bad had, in their own way, formed him into the man that he was, like the warp and weft that held fabric together, or the mixture of clay and water that was needed to make pottery. He had been shaped by life into the person who was at least close to being the man that he was meant to be. When he looked back and saw himself the way he imagined God saw him, he had not done too badly. He had served both God and man as well as he could. He could only hope that he had done enough – and if he had not, he relied on the mercy of God.

During those final years after he had returned from Britain, leaving Aethelreda behind forever, he had finally recognized a profound deficit in his life: his inability to forgive the person who had hurt him the most. He had preached to others the futility of living under the shadow of resentment, but he had never forgiven Pope Leo for his imprisonment, and he had never forgiven himself for his passive acceptance of his fate. He had wandered in a cloud of amnesic fog that had hidden his deepest resentments from his own consciousness for more than half of his life.

Pope Leo was dead. Whatever guilt he had carried with regard to his treatment of Paulos was between the Pope and God. Nothing Paulos could do would change that.

The Abbot heard his confession and pronounced his absolution, and Paulos knew he was free from the burden; but instead of the lightness of freedom, he felt like the bare stalk of a dandelion once its seeds had been blown away by the wind. He felt naked and vulnerable. It was as if the seeds which were ripened by his repentance and forgiveness had flown off to produce life in other places, leaving him rooted in place, waiting for death. Paulos prayed for the seeds of his ministry, wherever they had landed, to be fruitful. It was all he had left to offer to the Lord.

Once he had forgiven the Pope, he moved on to forgive himself. He found wisdom in his Abbot's advice that his anger had been a perfectly human and utterly reasonable response to having been locked away by the Pope. But his Abbot also reminded him that by carrying his anger inside him for all those years, it was only himself he had damaged.

He found wisdom in another source, too. Aethelreda's acceptance of their separation and her decision to look beyond her own personal needs and desires to the needs of her people had gone a long way in helping him to unburden himself of guilt. Her wisdom had helped to set him free from self-recrimination. If she had been able to move on from a place of regret and disappointment, so could he, with the Lord's help. In his final years, she had taught him how to live a life that was rich with joy and acceptance of things over which he had no control.

***

The day was about to dawn. Outside the abbey, the sky was just brightening on the horizon. The thin golden line at the edge of the hillside would soon spread and expand to fill the sky with the pink, red, and gold prism of morning light. The earliest songbirds were singing their ode to the return of the sun.

From his bed in his cell, Fra Paulos's breathing slowed. There was no window in his cell; nevertheless, he began to see a bright horizon, growing more luminous in front of his eyes. Beyond that golden gleam at the rim of the world, he knew there was a Lord who loved him and would welcome him into His presence. Summoning every last drop of strength, Paulos proclaimed, "Brothers, the best journey of all is about to begin!" Then, almost so quietly that Luke wondered if he had heard right, he added, "Aethelreda, I will see you soon."

Luke, who had been half asleep, was startled into wakefulness by the words. He took the old man's hand in his and murmured a blessing for his last journey.

Fra Paulos closed his eyes for the final time, and with a smile of contentment on his face, he breathed his last.